THE UNPRO TECTED

THE UNPRO TECTED

A NOVEL

KELLY SOKOL

Skyhorse Publishing

For Lucy and Milla, my greatest teachers and the loves of my life.

And Sean, the best chapter with pages yet unwritten.

Prologue

They were about to spend their first weeknight together at Lara's house, a June-sticky Richmond Wednesday. She and Will hadn't discussed it, of course, but both their first and second attempts to leave for dinner that night failed. A discreet zip-up duffel was pressed to the plaster wall just inside the doorway behind Will's battered messenger bag full of student essays and plays. Clothes re-fastened only to be unbuttoned again, sweat beading at their hairlines, bodies a tangle of kudzu limbs. Discarding the plan for dinner out, they sat on her angular Swedish leather sofa, Will wearing only a T-shirt and his boxers, Lara, lacy boy shorts and a camisole.

She opened a bottle of white wine—red in the summer raised hives across her chest—and poured ice water, too. Even the glasses perspired, leaving rings on the tray below the pitcher, bottle, and stems. Will rubbed the bridge of his long, freckle-darkened nose, the small creases, and two round indentations on either side from the glasses he wore almost all of the time. He'd told her that he couldn't remember ever not having glasses. He'd lost or broken so many pairs as a boy, he'd learned to just keep them on. His face could have formed around the frames. His eyes, gray and blue, flecked like zinc from quarry rock, shrank just a little when he took them off, giving him a startled, younger appearance.

They had at least forty-five minutes before the take-out Lara had breathlessly ordered would arrive. They were insatiable physically and as hungry for each other's conversation. Skin stories, life stories, always new in the retelling. He was still endlessly fascinating to her.

At Lara's father's funeral in late February, Lara and Will had stood apart. They'd hidden their relationship for the past six months, including the last of her father's life. Lara held her mother's hand amid her brothers, their wives, her sister, and young nephews and nieces. Her best friend, Karen, stood close enough that their arms touched. Eyes lowered, Lara had focused on Will's knees in gray slacks on the opposite side of the burial mound. She could have been looking at the shiny casket, wavy in the sunshine, still atop gleaming metal casters. But she thought of the dark black ink on Will's thigh, the hidden tattoo that had surprised her—a dangerous curl of water, the sharp plane, a hint of kayak on muscle.

Life in the open as a couple felt refreshing and dangerous. For the final months of her father's illness, Lara had spent so many hours with her dad at VCU Medical, then at her parents' home, or otherwise catching up at her agency, that time with Will now retained a furtive, grand-theft flavor, adrenaline metal and wet tequila salt. Being on the couch with Will at eight o'clock on a Wednesday was the antithesis of staid domesticity. His car, a Camry that seemed too small to hold all of him, parked in front of her row house on The Fan, behind her cherry-ChapStick-red Saab convertible, was a proclamation. And the way his thighs tensed and released as he sat forward or invented a reason to touch her were, well, delicious.

"Wine on a school night," Will said with a smile that revealed a row of crowded bottom teeth. She'd opened the plastic case once in his bathroom: a retainer at thirty-eight. "This is the wild life of the advertising exec?"

"Make Wednesday feel like Friday," she quipped, holding the wine bottle like a product placement. "Sip Sonoma-Cutrer and every night is a celebration."

"You without your clothes and nowhere to be. That's reason to celebrate."

"How un-cerebral of you, Dr. James."

"You're a work of art. My brain short-circuits when I'm with you."

When Lara sat back down on the couch, Will lifted her summer-brown runner's legs and laid them across his lap. The move was intimate and familiar at once. His cheeks pinked and his eyes crinkled. He ran a thickly veined hand through his hair, self-conscious. The thick brown strands stood taller, roots damp.

"That's a nice fit," she said, lifting one foot and pointing her toe to highlight the placement of his thigh in the bend of her knee.

"I'd say so." He took a swallow of wine and leaned over her, his lower lip slick, inviting.

As Lara set her glass down on the table, the phone rang. She waved it off. Ring upon ring nagged at her until the voicemail picked up. Then it started again. She wriggled out of Will's arms, the soles of her feet tapping her annoyance, and picked up the phone.

"Hello." She used a warding-off-telemarketer tone.

Her mother, as she'd feared and expected.

Lara held her pointer finger up to Will and mouthed, *One minute, sorry!* Aware of Will's gaze, she sucked in her flat stomach and walked down the narrow hallway to the galley kitchen.

"Hi, Beth, I mean, Mom." Her mother hated Lara using her nickname, though she insisted on the diminutive Beth, instead of Elizabeth, for everyone besides her children.

No words, just sobs crackled through the phone.

"Are you okay?"

She'd called sobbing or about to cry at least every third day since the funeral. The calls were regular only in their irregular timing. Occasionally a couple of days would pass between phone calls. On bad nights Beth couldn't be alone in the dark and Lara's phone rang moments after they had hung up. But never had Beth sounded this gasping, choking.

"T-turn on the news. ABC Nightly," Beth said.

A few minutes past eight seemed too reasonable a time for Beth to be so upset. She usually placed frantic calls in the middle of the night, after waking from a dream that Lara's dad had died and then realizing he was already gone when she rolled to the empty space on his side of the bed, to the fat fresh pillow monogrammed with his initials.

"What's going on?"

"Five babies . . . dead. Drowned. Their mother did it."

Lara walked to the living room and turned on the television. A static red banner across the bottom of the screen read: *Breaking News: Houston mother confesses to killing her children.*

"Beth, you need to turn off the TV. It's too disturbing."

"I can't. Those children. So helpless. I . . ."

Lara knew her mother lived to be needed, to care-take, even when she couldn't take care of herself. The day the hospice nurse set up a bed and care station for her father at her childhood home, Lara had sensed Beth's relief. He would die, nothing to be done there, but Beth could take care of him until that happened. One less empty room in her blown-away nest. Then he died and all of the nurses and their bright movements and swishy scrubs left, too. Beth mourned absence above all.

"Do you need me to come over?" *Please, please, please, no.*

"I don't think so, Jo-Jo." Lara frowned. Her mother's obsession with *Little Women* had ruined Louisa May Alcott for Lara and her three siblings. "You're all right?"

"Yes, Mom. More than fine." She winked at Will who'd been watching Lara as she spoke. Her row house was so small, Will would have to go upstairs to her bedroom for any privacy, to avoid her brisk walking and gesturing while talking. Regardless, he would have been able to hear.

By any comparison, Lara's 1906 Fan home was a leap from her Lower West Side apartment, which she'd left when her father's cancer was deemed incurable. A return to Virginia had not been part of her design. A twin bed, bathroom, and kitchenette above a New Jersey Indian restaurant was her start. Next, a loft in Queens, then Brooklyn, and finally, Manhattan.

Her dad's illness rewrote the setting. She'd traded NYC for RVA, another city of arts and monuments but one with a difficult past. Instead of a lease, a mortgage: gutters and pipes, all her own. Stamped Old Salem Brick exterior contrasted with sharp modernity inside. And she owned this space.

"I called your sister and brothers," Beth said. "They're fine. So are the kids."

"Of course they are." Lara's two brothers and their families lived in California, her sister, Bea, in Lynchburg. "You call if you need to." She hoped Beth wouldn't phone again while Will was there, but knew she'd answer anyway.

"Okay, goodnight. I'm sorry for the interruption," Beth said.

"'Night, Mom." Lara hung up and shook her head.

She slumped down beside Will on the couch and took two big swallows of wine. "I'm sorry about that," Lara said. "She's been having such a hard time since . . ." Her voice always broke on "Dad" so the word hung in the air. Cancer had taken her father, but it had given her Will James.

His glasses reflected the television screen. "That's fine, of course." When had he put on his shirt? The wrinkled linen hung open, unbuttoned. "And this story is pretty awful. A mother killed her own children, a baby on up to a seven-year-old."

"How many were there?"

"Five."

"Five? Between six months and seven years? It's not funny, but that's enough to drive anyone over the edge."

"It's criminal," Will said. "Some people shouldn't be allowed to reproduce."

She barked a laugh, appalled by the sentiment from the mouth of a writer, an educator. Of course he was only joking. His eyes were serious, mouth flat and straight. He took the remote from her hand and turned off the television, but not quickly enough. Before the screen blinked blank, beyond the yellow police tape, flat black eyes stared out from dirty dishwater skin, snarled hair tangled down below shoulders, a back hunched in surrender, wrists encircled in scuffed steel. The woman's flesh appeared as cold and pale as Lara's father's hand had when she held it the morning after he died, before the funeral home prettied him up.

"Now, where were we?" Will asked. His mouth on hers, lips rough and pressing, pushed the image away. His skin, the odor of Brut and sweat and sex, almost helped Lara forget.

Chapter One

1999

"No." Lara stomped the slush off of her boots on the mat just inside her father's room. She'd already cleaned them at the hospital entrance but she felt like stomping. She felt like stomping and holding her breath until she got her way.

The oncologist pushed past her, his goodbye a terse grip of her shoulder and an avoided glance.

"No," she said again, louder. "There is more we can do. I heard him, Dad. If . . ." *If you give up it's over.* But she wasn't going to say it aloud.

"It's not any use. We all know it." Her father's voice was a whisper.

He'd always looked more like a lumberjack, stocky, almost rect-angular in bulk, but it was his voice that could command a classroom or an auditorium or a bookstore. Not quite six feet tall, he gave the impression of height. But he wasn't a lumberjack. He wasn't a professor anymore, either. Her father was a whisper. The withering had begun before his diagnosis and it accelerated each time cancer was found in another part of his body.

Despite his quiet voice, his eyes were an unmedicated bright. She'd forgotten the real color and liveliness of his eyes before the drugs dulled them. Clear again, they appeared almost alien, retouched, without his thick eyebrows and dense lashes, chemotherapy's last trophies. But she didn't want to look right at them. She wouldn't let him convince her. Instead, Lara picked at flecks of orange glitter on the pumpkin and candy corn garland still wrapped around parts of the bed. Halloween was almost two weeks ago. It shouldn't still be there: festive didn't belong in oncology. And no one needed reminding about death.

"Beth, come on." Lara's will could out-muscle her mother. She'd done it for years.

"If it's what your father wants." This was Beth's form of declarative sentence.

"Teddy, Bea, we should all get a say. I—I can help with more," Lara said.

"La," her father said. He hadn't spoken that nickname aloud since she was a child, though he addressed every letter he'd ever written to his La. "La" had been Bea's first word. "We've talked to the other kids. And you've helped more than you should already."

"Dad—"

"I'm not going to beat this, but I don't want to die in this hospital. Even if you can't understand that, I need you to stop fighting me."

Lara wasn't fighting her father; she was fighting his cancer, fighting his dying when everyone else had surrendered. Ted Jennings had taught Lara how to fish, taught her to drive a stick shift, to negotiate a fair rate at the mechanic, how to follow up on a resume and land the job, how to slow her breathing while running, get over her first broken heart. One foot in front of the other, one stride and then the next. Find forward and walk through it, her father had always said. And now he was giving up.

"Fine, then I'm moving home."

Her father's back straightened at her words, but only just. "Absolutely not. You've only just gotten started in New York."

"You make your decisions, Dad. I'll make mine."

He was trying to look stern for her, but he smiled anyway.

She was only gone for two and a half weeks, long enough to pack up her apartment, sign over her only months-old lease, and empty her desk at DDB, where she wouldn't work anymore.

"I'll be back as soon as my dad gets better," she told the woman who shared a cubicle wall.

Standing inside the footprint of where her bed had been, Lara could touch three walls standing still. Without a mattress and bedframe, the space seemed even smaller somehow, where before she had felt infinite—the city, its people just beyond her touch, energy humming on the other side of the plaster. All of her kitchenware was miniature, New York apartment–sized: a four-cup coffee pot from a market for all manner of items manufactured to fit inside a postage stamp. Even the smallest apartment in Virginia would be twice as large as this one. She would be enormous and reduced at once.

As she surrendered her key, she knew she would immediately change her cell phone number. She wouldn't cling to the 917 area code like someone who could never move on. Holding onto it would be too sad. She'd only lived in the city for five years, not long enough to call herself a New Yorker, barely longer than the starry-eyed farm kids who arrived after college, ambitions bulging their suitcases, kids the city spat out by the hundreds. New York hadn't finished with her—that was some satisfaction. She left far more established than she'd arrived. Lara wasn't finished with New York. Still, she would never come back as anything more than a tourist; it was clear.

Her New York dream stillborn, she mouthed her goodbyes.

She didn't have time to wallow. Her father hadn't looked well before she left. She wasn't going to miss out on any more time with him.

Her dad sent her one email while she was gone: *Don't give up on your life because of me. Mine's already over. I can't take you with me.*

Her time in Manhattan was one long correspondence with her father, first on paper and then electronically. He typed the way he spoke, the way he wrote longhand. His letters were block-angled and sturdy, and his words, across either medium, were fluid, deep. Unrushed. The sudden brevity of his emails, once seven paragraphs or more, signaled his failing. Would she have realized sooner if he were still writing in ink, trying to move a pen in a trembling, tired hand? Could she have saved him?

Lara's response: *I'll be home soon! Love you, La.*

Two phone calls later, Lara was employed again. From account manager to assistant partner. Kathy O'Malley, a visiting professional Lara had met as a student at Syracuse, was starting her own public relations and marketing firm in Richmond on the heels of a campaign that helped turn around a national transportation franchise. Kathy wanted a partnership, offered Lara equal stake in the company. As she was paying for her father's experimental and expensive treatments, Lara had to pass. Still, Kathy never treated Lara like an employee.

Kathy and Lara picked their clients, focusing on who they loved and what accounts were profitable. No politicians—no money to be made there, no space for creativity. You could only do so much with red, white, and blue, and there were only so many ways to say, "I'm not like him, I'm like you." Strange how much easier it was to make products more exciting than people.

They hand-selected corporations, museums, restaurateurs, promoters from New York to Miami to brand and market. O'Malley Media was born and thrived.

When Lara and Kathy renovated the old shipping office in a corner of the massive Nolde Bros. Bakery, transformed it into O'Malley Media, the conference room was their showpiece. They punched through the outside wall and installed a ten-foot by eight-foot leaded glass window with 108 thick square panes. They peeled the paneling from the walls to expose the intricate chevron brick pattern. The room was light but private. From every vantage point, you could see the smallest detail on the screen that stretched down over the inside wall, in high resolution. For six months Lara searched for the right conference table. She decided on a large wooden door from an old fire-curing tobacco barn. She sealed it with polyurethane. Even the wormholes gleamed with every brush stroke. The twelve chairs around the conference table were nimble, small, and modern; they kept your posture in line and the client comfortable.

The December day Lara closed on her new row house, she drove the U-Haul from the storage unit to her parents' house first. All of her New York self fit into the small truck, furniture included. She had asked to take her dad to his last chemotherapy appointment. She hadn't meant to gasp when she saw him, helping him to the car, but she flinched at his papery touch, his cold fingertips. He'd always been ruddy in complexion, the same red she had tried to balance out in her own skin, but he wasn't red anymore. He was raw scallop-colored and nearly as translucent. It was disconcerting to see life and illness moving beneath his skin.

He shivered beneath three blankets during his last treatment, his eyes closed most of the time, the veins at his temples like a mountain range on a map.

"Goodbye, Mr. Jennings," the nurse said as she hugged him. Lara hoped she did that at every visit.

"Straight home, Dad?" Lara asked.

He shook his head. "We've got to make our last stop, like always." Ukrop's for a mint-chocolate chip milkshake, his weekly post-chemo treat.

"You sure?"

"It'll help get this horrible taste out of my mouth."

Once they arrived at the store, he refused to stay in the car, away from all of the people and their germs. "Not this time," he said.

He winced after his first bite. Unable to use a straw, he spooned the shake into his mouth. He shuffled more quickly to the sliding doors. As he hinged over the metal trash can beside the entrance, Lara gingerly pressed her palm against the knobs of his vertebrae after each retch. Neck burning, eyes stinging, she glared hard at anyone who stared— the women who shepherded their children closer to their sides. Lara set her mouth stiff, daring someone to speak. Her stomach shuddered. Anger was easier than watching the avian hump of her father's spine over the trash can that had to be filled with cigarette butts, half-empty beer cans, condoms, the poison that wasn't killing his cancer.

Thinned like the birds he so loved and shaped like the letters that filled his life, Ted was a spectacle for shoppers and passersby. Queasy to her bowels, Lara wouldn't show her father her revulsion. Once he was upright again, she dabbed bits of spit, flakes of chocolate and bile from the corners of his mouth with a Kleenex. She massaged his knuckles as she helped him back onto the sidewalk, closer to the car. Breathed only through her mouth.

"Brett, hold your sister's hand," a woman told her son, making a stop sign of her palm. She walked briskly to Lara and her father. "Can I give you two a hand?" She smelled like a fragrance department— too much, but it covered the stench of chemical puke. Lara was afraid he might faint. Could she catch him before he hit the concrete? She started to nod, but her father's head dropped. His grip tightened.

"We've got it covered," he said, releasing Lara's hand and walking on his own.

Lara smiled at the woman for not pressing it. Once the woman took her children into the store, Lara again offered her father her hand. He batted it away.

She hurried to the car and opened his door. He was winded by the third attempt to buckle his seat belt. As Lara closed the door she knew it was the last time they would drive home together.

Lara wouldn't speak with the gravel in her throat. He spoke for her. "You don't have to do this."

"I know," she said, turning on her blinker. "I want to."

"Since when does your mother have a better poker face than you?" he asked, turning to study her face.

She smiled, but kept facing the road. "Please, I play all my cards very close to the vest."

He cough-laughed. "I'm dying, La-la. I know that. But if I didn't, I'd realize it every time I looked at your face."

"Dad . . ." She couldn't refute him. She was trying so hard.

"You're trying so hard," he said. Had she spoken aloud? No. "You always try so hard. Your mother lives for this stuff. Don't deny her." He touched her shoulder. His fingers were the weight of a child's.

"You're not getting rid of me," she said.

"I don't want to. But go home. Get settled. Let your mother and the nurses perform the laying on of hands. Come back and read to me later. I'm going to ask a lot from you, things that would be impossible for your mother or Bea or the boys."

"It's a deal."

Her relief was acrid. She'd hate herself for it later, how he made her special and also dismissed her. But once back in her U-Haul she rolled down the windows to the damp winter cold. At her sink, she scrubbed her hands raw to get the stink of cancer and chemo and hospital solvent out of her skin.

She scheduled movers to help her with the larger furniture the next day, but she placed each box in the center of the rooms in her new house and hung her clothes on the single bar in her bedroom closet. The rooms in the nearly century-old home were small but many, with an antiquated parlor for receiving guests, even a tiny maid's closet between the back door and the cramped kitchen. The textured plaster walls were painted in dark plum and earthy tans. The stately crown molding was peeling. She would start painting the next day: White Dove high gloss for the molding and trim and doorways, Fresh White for the walls. Clean, bright. Polished. She could work miracles on her home, but not her father's health. Home improvements were visible by the day. So was his decline.

Each time her father failed, weakened, lost himself, Lara felt the match strike of hunger, of want. She had a lifetime's experience of suppressing her appetite. Her college roommate, Karen, called her on it freshman year when they stumbled from their first frat party to Pizza Mart. Everyone else gulped their pizza, slopping oil. Lara dumped the cheese in the trash, blotted the remaining oil, and savored her allotted three bites. Her stomach twisting for more pizza, she was fed by her self-control.

"I don't know how you do that," Karen said, her freckled cheeks and nose red from a night drinking keg beer.

"I was a fat kid a long time ago," she said matter-of-factly. "No bite will ever taste better than the first."

The burn of loss she used as fuel. If necessary she could run so far and so long that food turned repellent. And boys, then men, could make her feel even better than food—sinew, hips against her, and the artful use of tongue. So could winning, success. The strategy worked for years.

She couldn't keep her father alive. His looming absence became less deniable by the day, with every soiled sheet, his wan complexion, the way his clothes seemed to grow larger on his frame. This loss had incisors that tore deep and down. She was unprepared for this hunger.

New Years Eve at her parents' house, Lara's father looked less ragged. His downy strands of remaining hair had been combed to one side. He had his glasses on, his favorite pajamas. She kissed him on the cheek.

"Grab the bourbon from the freezer," he said.

She narrowed her eyes but smiled.

"And pour us both some," he directed. "I've made it through the year," he said. "A new millennium. That's something."

When she returned with two rocks glasses, each with two fingers of Black Maple Hill and three ice cubes, Ted almost looked like himself, except that he took up almost none of the bed. At least his bodily failures now happened privately. Lara didn't miss the traffic flow of the hospital or the way it was clear that her father could never really rest with the bed articulating to try and prevent blood clots, and the regular check of his vital signs. Home was so quiet without the machines and cuffs, the whirring and beeps.

They clinked glasses and sipped.

"What will we be reading tonight?" Ted asked.

He'd banned poetry. Poetry, he'd read himself, aloud, when he had the energy. If it weren't the poet performing the reading, Ted Jennings wanted to shape the words with his own mouth. He asked for narrative. Transportation but with depth. Lara had searched for hours. Afraid her choice would not measure up.

"*A Prayer for Owen Meany.*"

"Cheeky. Let's confront the many deaths and humors." He tried to yell, like Owen, in all caps. He achieved conversational volume.

"Always the comedian," she said.

In the stillness, Lara had to watch the flutter of the bedsheet as her father's breath hitched, when phlegm strangled his glottis. The quiver of his mouth after a cough, the phlegmy, then crusty, dry corners of his lips. The green hue of the sweat that beaded on his scalp after a hack, the few remaining strands of hair trembling like antennae. His wheezing attempts at breath, how his lips darkened purple to navy, and the hollows under his eyes. Even his skin had thinned.

So she read. When she read, an hour could pass under the spell of story. She trained her mind on inflection and meter and cadence and performance. As she read, her father's breathing would slow, as the hospice nurse silently slipped him more morphine.

Chapter Two

2000

In mid-January, after she had unpacked, repainted, and recycled her packing boxes from New York, Ted asked her to box up the books in his offices at home and on campus and to deliver certain titles to different members of the faculty. The fourth delivery was to the younger member of his department, Ted's favorite. Will James.

Lara studied the Post-It note, trying to camouflage her difficulty in reading her father's palsied script. "Both of these to office 206, right?"

"Yes, those are all for Will James. Hopefully you'll get to meet him."

"Why do you want to get rid of these now? Why not after—" She winced.

"They aren't doing anyone any good here. The pile just over there is for you but, of course, pull out any other titles you want. Have at them." She knew, eventually, even as she looked at him, that she would confuse his smell with the must of an old page behind a thick cover rarely opened. She would open them like spell books and try to conjure him. Yes, she knew she'd find deep gratitude for the stack later, but their presence reminded her of the inevitable. She tensed her jaw to keep from quivering, swallowed the thickness at the back of her tongue.

"Before you start missing me," he said, a cough catching on the double *s*, "I need to ask you an unforgivable favor."

She couldn't read his slack face anymore. All of his normal reactions and tells had tumbled into the deep lines. "Murder?" she asked. "Black market organ purchase? Name it, Dad."

"When you bring the books to campus, there's something else I need you to deliver first."

She frowned at this alien coyness. He ticked his head toward the books he'd set aside for her. The second one down had an envelope wedged between pages. She stood and retrieved it. The envelope was heavy in her hand, thick, with several folded pages inside. The outside said only *Ellie*, in smeared ink.

His fingers danced on the bedrail. "Eleanor Edwards," he said, his voice thickening, an involuntary twitch of a smile. "In the biology department. Give that to her. Please, La."

Holy shit, he had a girlfriend. Her perfect, always-putting-up-with-Beth father. The revelation was almost a relief, except where the bottom dropped out of her belly. "Alright," she stammered, shifted her weight, unsure just how much she really wanted to know. She composed herself, closed her mouth.

"It's not what you think," he said, closing his eyes. "Or maybe it is." She hated this unnerving eyes-closed talking. "We've been close for a long time."

"Dad . . . I really don't—"

He cleared his throat, opened his eyes, and fixed an almost familiar gaze directly on her for the first time in so long. "I wouldn't ask if I had any other choice. I'm so sorry to burden you with this."

"I'll do it," she said, unable to resist. "Does Beth know?"

He shook his head. "I've always told myself, justified it, that everyone deserves one big secret. Believe it or not, our companionship helped keep me grounded here, with all of you. But now . . ." Even he didn't say, *now that I'm dying*. He sighed and studied his IV.

"Don't you dare say a word to her," Lara said, going for humorous conspirator but landed on wounded sharp. Beth, crazy, over-the-top Beth deserved better than the truth, and Lara knew that she'd splinter into too many fragments, pointy and long-lasting, if both her husband and their life together was taken away. Lara bullshit-smiled at him.

"Thank you, La. You really are the toughest of us all."

Yes, Lara knew the truth, at least some of it. Did that keep her life from turning into a lie?

The woman's long fingers trembled slightly as she accepted the envelope from Lara, but that was the only break in her composure. Her eyes were dry and bright, elegantly whiskered with lines from the outside corners.

"Thank you," Eleanor Edwards said. Lara nodded and backed away. She wanted out of this office, away from this woman who likely knew her father better than anyone else. "Lara." She paused. "I've heard so very much about you." It had never occurred to Lara that her father would have discussed his children with her.

"You have an advantage there," Lara said, but not with cruelty.

"He wouldn't admit it, of course," Eleanor continued, "but he's thrilled you're home."

Lara had been so confused. Was she doing the right thing by moving back or was she just giving him the okay to die? His mistress, whatever she was to him, had validated her choice, answered the question she couldn't ask her father. She could be generous, too.

"Is there anything you want me to give him?" Lara asked.

"No, dear. This is your time with him," Eleanor said.

Lara walked back into the hallway, dizzy. Of course he had been drawn to her. She was refined. Intelligent. Calm. None of those words could be used to describe her childhood home. And Eleanor loved him enough to back off when she'd probably never see him again. Noble, even.

Lara would keep their secret, not just from her mother and siblings. She would keep this secret, the last part of her father that would remain hers alone. She'd never kept a secret as big as this one but she knew once she fought the first impulse to tell, it would get easier.

The peace she felt was surprising. She'd expected a snarling roil in her gut, but instead just a steady beat of heart and breath as she headed back to the car. The box of books on the passenger seat—no real trunk to speak of in Sadie, her Saab—would be harder to deliver than the letter.

Lara didn't know the Ted Jennings that Eleanor would recognize in his letter. Lara always knew her father in the context of books. He was never without at least two, whether they were slim chapbooks of up-and-coming poets, or a field guide, *Walden* or Whitman. At home he drummed his fingers against their covers while someone, usually her mother or brothers, was speaking. He showed Lara how to search for themes in a text. How to learn a word's meaning through context.

"A word is never fixed, La," Ted explained. "It never means just one thing. It reinvents itself in company."

"Like I do with friends and clothes," adolescent Lara had quipped.

"Sort of." He had smiled.

Ted had three to-read piles—one in each office and one in his bedroom. He refused to put an unread book on a shelf—a title would get lost that way. He couldn't read in order, either, because some new tome would arrive and take precedence over what had surfaced at the top of the stack, piles perpetually the same height. Until this morning. Only Lara's small collection remained at the house. The rest she was giving away as her father instructed.

Fortunately the faculty parking lot was just around the corner from the English building, because the box was unspeakably heavy. She had to set it down in order to open the exterior door and again once partway down the hallway. Her shoelace had slipped out of its knot. She wanted to be in and out, stealth, not bumbling down the corridor. She passed the door with her father's name beside it. English Department Chair Theodore Jennings, PhD. She was eight the first time she could reach, bump her fingers over the letters of his name. Richmond said they would save his office for Ted until his return.

"Such a waste," he'd said. "They should give an adjunct a home."

The realization that her father would never again open this door was physical, sharp, a bramble wedged deep into the soft webbing between toes.

The connection between Lara and her father had never required effort. She was content in the silence of his office, pleased to share the adult space, his natural habitat. He sat at his desk and doodled with a pen while his mind unlocked the puzzle of a poem, worked to make it new for his students. Lara would lay a piece of paper over the dust jackets of his books and trace the cover art. She copied the prints he hung in his office: Agasse's giraffe, Audubon's cardinal and ibis. With a fat pink eraser, she could undo any error. Even into her twenties, Ted Jennings was Lara's quiet place.

Lara knew that if she opened that door, her father's office, with the décor he hadn't changed in twenty-five years, she would never be able to close it. Better to leave the door shut and keep walking. All she wanted was to drop the box of books and get out of the English building. Her father's office and the long empty hallway felt like the inside of some cavernous sarcophagus missing her father's body.

Finally she heard signs of life: a voice from the open door two offices down, low and rocky, turbulent. "Melody, this is the third extension you've requested this semester."

"But, Professor." A high, juvenile voice.

"I have all of Dr. Jennings's notes here. I know his recent leave has been difficult on all of you, but this pattern was established months ago."

"If I don't pass, I don't graduate."

"I'm aware of how that works," the man said. A smart ass, nice. She could see why her father liked him.

"Please, Dr. James, I'm so overwhelmed right now."

"Send me what you have started and I'll give you my answer by tomorrow." Tough, but fair. Check. A chair squeaked. The girl looked surprised to see Lara as she exited. Lara set the box down in the office doorway, her biceps shaking, and looked up at William James. She had assumed he would be white-haired and bulldog shaped by his voice.

"I'm—"

"Lara Jennings," he interrupted. "It's your eyes; they're the same as Ted's," he said. "And, of course, the books."

He stepped around her and grazed her lycra-coated thigh before hinging over and easily hefting the box of books from the floor. "You carried these all of the way from your car?" he asked with a nod, impressed. "Sorry, where are my manners? I'm Will," he said, one large, calloused hand extended toward her.

Her urge to cry abruptly receded, but her body, her mind, all of her senses stretched wire-tight. She was sure to be shocked, static electricity, if they touched. The air between them held a charge. His eyes cased her body like a thief. It was all so confusing. She shook the offered hand anyway, enjoying the thickening tendons the length of his forearm. She pulled away first.

"He wants you to have these," she said.

"Thank you." It was hot, his refusal to pretend that there was no need, that Ted would be fine and wanting his books back. The lack of sentimentality, sexy. "I'm going to hate it here without him," Will said with a slow, sheepish smile and shrug of his shoulders.

"Yes," Lara agreed, even though she knew Will meant work and she meant the world.

One morning just after Valentine's Day, Ted's breath refused to calm. Lara saw death on the faces of the nurses, and in her mother's troubling of the tchotchkes she stashed all over the house, her sweepstakes talismans.

"Read," he said. She had never seen her father afraid.

Lara rested her hand on his bed, aftershocks of spasms radiating across her skin. She read. He coughed. Sputtered. Choked. Each inhale startled her, as the exhale preceding it had hissed with finality. Ted stopped speaking sometime mid-morning. His eyes were open and wild, searching but unfocused.

Her mother lumbered into the room but never lasted more than a few minutes. *Not helping, Beth.* She was a disaster. Wailing and hurling questions at the air. Her behavior was more disgusting than cancer, more embarrassing than Lara could imagine. This moment wasn't about her mother. One of the nurses, Mallory, held Beth in her thick, dimpled arms. Her hair was bright silver, cut short.

"He isn't in pain," Mallory said. "He doesn't feel this. The major organs fail in turn. When he stopped eating, he stopped because he wasn't hungry. His stomach, his intestines, those went early. Now his brain is slumbering. Other organs are more stubborn."

"Like they've all been handed pink slips," Lara said to the other nurse, Alexa, who increased the morphine drip. She was younger than Mallory, somewhere between Beth and Lara's age. "Each organ. Laid off. One by one."

"Yes, kind of like that," Alexa said. "He knows nothing of the pain you're in watching him go."

"Does he know we're here?" Beth asked, words muffled against Mallory's shoulder.

Mallory stepped back to look Beth in the face. "He knew you were here this morning," she said. "He's moved on now, but we'll make sure he isn't alone. This probably isn't how you want to remember him. It's certainly not how he would want to be remembered."

"I—I should call the other children," Beth said, looking to Mallory for agreement.

Mallory nodded. "Let's go in the kitchen, make some tea, call your kids." Beth let her lead out of the room.

How dare she. No wonder he'd needed someone else. This weakness, at a moment that begged for strength, made Lara sick. It was better with her mother out of the room. Lara had to make up for the defects, the failures of the rest of her family. Her father deserved at least that much.

Lara kept reading, her eyes trained on the shaking text on the page. After Irving, he had requested Coetzee's *Disgrace*. It had made them both uncomfortable enough to forget why she was reading. He could no longer hear, but she couldn't stop reading. Her father was a blur of pain and death in her periphery. She wanted to sprint out of the door out onto the lawn across the road; she wanted to run and run and run until she couldn't take another step, run until she could look behind her and realize the threat was only a blur. It was hairy-throated, wet teeth, ankle-itching feeling, her need to run.

She wanted to run like the first day she learned she was fast. Her thighs had burned as she ran away; they burned in the middle where they rubbed, the seams of her shorts thick and driving up to her crotch. The boys were fast, vulpine Scotty Broderson leading the pack, their bodies lithe and lean, legs gaping with air between them.

"Come back, Lardo," Scotty taunted through braces. Lardo Lara. No one's name was safe from ridicule—all could be bent and boy-handled and hawked back, a linguistic loogie. Lardo. On the eighth day of sixth grade, Lara was nearly expelled for kicking Scotty in the groin.

He'd spotted her tugging down her shorts to try and hide the bulge where they met. "Lardo legs," he yelled in the courtyard, drawing the attention of the entire middle school.

She walked toward the steps back into school. Scotty blocked her. "Hey, Lardo."

"Shut up," she'd said and shuffled sideways. So did Scotty. Her face was hot. Her nose began to run.

"Lardo. Lardo!" He'd yelled, his cheeks puffed out. He swung his arms like an ape, pretending he had a fat stomach even though Lara's tummy was flat. She carried all of her weight behind her and below. A chant shivered through the crowd. Kids, most of them taller than Lara, closed in.

"Shut up," she said again. And then she struck, Keds to crotch. As he crumpled to his knees, his navy Lands' End backpack tumbling down, the assistant principal dispersed the crowd.

In his office, later, her mother thin-lipped and taut-belly pregnant beside her, the assistant principal had said Lara would not be expelled. "You can't let yourself be baited into violence. If someone wants to make trouble, walk away."

Walking, she could still hear the names they called her, but if she ran, she was quick and she could run long. The boys got winded after a few blocks and had to stop.

The same urge to flee prickled under her skin now. She wanted to be out. She wanted to escape. She couldn't watch this. She couldn't watch him. She was the only one there. The front door had slammed. Beth was moaning in the backyard. She wouldn't leave him to the nurses and their polite discretion. If she looked up from the book, the wrestle with death would chase her from the house, too. She kept on. Lara never tired.

Ted's death was not peaceful. Or brief. His chest convulsed. His hands opened and closed like he was falling, reaching for something he would never catch. His head flopped, side to side, his eyes unblinking. She kept reading until the only sound in the room was the scratch of her hoarse voice. She held his hand until it stiffened, cooled in her own. Then she ran.

Chapter Three

In early July, Will took her to his cathedral, the James River. Although she'd spent her childhood on its banks, fishing with her dad, she always avoided the rough water and the algae-glazed rocks, the places where Will felt at home. He'd suggested a tandem boat for her first trip.

"I'll feel like a child," she said.

He relented, then cinched her life jacket tight, fat strips of nylon under her arms, the click of plastic buckles under sure fingers. He bonked the crown of her matching orange helmet, then took his shirt off before donning his life vest and rolling up his shorts. Her first lingering view of his tattoo—a wonderland beneath the staid clothes—ripped from a style guide for creative writing professors. An image of strained thigh, a line of white skin, tanned knee, swirled blood loud in her ears. She could barely hear his paddling instructions: how to turn, how to stop, how to recover.

"Go where the water takes you. Don't fight it." His summation.

Her bikini bottom wet in the seat of the kayak, she pushed off after him. He paddled an olive Perception and rented Lara a citrus FeelFree. She paddled flat water, fast, hoping to impress.

"Take it easy. It'll get exciting on its own."

Her kayak bumped over the first small cascade of rocks. She wanted to pull her legs out of the foot brace, felt cut in half, as she whirled in the eddy beneath the rocks. The reflecting sun off the river spun and blurred into watercolor. *Breathe.*

His arms swept long, languid strokes; his paddle barely splashed. They approached the next rock steps, Will in front. Above Lara was the pedestrian bridge where she'd jogged over so many M&M–colored boats. Cool shadow. Will skimmed over the rocks, bow just off-center, graceful. Lara hit the next rock sideways, jarred, then dropped over the second set, capsized on the third.

Her paddles flung up and out, her grip slackening. "Will!"

River water fire-hosed her mouth. Her head bounced against rock. She flailed her arms, tried to right herself, but kept falling, crashing. A muffled crack of paddle against stone, her hand wedged, open. She clawed at the algae, grasses slid through her fingertips. Water up her nose. She threw her hips around, had to get out. Stuck, she couldn't move her legs. Muddy brown, all she could see. Hysteria. *Don't swallow the water.* Lungs afire.

A softer collision, her body wrenched. Bright sun. Will's arms around her, his breath on her cheek. "You're out of the water."

He lifted her Raggedy Ann body from the cockpit and helped her to shore. She vomited river mud and snot; his hand on the back of her neck, his other arm holding her up. His arms, those thighs, fresh air into clotted lungs.

"Too much, too soon, perhaps," Will said before swimming to rescue the lost paddle, and Lara's security deposit.

—

That evening, finally warm and dry, Lara's doorbell rang. Her heart pitched—maybe Will was surprising her with dinner. She tightened her robe and wanded mascara through her lashes before heading to the door. A second impatient ring, unlike Will. She opened the door to a teary, extra-frazzled Beth.

"Mom, what's wrong?" No way her mother had heard about her misadventure on the water. Beth trundled inside, her hair scattered and messy. Lara could barely remember her mother without gray hair. Beth's was not a dignified silver. Her roots were suspended in perpetual grow out, and the ends splayed, shaggy from a bad layered cut. When Lara was a child, Beth wore her hair short like a French woman, a confident woman's haircut.

"It's your sister." Her body a sigh. "Paul left her."

"Oh." Lara walked into the kitchen in search of wine. Her cell phone lay on the counter; no missed calls. "Is she okay?" Lara asked, opening a bottle. "She's not surprised, I hope."

Over the bouquet on her sister's wedding day, Lara had smelled the proximity of divorce on the groom's bourbon breath.

She poured two glasses, though Beth would only take a sip or two.

"Stop being so sharp." Sharp, her mother's favorite reprimand. Sharp meant focus, intensity, not suffering fools. Lara was proud of her sharp parts. Bea was married at twenty-three, had two babies by twenty-seven. What could she possibly expect? "It lasted almost six years. That's respectable for a starter marriage these days."

"And now she's stuck with an ex-husband and two kids to raise."

If you were a cliché, could you tell?

"What about you?" Beth led an offensive. "All you focus on is work and whatever race you're training for next. Time is running out for you to start a family."

Wine, cool and oaky on Lara's tongue. She was thirty-two and all of her clocks were digital. No ticking hands. She wasn't ready to admit how stupid in love she was with Will, so smart, sexy, aloof. She hadn't even told him, though she'd fallen harder than her kayak off the rocks. Beth stood no chance in this linguistic arms race. "A baby is hardly an accomplishment. Any dumb mammal can give birth."

Lara's words landed hard on Beth, forced her gaze down. Silence.

Lara had finished third grade when Beth told her and Bea that she was pregnant again. Lara had said, "No one else's mom is having babies anymore."

Beatrice was Lara's baby doll. She could change Bea's diaper, with her mother's help, but she could also escape her babyness. She knew how to get herself shooed away for causing trouble or over exciting her sister. She crafted the perfect wounded affect to hide her thrill in exile, back to the big kid room with choking hazards for toys and a step stool so she could get her own glasses of water. Beatrice needed their mother for everything, whereas Lara could balance her neediness and her self-sufficiency. And she got her mother all to herself before bedtime.

But once the twins were born, she was expected to help. She had never resented Bea the way she hated the boys. By age twelve, Lara was done with babies. For good.

When, as a teenager, Lara complained to her father of Beth's nosiness, her pestering, the constant "what are you thinking nows," Ted had admonished her. "When your mother had you, then Bea and the boys, everything else fell away."

"Like she fell apart?"

"No. Like nothing else could compare to what being a mother felt like to her. Her teaching, nothing else makes as much sense to her as you four do. Trust me, it took me a while to parse that out."

Her mother was quiet through the remainder of Lara's glass of wine. Then she gathered her purse and rain coat and stood. "Get this out of your system now. Bea's driving up in the morning. She needs you."

Need. The word tasted like aspirin left too long before swallowing, dissolving too early on the tongue. Lara agreed to go into work late, after a stop by her mother's the next morning, as she eased Beth out the door. Lara imagined that if her father were alive he would have been on her side. But would he? He had been such a natural with Bea's boys. They were immediate favorites, even when they spit up on his starched dress shirts.

A beep from the kitchen, her phone, a message from Will: *How's my love tonight? May I come over and check on you?*

Love. She waited half an hour to respond. *Of course.*

The following morning, Lara arrived at Beth's house with a briefcase full of her best sisterly intentions. She was sad to think of her sister alone with two small children to raise. How taxing and self-denying that had to be. She wouldn't let Bea see how she really felt.

Beth answered the door in her robe. "Behave," she said as Lara walked into the house.

"Of course," Lara whispered.

Bea's eyes were pouched from too many tears and too little sleep. Her hair frizzed up above her crown from a restless night and no brushing. Bea met Lara in the foyer, wearing a sloppy man's T-shirt and threadbare pajama pants. Lara reached out to hug her sister, but Bea was wary.

After a mumbled hello, Bea told her, "I'm not interested in you being *right* right now."

Bea was as tall as their father; Lara's heels almost leveled their eyes. She had always envied Bea for looking like a beautiful version of their dad—burnished gold hair, tall and strong. All Lara could claim were his eyes, dark and deep. The rest of her face, her stature, was all Beth. Bea troubled her gold hoop earring, shifting it back and forth. That beauty was still evident beneath her puffy skin and morning breath, but Bea would have to get it together or she'd be single for a very long time.

The boys thundered downstairs, a hydra of noise and limbs. Missing teeth and that grassy, verdant boy smell. "Hi, guys," Lara said, reaching out to ruffle their hair, but they ran through the living room and into the kitchen where Beth had arranged cereal bowls and glasses of milk.

"It's so good to see you," Lara said. "I'm sorry about all of this."

Bea sank into the couch. "Thank you for coming over."

Lara couldn't help herself. "He's at least going to share custody, right?"

Bea took a deep breath. "Yes, some anyway. But I get primary." She smiled.

Lara was baffled. They looked just like her soon-to-be ex-husband. Two living, breathing bodies of reproach, reminding her of her childish mistakes with each chewed sippy cup and runny nose.

"Of course he'd stick you with the boys."

A tremor shook Bea's chest. She turned away from Lara, clenching jaw and eyes shut. The hand at her ear shook. Beth moved to sit beside Bea, sandwiching her hand between her palms. Bea's eyes looked far away once she opened them.

"Lower your voice. I don't want them to hear any of this. And I couldn't bear to be without them for too long," Bea said.

"So are you going to move home?" Nothing would please Beth more than Bea trading Lynchburg for home. *Marmee's aching for her Meg.*

"Lynchburg is home now," Bea said, studying her lap.

"Sometimes we have to make the best of a bad situation," Beth said.

Just like their mother, Bea insisted on blooming where planted no matter how poor the earth. Sloppy women making sloppy, reactive decisions. "I like it there."

Will proposed to Lara during the last month of Bea's state-mandated separation. The looming divorce was the perfect excuse for a simple elopement. They spoke their vows in University Chapel before the chaplain and cemented them with a heavy make-out session against a tree beside Westhampton Lake, a crunch of crimson leaves beneath their feet, sun-warmed bark against Lara's back. No frilly dress or fattening cake. No awkward silence where the father-daughter dance should be. The only song Lara could have imagined sharing with her father, Doris Day's "Again," had been the soundtrack for his funeral. An ending isn't a suitable beginning, however true the sentiment: a memory may last forever, but the moment is evanescent.

Lara had a new family of two, and her initials wouldn't even have to change.

Chapter Four

2004

Every morning for fourteen years, Lara had popped a small round pill from the foil blister pack and swallowed it before she brushed her teeth. No day started any differently. For nearly a decade and a half, Lara ensured she did not get pregnant.

If she needed antibiotics for a sinus infection, Will wore a condom. Of course they made love, and often; they just wouldn't make a baby. Her body listened. She made no mistakes. She kept it from doing what it wanted, what it was made to do. But now she was ready; her body would understand. It was time.

Lara couldn't point to the date when she started seeing babies everywhere. Or when her response to infants shifted from *ugh* to *maybe* to *yes, please, please, yes*. Every celebrity was having babies, all of her friends had babies, even the holdouts. She found herself making faces at a fat-cheeked little boy while in line for coffee. Each time his dark, toothless mouth spread open, she wanted to make him smile again and again, bigger next time, like an addict chasing a high. Once she indulged the maternal fantasy, it took hold.

Calories in minus calories out. Hours billed, copy approved, strategy implemented. After the heady, hectic O'Malley start-up years, Lara's days had become a long string of transactions, most of them repetitive. The clients changed, sure, just as she varied her running distances and mixed up her routine by lifting weights, experimenting with plyometrics. She and Will had traveled and stretched out their honeymoon well past their return home. Daily life stayed the same. She missed having someone in her life that she wanted, needed to impress. She missed her father's warm palm on her neck. His words: *you're marvelous. You've made your mother and me so proud.* She missed his gaze, the way it made her feel known. His eyes had not reflected Lara; they had given her shape. She had looked everywhere inside her world for that kind of knowing since. It hadn't been born yet.

Will had agreed to her stopping birth control. The conversation hadn't lasted more than a few minutes. They sat in the rectangular backyard, bracketed on three sides by high fences, beneath the cross hatch of wires and utility poles that graphed the night sky. She'd been reviewing her notes from a meeting earlier that day. He sat grumbling over student work.

"You're serious?" He set down the papers he'd been grading.

"Yes," she'd said. "Why not? Let's give it a try." She held her breath until he answered.

"I'm game if you are."

He'd been surprised when she told him that she wanted to get pregnant but didn't fight her on it. "You were the one who sold me on the benefits of childlessness. But if it makes you happy," he said. She had been prepared to argue. Every conversation was a pitch, if you looked at it properly, a move toward a desired outcome.

"I'm thrilled you came around," he said. He picked up his papers with a smile.

Flouting the ob-gyn nurse's recommendation to wait at least three months after taking her last birth control pill before trying to conceive, Lara surprised Will in his office.

Already she had a secret. Will didn't know the remaining pills punctuated the bathroom trashcan. Unlimited and encouraged, unprotected sex with her *sexyashell* husband was too good to resist. His body, beneath the too-large button-downs he wore, was long but not lanky, solid but not bulky. He had a body molded out of doors. Safe. Sexy, if stolid.

She had only spruced him up over the years: buying his clothes, matching those oversized shirts to pants, swapping smelly Tevas for polished loafers. Otherwise he would wear the same jeans, oblivious to fraying hems and pockets. The strong jaw and navy eyes were there from the start, only obscured by unruly, pine-bark brown hair. She loved to twist the few graying curls at his neck around her fingers. He looked too big for any chair, his knees always angled up. In his lap, the branches of his arms, Lara was small.

The University of Richmond English department was mid–reading period, in between semesters, with no active classes. She saw no one else as she passed the sky-pointing Boatwright library, its gothic spires looming above the old-growth deciduous trees; the cathedral openings in the cement could house a luminous Rapunzel. When the campus echoed with students, Will often hid in the stacks, reading and writing, away from hands knocking on his office door.

Like the brick pathways around the secluded campus, the high-ceilinged hallway to Will's office was empty. No hum of fluorescent lights in the corridor; like students, much of the faculty were away. The clack of her heels against marble turned her on. Will's door was cracked; a triangle of light spilled out onto the hallway floor.

"Professor James." Lara knocked and pushed the door in one motion. "I need your help with something."

He looked up at her over his glasses, then took them off. After laying a book down, he ran his hand through the curls that flopped

31

over his forehead when he bent over reading. He smiled and leaned back into his chair. She would trace her finger over the line that formed between the corners of his eye and lips when he smiled, the attraction as immediate as the morning they met nearly four years ago.

"A midday visit from my busy wife," he said. "What have I done to deserve this?" He spun the gold band on his finger. Thoughtful, nervous, aroused—that's when he wound his wedding band.

With her back, she closed the door, her whole body smiling. She pressed the thumb lock, muffling the click with her palm. He raised an eyebrow. She stretched her legs long as she stepped across his office, stood between him and his desk, and then perched on the edge. Despite the papers, folders, notebooks stacked on the floor, and the shelves heavy with journals and texts, the only items on his desk, ever, were his laptop, an elementary-school marbled composition notebook, and whichever novel he was reading, today Hesse's *Journey to the East*. Two framed photographs. One of them from the weekend he proposed and the other a black-and-white shot he took of her asleep in the car after their first marathon.

"I'm here to work on the joint project we discussed," she said.

He shimmied her into his lap. She fulfilled the promise she made to the lines on his face and his eyebrows, threaded her legs around his hips, ankles gripping the leather seat back, came out loud. Before returning to her office, she smoothed her black, bobbed hair and reapplied lip gloss in the reflection of his doctoral degree from the University of Virginia.

"I would have agreed to a baby a long time ago had I any idea," Will told Lara two weeks later. They had made love every day since her unannounced visit to his office.

Her body, when regulated by birth control hormones, operated with military precision. Her period started no later than the eighteenth of each month, and the bleeding ebbed by the twenty-second, the twenty-fourth on the outside. Off birth control, her body was less predictable. Will could have gotten her pregnant any of those times, hard to tell.

The calendar didn't hint to Lara that she was pregnant; her gag reflex proclaimed it. Lara was awake and preparing to leave for the day, before Will came downstairs, their normal routine. She sniffed the milk twice before pouring it into her travel coffee mug. It smelled off, too grassy. She cooked her hurried breakfast of egg whites and wilted baby spinach on the gas, stainless-steel cooktop, flopped open the *Richmond Times-Dispatch* while standing to eat at the marble counter as she did every weekday. She stabbed at the eggs and spinach and moved a bite into her distracted mouth. At once, the eggs were scalding and gelatinous. They slid around her tongue, runny and revolting, the texture of snails. They held a taste of the fork, metallic and gritty. She lunged to the sink and spat.

"Oh, God," she said aloud. Despite the leather briefcase on the slate tile floor and her Italian leather heels, Lara was twenty-two again and unmarried and unprepared, her life circling the garbage disposal in the deep sink. So fast, too damn fast. She wanted this, to be pregnant. That was the whole point, after all, but maybe not just yet.

What about work? Motherhood changed a woman. The most organized, confident employee returned from maternity leave disheveled, distracted, late each morning. Lara worked, even when she wasn't working. Ambition had been her child for decades—fed, strengthened, followed. Could she both mother and succeed?

The transition from JV to varsity sex, the hormonal goalie pulled from the net, was so much fun. A baby, though, growing inside her already? Stretch marks, a big ass, swelling breasts, a third person where two were just fine, more than fine. What she'd wanted, so readily obtained. Too easy. Giddy, quaking, Lara swung the spectrum.

Will walked down the steps. Lara flipped the switch for the disposal, ran the faucet, and scraped what was left of her uneaten breakfast off of the plate and away. His aftershave wafted into the kitchen before him. *Overdid it a little this morning, honey.*

"Good morning," he said, leaning in for a kiss. She gave him her cheek and held her breath, not ready to tell. He walked to the refrigerator. She filled her lungs.

"Good morning to you. I'm on my way out, but there are eggs on the stove." Her keychain clinked as she reached into her briefcase.

"Thanks, I'll call you later."

"Bye," she said with a wave and walked out.

On her way to work she went to CVS. A swoony head and upset stomach could be payback for the extra glass of wine last night. No reason to panic or think she was pregnant if she wasn't. Her heart double-timed as she walked over to the pregnancy tests, past the condoms that had once spiked her pulse, prickled her cheeks. She selected a pink and white two-pack early pregnancy test kit that boasted, "results up to five days before your period."

She dropped a 20 oz Diet Coke, two bottles of Essie nail polish, and an *InStyle* magazine into the basket to make the purchase casual. Nonetheless, the red-smocked checkout girl smiled at her and said, "Good luck!"

Lara balled up the bag and shoved it into her briefcase. She crumpled the receipt and threw it into the trashcan just outside the sliding glass door.

At work, she forced herself to scan her inbox and chitchat with her assistant and junior executive before going into the bathroom, test kit in her pocket and a bottle of water in hand. Lara checked for feet under the three stalls, as though she were about to sneak a smoke in the high school girls' room. Seeing none, she ducked into the center stall, set the water bottle on the floor, and read the pregnancy test directions. *Should be fairly simple.*

She tore open the first test stick, squatted, and peed, counting *one-one thousand, two-one thousand, three-one thousand, four-one thousand, five-one thousand, six-one thousand, seven-one thousand* . . . Her fingers were wet and warm. Pee splattered the toilet seat, but the indicator line filled; processing.

Two minutes, the instructions said—at least two minutes but not more than ten. She placed the stick flat on top of the metal waste bin, and then she emptied her bladder and wiped off the seat. She looked at her watch. *Wait till one and a half, and then you can look.* And there it was, less than two minutes: a dark pink cross, a plus sign, bled up into the test result window.

She ripped open the second stick with her teeth, gulped the contents of the water bottle and peed again. Same result. She took a picture of the test stick with her cell phone. She threw both away, wrapped three times around in toilet paper and jammed into the bottom of the trashcan. She included no subject line or explanation when she emailed the photo to Will.

Her phone buzzed before she got it back into her pocket.

"Wow," Will said. "Already?"

"Yup." *Already.*

"We did it."

"Looks like." *A baby.*

"I love you, Lar."

"You, too. Gotta go." She hung up. No one at the office could know. One of the junior executives would measure her office, picture herself at Lara's desk the second word whispered around. Career suicide.

Less than a month later, Lara and Will had their first prenatal appointment. The doctor raised Lara's blouse and lowered her skirt before squirting cold gel onto her still-flat stomach. Miles after miles run, planks held, and calories meticulously counted bought the shadowy ridges between her abdominal muscles, the definition from her hipbones down to the center of her thighs. Slowly, the softening of this sinew appealed to Lara. She imagined her belly sprawling and was not repulsed.

35

The balding obstetrician removed the Doppler machine from the outside pocket of his lab coat. He patted the top as though it were a microphone, gold class ring heavy on thin fingers. "Is this thing on?" he asked with the head bob of a lounge comic.

Lara and Will laughed on cue, too loud and tight-throated.

"So put it on already," Lara said. She slipped her hand off of the examination table and Will filled it with his own. Will studied the doctor as he spread out the gel across Lara's pubis.

"It's early, so it can take me a minute to find it," the doctor said as he pressed the Doppler against Lara's abdomen, just above her pubic bone. Quiet. "Don't panic," the doctor said. He slid the Doppler to the side.

Galloping hoof beats. That's what the heartbeat would sound like. She had looked it up online.

The doctor tried her other side. Nothing. He repositioned the Doppler farther up. *Whump, whump.* Lara gasped.

"That's you," the doctor said. "Too slow."

"Oh."

He moved the Doppler again and again.

"I'm afraid I'm not picking anything up. I'm sorry."

"And you're sure it's on?" Will's voice cracked, despite his stab at levity.

The doctor nodded. "I'll keep checking for another minute or two. But if I don't get anything, I'll send you over for an ultrasound to confirm." The last phrase mumbled.

"Confirm what?"

"Fetal mortality."

In the ultrasound room, Lara and Will held hands, fingers a loose knot. Lara lay on the table. Will stood beside her, against the door to the bathroom. Between Lara's knees, splayed wide by the stirrups holding her feet, the hugely pregnant ultrasound technician prepared what looked like a giant white dildo, sheathed in a condom and dewy with lubricant. She slid it inside Lara. Each time the transducer bumped up against it, Lara's cervix burned. The doctor, with his back to Lara, faced the monitor. On the screen was a gray tadpole curled up like a shrimp without its shell.

"The heartbeat would register as a flash," the doctor standing next to the tech said, his hands in his pockets.

"Flash of what?"

"Light."

"This has all happened so fast," Lara said. The tangle of emotions in her stomach, heart, and mind wouldn't straighten into a line to follow. Much ado about nothing and yet, something big.

"We'll step outside," the doctor said. He and the tech closed the curtain behind them before exiting.

Will let go of Lara's hand and collected her clothes. When he turned his back, Lara wiped the paper drape between her legs to stop the fluid and lubricant that dripped out of her. She removed her feet from the stirrups and awkwardly dismounted the table. Will stood still, his arms full of her clothes.

"I'm sorry," Will said.

"Me, too."

"We weren't prepared for it to happen so fast," he said. Lara shivered, still naked from the waist down. Too bare.

"I'll take those," she said, reaching for her skirt, underwear, and shoes.

"Oh, of course." He handed her the panties. She waved for the rest. He studied her as she dressed. He unfastened the sling backs of her shoes.

"I can do that," she said. She needed to get dressed so he could hold her, so she could cry on his shoulder, not with him as an observer. Shoes on, skirt straightened, Lara stepped to Will. He placed his hands on her shoulders and kissed her forehead.

"Let's go see what the doctor has to say," Will said.

Lara and Will met the doctor in his office.

"What does this mean?" Will asked.

Lara stared at the papers on his desk, avoiding the posters of the different stages of fetal development framed on the walls.

"This is quite common," the doctor said, massaging the bridge of his nose. "Most miscarriages occur before you're even aware of pregnancy. It's the gynecological equivalent of a throat clearing."

Again, Will. "What next?"

"Lara, you'll likely miscarry on your own in the next week or so. If you don't, please call. We have options to speed things up. It's healthier, though, for you and your body to try and let it happen."

Four days later, Lara's uterus clenched, coiled tight into a fist. A baby, reduced to gray and red clumps, fell hot then cold against her inner thighs. Her belly flexed, a strong internal ball, the outsides as firm as India rubber, as it squeezed and released.

Lara tried to change the first pad standing up in the white-tiled and sleek gray-walled bathroom. She never wasted the time to sit down on the toilet for a routine tampon change. Pull the string, shove it in the wrapper, drop in trash, insert new one, wash hands, and move on. She never wore pads in the daytime, though, so this wasn't routine. She yanked down her pants and underwear. Pubic hair, wet and gleaming, red and purple, clumped in curls. Between her legs was a crime scene. The skin where thigh met pubis red-smeared, her legs stuck together. Bright drops of blood dripped from the lip of the toilet, landed, splattered on the white tile beneath her feet, splashed and stained. It was the blood of fairy tales, the doomed virgin lip, a puncture from a spinning wheel.

She needed four overnight-sized maxi pads to dispose of it. The amount of blood and the speed and rhythm of her body pushing out the tiny dead baby, now in pieces, startled Lara.

Her first on-purpose pregnancy ended before it began.

Chapter Five

"It was too soon, anyway."

Lara said it over and over, to Will and to herself. She wouldn't be the woman who let her quest for a baby take over her life. Her first instincts whispered she was not ready to be pregnant right away. She wouldn't go overboard because of an early lost pregnancy immediately off birth control.

The day after her miscarriage, while Will showered, Lara stood in her bra and panties before the full-length mirror on the back of the closet door. Bikinis and cover-ups had been shuttled to the attic in October. Her fall wardrobe was punctuated with clothes intended for layering, loose T-shirts, skirts with stretch, light sweaters. She slid her hands down from the top of her rib-cage to the lace seam of her underwear, turning to see her body in profile. Her belly was flatter, though what bled out of her had not held the mass of a lime. She missed the swell that could have simply been PMS, the same bump she couldn't wait to get rid of each month.

Will appeared in the reflection beside her, his chest and arms bare, pink and beaded wet from the shower, a towel knotted at his waist. She blinked. Then she smiled.

"You sure you're okay?"

A minor setback. The old Lara would have led him by his tousled hair onto their bed.

"Of course," she said.

The soft space where her thighs met was a wound. She smiled bigger, ruffled his hair in her hand. He patted her ass and turned away.

She'd fooled him.

Move forward. Onward and upward.

Each month she Googled early pregnancy symptoms. Initially she logged in only from work. She experienced psychosomatic breast tenderness. Or slight cramping that could signal embryonic implantation.

As soon as the doctor cleared her to start trying again, Lara concealed her fixation. She could find the feminine hygiene aisle of any pharmacy blindfolded and spun, like swinging at a piñata or pinning the tail on a donkey. Pharmacy layouts were orderly and specific—an entire aisle, both sides, devoted to toothbrushes, toothpastes, plaque rinses, mouthwashes, shelf above shelf of all things oral hygiene. The shaving aisle was his and hers, razors and shaving creams; aftershave on his side, Nair and tweezers on hers. Deodorant stood sentinel on the end caps.

The feminine hygiene aisle broke the code of the rest of the pharmacy. At the start of the aisle on the left was baby formula (at the Rite-Aid it was kept locked behind plastic shutters). Above the formula were breast care supplies, bottles of witch hazel, Lansinoh creams, and nursing pads. Bright yellow and green tubes of Preparation H. Below the formula hung bottles and pacifiers. Across from the formula were the condoms—no wonder men never wanted to wear them, reminded of what they were trying to prevent—lubricants, pregnancy tests (also on lockdown at Rite-Aid), ovulation kits, and tubes of Vagisil and Monistat yeast infection remedies.

Beside the bottles, maxi pads crowded into lumpy rectangular containers (pads for light days, regular, heavy, overnight, overnight extra-long with wings, even thong-shapes). Next were the clean-edged, neat, square boxes of tampons. Self-contained, crisp and in control, and available in light, regular, super, with plastic applicators, cardboard applicators, no applicators, braided strings, and—*New!*—colored wrappers. As a teenager, she'd buried the tampons in her cart under a magazine, the box too garish a blue, one that glowed. Still, she loved the way it bothered her mother when she plunked the box down on the counter at home. *Take those upstairs, young lady.* Her mother would have fainted at the thumb-worn sex scenes in Lara's *Sweet Valley High* books and her V.C. Andrews collection.

Lara ventured into Rite-Aid three-and-a-half months after her miscarriage. She could only ask a thin, pimply stocker to unlock the pregnancy tests once. She would have left and gone elsewhere if she did not have a mid-morning meeting. Her bladder was full to bursting.

"Which one?" he asked, his back to her.

"Whichever is the cheapest will be fine," she said, scrolling through the emails on her phone.

He slid out a box and re-locked the shelf with a key that hung from a blue lanyard around his neck. "Store brand, you get two for one," he said, handing her the box.

"Great, thanks," Lara said with a twitch of a smile. At least his eyes never strayed off her business casual cleavage, trimmed in lace.

She raced to the office, her bladder aching. Once inside, she walked past the bathroom to her desk, waving at each person she encountered. She booted up her desktop and found the client folder for an upcoming meeting, then set it on her desk. She shoved the test kit box into her pocket and walked to the bathroom, pelvic muscles clenched.

She flooded the stick with urine and then read over the instructions—again—while the stick processed. *One line, not pregnant. A plus sign, pregnant. Lines do not need to be of equal thickness or density.* This last sentence hid in tiny print inside a small pink rectangle in the corner of the instructions.

Two minutes. Nothing. The test stick was blank. *Must've been a dud. You get what you pay for.* After burying the defective test in the main bathroom trashcan, beneath paper towels and makeup removal wipes, she opened the second test and tried again. One thick blue line. After yanking a strip of toilet paper six squares long, Lara picked up the stick. As she turned it to wrap it up, she saw a shadow of an intersecting blue line. *Wait.* She turned the stick again. The shadow disappeared. She opened the stall door for light, checking that no one had entered the bathroom unheard. Instead of harsh fluorescent bulbs above and around the large mirror, Lara had selected four slim pendants. Their lights shone in triangular glows, soft on the eyes and face.

Lara leaned over the sink and toggled the stick. The shadow appeared again, still faint, but there. She climbed up onto the counter, glancing at the door for any movement. She twisted the stick under the dim glow. At one angle there was a plus sign, a cross, no question. Turned another way, there wasn't. It had been four minutes since she set the stick down. She would come back and check in three more minutes. She wrapped the stick loosely and put it in a trash can. It was empty. She was bold.

Her phone was ringing as she reached her desk. She picked up before she sat down. "Hello, O'Malley Media. This is Lara James."

The breath, before speaking, heralded her mother.

"Hi, Beth . . . Mom," Lara answered. "I'm headed into a meeting. Can I call you back?"

Beth knew better. "Honey, I know you're busy. And I'll let you go." In an hour. Beth, like her favorite little woman, was a skilled manipulator; on the phone she spoke without pausing for breath, a verbal blitz of guilt. "I just had the nicest talk with Teddy. It sounds like he's bringing the girls back east for a visit. Wouldn't it be nice to get you and Bea together while he's here?"

Teddy always gave such nice conversation. He should, he had a safe 2,000 miles between him and Beth. Lara corralled her mother off of the phone in seven minutes, a personal best. Later she would call Bea to see what Beth had told her about Teddy's possible visit. His family trips east were often discussed and rarely executed.

It was too late to check the test, but Lara went into the bathroom anyway. The result was invalidated by the clock, but the shadow remained. Time to go digital. The extra seven dollars had to be worth the clear "pregnant" or "not pregnant."

She washed her hands and breezed into the meeting, grateful for Colonial Bean, a home-grown roaster and coffee shop with Starbucks dreams and a start-up budget. She had already begun positioning Colonial Bean as the subversive's coffee, through placement in RVA essays and tastings at the mobile arts parties held on the Fan each Friday. Lara would make the bitter beans expensive, hip, effortless.

The women on the Babycenter.com "Trying to Conceive" message boards told her about ovulation test kits. She first visited the site after her miscarriage while researching prenatal vitamins, convinced she'd been deficient in folic acid or other nutrients critical to fetal development. After her Google search led Lara to a Babycenter Q&A thread between expectant mothers, she spent more than an hour clicking through "Preparing for Pregnancy" pages, "Birth Clubs," and the pregnancy message boards organized by trimester: 0-3 months; 3-6 months; 6-9 months. She nervously clicked on the "Trying to Conceive" message board. She acquainted herself with the acronyms, everyone hoping for their big fat positive (BFP) pregnancy test result and the move to the pregnancy (PG) boards. She lurked for a week on the board before picking out a handle, AdGrl, and timidly entering the conversation.

She started with three ovulation test kits and began testing five days after her period. The all-caps message on the screen of the test kit determined her mood for the day. YES! days were good. NO days were bad. Too much sex, or sex on the wrong days, could hinder her chances of getting pregnant. Lara confined her moods to the bathroom walls, the test stick in her hand. Then she crafted her appearance, first in the closet, then in the bathroom mirror. She invented new ways to casually initiate sex on the YES! days and satisfy Will outside of intercourse on the NO days. Spontaneous and horny sex was fantastic. They'd had that for years, though, and could certainly go back to it again as parents. That had always been the easy, natural part of their marriage.

Lara also couldn't resist the early pregnancy tests. Five days was too early. She used them two days before her period was due and tested until the bleeding began. If her period was light, she tested for an extra day or two. She hid her receipts from Will and started alternating which pharmacies she visited, like a pill-popper. She couldn't stand the judgment in the checkout girls' eyes.

For seven months she tested. Lara could pee on command. And she no longer drenched her fingers in urine. She became an EPT pro, a field market test expert. She intended to pitch O'Malley and her services to First Response. No one knew their products better.

She would close her eyes, turn away from the test stick for the two-minute processing time. At home, she could walk into the backyard with the kitchen trash in exactly two minutes and fifteen seconds. At work, she could respond to three emails. Each time the digital screen on the blue-and-white test stick flickered "not pregnant."

Next time. It'll happen next time. She told that to Will, too.

On the evening of *Richmond Business Magazine*'s Forty-Under-Forty awards party, always the Saturday after Valentine's Day, Lara held the glass statuette six inches from her chest as she walked onto the step and repeat for pictures. Yes, the pose looked forced and awkward in person, but Lara had orchestrated enough of these events to know that every woman's arms photographed better when they held space under the armpits. Better definition that way, no skin-on-skin spillover. She knew that the way she knew a half-smile made for a prettier face on camera, too, as it highlighted cheekbones but didn't squish eyes or show enthusiastic acres of shiny gums. This savvy was one of the main reasons she had won the award for Richmond professionals, under the age of forty, on the rise.

"First the individual shots, and then the group of award winners together," the event coordinator, Tim, PR Manager for the Better Business Bureau, said. "Lara, of course, you already know that."

"I'm on the other side of the camera. It feels a little backward," she said. Left foot forward on the x, right leg angled back, Lara smiled for shot one.

Will stood several feet away and watched. Lara had selected his suit for the evening around the drink she knew he'd hold. Brown hand-stitched Oxfords, nearly the same color as the whiskey, neat, in his glass. Sexy professor, closely tailored suit, small pocket square, no tie, under a beautifully cut shirt, top button open.

He used to ask her what he should wear. Now, he arrived home to find his suit, shirt, belt, shoes, and cufflinks laid out for him on the bed. Early in their marriage he'd balked at the designer clothes, the price tags, the sweatshop foreign labor forced to produce an item as cheap as possible for maximum profitability. Everyone wants the best; Lara worked her ass off so they could have the best and enjoy it. She had him as soon as he tried them on. The compliments he received, acknowledgement of her sartorial savvy, followed by a taunting raise of her eyebrows quieted him. Item-by-item she replaced his pre-Lara wardrobe. Now he complained about wearing any shirt his mother or sister bought him as a gift: "Bites a bit at the shoulders . . . Doesn't move with me . . ."

"Welcome to the dark side," she'd said.

Will stood taller with each photograph taken of her. Flashbulbs became her, he'd said.

"That should do it," Tim said, stepping away from the camera. "Congratulations, Lara. Well-earned and well-deserved."

She faked wiping sweat from her brow. "Thanks, Tim. Snuck in just under the wire. I was afraid I'd age out," she said. She wore thirty-seven well. Until her ovaries were labeled geriatric, Lara had welcomed each new year.

Tim assembled the other award recipients and organized them by height for the group picture. Each face and name was familiar, at least cursorily. Two web designers, two doctors, three realtors. She was the sole advertiser. Granted, Kathy, her boss, had been one of the first classes of Forty-Under-Forty awardees a decade or two before. Lara walked over to the far right side of the first row before Tim had to direct her.

One of Lara's coworkers and a professor friend of Will's stood with him and shared a toast, to her, presumably. Over the chatter and the shuffling of bodies for the perfect composition, Will's friend said, "Quite the dynamo, Will. What hasn't she done in this town?"

Will coughed. He leaned his head to his friend and said, "She looks like my wife tonight. She certainly sounded the part at the podium." He punctuated his sentences with his Balvenie.

"I'm sure you're very proud."

"Oh, of course. And relieved. *This* woman I know. Lara's become so baby obsessed that sometimes I wonder who spirited her away." His voice was brown-liquor loud.

"Most women do succumb to the biological clock. Eventually."

"I didn't marry most women."

Lara lost control of her face and her pose, but recovered before the last photograph was taken. She refused to give Will a scene, at least not here. Straightening her dress, she walked over to the threesome.

"Thank you so much for coming tonight, Susan," Lara said to her account exec. "Jerry, what I have yet to do is to get Dominion Power to see the light and switch to O'Malley. But don't worry. That's on my schedule for tomorrow at nine." She took Will's scotch from his hand and slung it back. She handed him the empty glass and smiled at his discomfort.

As she stepped through the squeaking automatic doors into Ukrop's grocery store, Lara's cell phone vibrated. She dropped her purse into the front of an aloe-green cart and slipped her phone out. A text from Kathy: *Revisions approved by client. Nice work. How?! Drinks on me.*

That afternoon, Lara had placated the Richmond Restaurant Consortium and renegotiated their fee. The brother and sister founders of the RRC, both chefs, were equal partners and owners of a group of six area restaurants. One sibling would approve an advertising initiative and spend; the other would call to argue with the concepts. When Lara billed them for the time she incurred making changes, they had threatened for a month to fire the firm. Renegotiating had cost her another month of sixty-five-hour weeks but would show in her bonus. And she liked the reminder of just how good she was.

Will had asked her to try and cut back a little, to use her junior executive to handle more of the copy editing and detail work, but Lara had helped build this agency. Until there was a more important role in her life, she enjoyed giving so much of herself to it. When she worked, she could push everything else away. She walked into the grocery store with a work buzz.

She plucked the grocery list out of her purse and told herself she would think about her work success, fill the cart, and get home. Her list was short: a bottle of Sancerre to enjoy with salmon steaks, polenta, and bok choy. She wasn't sure when she and Will had begun their celebratory dinners for each other's career successes, but the victor always developed the menu and cooked. Will would clean up and leave the last glass of wine to Lara.

She picked through the organic produce section for the bok choy and selected two plump, wild-caught salmon fillets from the shiny ice of the seafood counter.

"He loves me, he loves me not," a little girl said, plucking the petals off a carnation. She sat cross-legged in a patterned T-shirt and matching skort in the belly of a shopping cart. Lara smiled at the dark brown French braid, tied with a bow, that touched the little girl's shoulders, blunt bangs cut just above the child's eyes.

Lara wondered if she would cut her daughter's hair into bangs. She, her sister, and two brothers had nearly identical bowl haircuts for the better part of a decade. A short cut must be easier to manage, but there was a beautiful unruliness about a girl with long, curly hair. The little girl was halfway through the petals of one purple-dyed carnation when her mother's hand swatted her small fingers.

"Stop that." The girl jerked backward. Her eyes filled.

Lara's stung, too. She kept walking.

She resented the women with too many kids, who were forever shouting down aisles for Bobby or Kerrie who'd run off, sure. If you couldn't keep track of your children, you'd had too many.

The second tier of resentment embarrassed Lara. She held the grudge tight and couldn't smother it. She despised the teenage mothers with their second-skin jeans and the roll of flesh that the too-tight and too-short T-shirts only barely covered. They became one person to Lara: a gum-snapping mess balancing a cell phone between her shoulder and ear as she barked at her child to be quiet, loaded her cart with formula—certainly never attempting to breastfeed—and other processed junk food. Lara no longer shopped on the first or last days of the month. Watching a careless young mother count out stamps or swipe an assistance card to pay for formula and diapers enraged her. At least she could feed a child.

—

After a year of failing to get pregnant on their own, the clinic tested Will's fertility first. Some scheduled masturbation, a preserved sperm sample, and he was done. When Lara and Will waited to receive the results, they were seated in the doctor's office instead of an examination room. Two folders lay in the center of the large desk. One was labeled *William James.* The other, twice as thick, said *Lara Jennings James.* She had signed documents outlining the privacy accorded to her files but she hadn't read them thoroughly. The doctor wouldn't open hers in front of Will, would he? She didn't need to look at her ob-gyn history. The paper looked like a rap sheet. The black and white boxes bisected for yesses. Abortion: one. Spontaneous abortion/Miscarriage: one.

When the doctor entered his office and clapped Will's shoulder, saying, "Good news, all of the results on your specimen are healthy and normal," Lara chewed on the inside of her lip. A witless traitor in her marriage, Lara expected the problem to be, if not his alone, at least a burden they would share.

Will's wide grin and taller posture as he heard the news reproached Lara. His normal and healthy sperm count, motility, and even shape fingered her with blame. She smiled, though, saying, "Guess it's my turn." She was the broken partner. His reproductive perfection struck her as unfair, even cruel.

The doctor nodded. Will feigned sheepishness, raising and dropping his shoulders, but was clearly relieved, lips smooth and slack, teeth showing. He straightened in the chair. Will patted her knee.

"I've gotten pregnant before," Lara sputtered. She'd simply assumed there was a problem with his sperm, but that did not have to stop them from having a child. Weren't there sperm banks all over? Why didn't it bother her to think of subtracting Will from the mother-plus-father-equals-baby equation?

"Right," the fertility doctor said, "and I'm confident you'll be pregnant again."

Before she could work through any of her thoughts, she blurted, "No. That's not what I'm talking about. Before . . ." She waved her hand. "Him."

She'd never lied to Will about her first pregnancy; she'd just omitted that most private part of her pre-Will life. Even so, she'd felt like she had something to hide.

Will's hand slid off her knee. He swallowed hard and looked away. The doctor coughed, adjusted the knot of his tie. "Finding out the sperm motility and count are normal and healthy is good news. We've checked off one box in this process—the easiest one to test, unfortunately. This earlier pregnancy, it was terminated?"

Will waited, along with the doctor, for her answer. She nodded. She needed some water. Will folded, head held in his hands, a bundle of too large joints without muscle.

"When was this?"

"I was twenty-two," she answered, staring at her feet. This moment was worse than her imagined conversation with her father at the time ("Irresponsible, careless, too young, a disappointment . . ."). Lara knew she'd question the first abortion one day. Even so many years ago, with the decision, the urgency so clear in her mind, there was the whisper of another life, decades beyond her: *You'll blame yourself.*

Who else could make it, she had answered, sure of herself; no way she could carry a child and give it up. She had no intention of telling the baby's father, an agency intern just like her. They were children themselves. And it was impossible for her to slink off somewhere and have the baby, give it up, and pretend she had been traveling in Europe. Her parents couldn't afford that. Even if they could, she'd actually have to tell them. College, graduate school, everything she'd worked for, all a waste. She hadn't insisted that he wear a condom. And she'd only been on her pill for a few days, too few days. She had to be unpregnant.

"Yes, that was during your prime fertility years," the doctor said, and Lara's ears flamed. "More than a decade has passed. Things change."

"What's the next step?" Will asked, his voice a croak. Lara wasn't sure whom he was asking.

"Excuse me while I grab some information about additional options," the doctor said in a rush and walked out.

Will stood. He raised Lara's chin with his thumb. "What else don't I know about you?" His voice was stern.

"I'm sorry, Will. That was a lifetime ago. I've barely thought of it until we started all of this," she said.

"No more secrets, Lara."

"That was my biggest one. I promise."

Chapter Six

2006

She hadn't told Will of her scheme. He'd questioned her sudden interest in worship—they both loved their long Sunday jog and the volley of trivia from the paper as they passed sections back and forth. Church was for weddings and filling Beth's pew on Christmas and Easter, but he came with her anyway, though Easter was two Sundays away.

St. Paul's Episcopal Church pointed skyward in downtown Richmond, on Grace Street no less. There was no peeling clapboard, never a yellow mission bus parked in view, no Latin chanted or divine human vessel cloaked in chastity. The Greek revival architecture echoed the capitol building: a thinking woman's church.

Lara didn't know how it was done. She had walked by the side altar a hundred times but she hadn't paid much attention. In her youth, she daydreamed in stained glass from her seat in the pew. She blended the crayons carried in the church tote bag to mimic the watery blues of angel robes, the blood red of flowered fruit. As an adult, she rolled the wafer around in her mouth as she walked, trying to remember if she was supposed to chew or allow it to dissolve, and studied the tile leading back to her seat. Once or twice she passed a couple of people in line at the side altar after communion. She did not wonder why the elderly were waiting—prayers either accelerating or delaying death and its relentless mortifications. She couldn't help speculating what anyone in line below middle age had wrong with them. Bad blood work? An addiction? Even so, what did they expect the so-called lay healers to do? The woman on the right was the top real estate agent in town; the woman on the left, a prominent lawyer.

This Sunday: what the hell. She'd embarrassed herself before science more times than she could count. What could it hurt to kneel on the steps, to see if God could right what was wrong with her? Perhaps she'd earn points for effort. She nodded as the priest placed the host in her outstretched palms.

"May the body and blood of our Lord Christ keep you in everlasting life."

I don't ask so much as that, she thought. She dipped the wafer in the chalice of wine and placed it on her tongue. Will paused to let her walk in front of him, but instead of taking the left turn that would bring her back to their pew, Lara walked straight ahead into the side altar and took her place in the line before the realtor.

The host was gummy on her dry tongue. She studied the motions each of the women before her made. The healer/realtor motioned for Lara to step forward. The exchanges between the healer and the two people in front of her had been quiet and quick. No writhing on the floor. No strange tongues spoken. Lara stepped forward, knelt atop the hand-crocheted pad cushioning the wooden steps.

The woman placed her palms on Lara's head. "What afflictions do you bear today?" she asked.

A sob contracted Lara's ribcage. "I—I can't have a baby. Can't get pregnant and stay that way."

"You are brave," the woman told her. "Father, we pray that you ease this woman's suffering. And if it is your will, that you give her the gift of children."

Tears rolled down Lara's cheeks. She flicked them away.

"Amen," the woman said.

"Amen."

The healer dropped her hands to Lara's shoulders.

The walk from the church was as clipped as their conversation. Three times Will opened his mouth and shut it before finally speaking.

"What was all of that?" Will asked when they were back in the car.

Lara looked at him, shrugged, but didn't answer. She was hardly sure.

"I thought privacy through all of this was so important to you." He stared straight ahead. His face was pink in the rearview mirror.

"I think that's a thing of the past, Will. My sex organs have established visiting hours at this point. I had needles stuck all over me last week. I'm on every hormone imaginable. Why not try this? What else do I have left to lose?"

"Pride."

"Please, that left the building months ago." She was more humiliated before her husband than the stranger who'd laid hands on her. She wouldn't ask Will to come to church again, especially not so close to Easter: too many freshly brushed heads, pastel bows, and bunny purses, children with white wicker baskets.

"Shall we consult astrology next time?"

"You've made your point."

At thirty-nine years old, all Lara James wanted was a baby. The last two years of baby lust overpowered the previous thirty-seven of pleased childlessness. Her old self would be ashamed of her. Lara didn't care. She doubted the doctor behind the heavy doors, her husband, God, the universe, knew how much she wanted a child, what she was willing to offer in return. The defined curve of her bicep went underused. Her calves could bounce and dance. Unbidden, her hand curved into a loose cup, ready to support the warm, pulsing weight of a newborn skull. Iterations of the word *baby* or *child* tickled the soft inner flesh of her lips, waiting to be flung out into the world.

Lara still would not admit how desperate she was for motherhood, not out loud, even sitting quietly in the lobby of the One Hope Fertility Clinic. The calendar on her phone blocked out two hours for an "off-site meeting." Between Lara and Kathy, *off-site* meant anything from a lunch to woo potential clients, to Pilates, maybe a bikini wax. The dog-eared paper planner inside Lara's smooth briefcase read only: *O.H. blood draw and intro.* Her bank statements and health insurance forms, the step-by-step guide to filing fertility treatment reimbursement requests spoke the truth: $647 for six months of Clomid; ten ovulation test kits; eight double-pack home-pregnancy tests; co-pays to her ob-gyn; then the $275 out-of-pocket fertility consultation fee. A baby? Priceless. Will wouldn't look for those expenses; finance was Lara's domain. Nonetheless, she alternated between paying with credit and debit cards and handing the pharmacist cash.

Whenever Will asked if she'd told anyone, Lara responded with a question of her own: "Why, when there's nothing to tell?"

Besides Will, no one knew Lara had been trying for eighteen months, but Kathy had called her on it six months ago.

She had walked into Lara's office, closing the perpetually open door behind her. Kathy O'Malley was tall with shoulder-length silver hair wrapped in a chic twist that made her taller still. Lara instinctively stood at her approach so she would not have to crane her neck up to meet the bright eyes beneath the rimless glasses, bifocal line engineered to be invisible.

"Getting blood work done all the time," Kathy had said, toying with the sleeve of her tailored Tahari pantsuit. "You've either got cancer or you're pregnant. Which is it?"

She lied. "W-Will and I are thinking about having a baby." Lara had met Kathy fourteen years before, during her internship at New York's DDB, Inc. where Kathy had been a partner, a mountain above Lara's pay grade. For nine years they'd worked together, with office doors open. When Lara couldn't, after six drafts, write her father's obituary, Kathy had penned it for her. She trusted Lara.

"Glad it's not cancer," Kathy said and walked out.

Now at the clinic, Lara pulled the Sunday *New York Times* from her briefcase. Her favorite sections she reserved for waiting—for a client, a table, her reproductive future. She routinely scanned travel destinations, tallied the caloric hit of recipes, and now she underlined books in the review section so that she could ask Will about them over cocktails at the reception following his seven o'clock lecture.

The waiting room at the One Hope Fertility Clinic could be confused with a plastic surgeon's office with its piped-in classical music and occasional arias. She'd already sat through one full loop. But rather than breast implant samples and pamphlets explaining injectable fillers, leaflets on donor eggs and *Is Surrogacy Right For You?* sat in crisp-edged piles on the marble-veneered tables. Who designed their collateral materials? Those pamphlets were to be read in private. A woman would slip them into her purse only once she was called up and out of the deep-cushioned leather chairs, their legs, wooden, carved into claws. To promote fillers and injectables, Lara would shoot drab before photographs and glossy afters, pictures of women whose faces stopped smiling once they did, no wrinkles to prolong the sentiment. Fondling a gel or silicone breast implant could be calming or thrilling. You could slip one into your bra and instantly see the results. Fertility was a trickier business.

There were twelve chairs in the room, but only three other women. Had the women in these seats arrived at her office for a market test, Lara would have rejected the sample: too white, too wealthy, too old. Too similar. Lara wasn't the oldest Infertile Myrtle present but wasn't certain if she was the youngest. *Maybe we're all the same age. Maybe they've been at it longer.* The other women had given up Botox so long ago that the curves had sunk back into their faces. Or maybe they were hopeful they were pregnant and had summarily stopped coloring their hair, roots splintered and frizzy, ends dull and brittle. Lara touched her hair, still a smooth, meticulous blunt line at her chin.

Lara's phone buzzed, a text from her assistant: *VCU Medical wants to add website re-design and TV spots to 2 pm mtg.*

Got it, L, Lara typed with her thumbs, her gleaming, though short, burgundy nails flashing. While the meeting wasn't for two hours, Lara had already cast the actors for the promos in her mind. Local, cheap, but good. VCU Med was the last place Lara had seen her father coherent and alert. They had taken such care of him. Even when Lara had adjusted their billing from a deep discount to her full going rate, Charlie in marketing remained a steady if demanding customer. She drew the hospital file from her bag. On a piece of notepaper, she added to her list of reminders, writing, *Highlight pioneering mammography technology.* Beside a second bullet-point, she scribbled and starred the words *bariatric surgical wing.*

The notepaper had been a cheeky gift from her father upon Lara landing her first Madison Avenue internship while in graduate school. The thousands of sheets he had embossed with her maiden name and a stanza of poetry survived him by five years. She ran her fingers over the text. *Lara Josephine Jennings.* Below her name:

Advertisements can teach us all we need;
And death is better as the millions know,
Than dandruff, night-starvation, or B.O.

She closed the file, placed it in the lap of her black pencil skirt, and lifted out her planner, though she knew the day's contents. She flipped through the tabs, unseeing. The wooden door separating the waiting room from what lay beyond squeaked open. Each woman's head snapped up.

"Mrs. James, the doctor will see you now."

Lara stood, a pinch from her throat to where calf tapered to ankle.

On a Monday, Will slipped one arm around her waist and used his other hand to sweep the hair off of Lara's neck. She huffed and ripped out her earbuds. His breath raised gooseflesh on her neck, still sticky from her jog. He pressed himself against her. She balanced on one leg, the other foot raised on the wooden fence surrounding the deck as she stretched her hamstring. She leaned back on him.

"You can't expect me to control myself when I see you like this. Your legs in those shorts are amazing."

He was right. The three-inch inseam emphasized the tight musculature of her thighs; sweat traced the knot of muscle that tapered into her knees. Even flat-footed, Lara's calves looked like she stood *en pointe*, her hamstrings curved in a smooth c-shape. She didn't stretch in front of reflective surfaces by accident.

Lara slid her foot off of the railing and turned to face him, his arm still encircling her. "I must smell atrocious, though," she said as she waggled her eyebrows.

"It's all pretty hot from where I'm standing." He tugged at the end of her ponytail. Her neck stretched open before him. She smiled as his teeth grazed just below her chin. He pressed her back against the railing. Her lips caught his.

His erection pressed into her belly.

"Nooo," she whimpered, more than groaned, and tipped her face back from his.

"I know, I know. Stupid neighbors. Let's take you and your runner's high inside." He grasped her hand.

"It's not that, Will. We can't, remember? Seventy-two hours with no . . . you know?"

Her hand fell from his. He pressed his eyes closed and sighed. For a breath or two he kept his eyes closed, before opening, and spoke. "Seriously, Lara, I thought people stopped having sex *after* they had kids." His jaw tightened.

She tugged his hand into hers. "It's just for a few days," she said, running her fingers over his knuckles.

"This time anyway," he mumbled just audibly, pressing her hand against his straining fly, penis hard beneath.

She dropped his hand like a scalding pot handle and stepped back. He held his blue gaze level but ran a hand over his newly-lined forehead and through the hair that was only beginning to thin. His head was cocked barely to one side. She searched his face for signs of remorse.

"How did I end up alone in this?" She turned and stalked into the house, allowing the screen door to slam behind her. She braced her hand on the countertop and gulped air, trying to force away the tears she knew would come. She was the infertile one, after all. The nurses at the clinic warned her that the fertility treatments and hormones amplified emotions. It wasn't her fault that her eyes were wet more days than dry. She had tired of the way Will responded to her tears. At first, they cried together, one body, arms holding fast, breathing freighted with loss and failure. Now he put his hands on her shoulders, more like a father than a husband, trying to calm her down. Even in their home they stood on opposite sides of an invisible crevasse.

The screen door wheezed as Will opened it and stepped through.

"Look, I'm sorry," he said.

"It's not fun having to be the bad guy here. You know what day it is as well as I do."

His arms enfolded her again, but this time there was nothing amorous in his embrace. She held herself rigid in his arms.

She mumbled against the pressed cotton of his shirt. "It has to work this time."

"The insemination's going to work, Lara." She pressed her hands against his chest to find some distance. His eyes were a dark, liquid blue. "And even if it doesn't, we're going to be fine. Aren't we?" He held her forearms when she tried to slip away. She wiggled loose.

"Giving up already?" she asked.

"Of course not. I'm worried about you. About us. How can I help?"

"I need to call in to work," she said.

Instead, she walked into her office to check her messages from the women on the BabyCenter "Trying to Conceive" message boards. There was one new post since she'd checked the night before.

```
From: BBYDrms
Subject: Breakdown
Hi, ladies. Hopefully this message will save you from
what happened to me yesterday. Please tell me I'm not
crazy. I went to Walmart (out of detergent but that's
not important) and saw all these moms loading up carts
with markers and pencils. This little girl kept open-
ing and closing a Trapper Keeper (remember those?)
and there were rows of backpacks and lunchboxes. And I
just started sobbing. Right there. In Walmart. It hit
me that I may never have that. I may never go back-
to-school shopping with my own child. I just left the
cart and ran away.

From: AdGrl
RE: Breakdown
No one understands what this is like. Ur not crazy.
It's hell.
```

With each failed attempt at getting and staying pregnant, Lara engaged more deeply with these women. From the first miscarriage, the six months of trying au natural, to the blister packs of Clomid, and now the ninety days of injection, Lara spent more and more time on the boards each day. These women she would never meet were her secret community. She knew how insane that sounded, but only the anonymous women on the boards knew what she was going through. They each supported one another, always ready to try and offer hope when someone miscarried or when insemination or egg harvesting or fertilization failed. That communion was natural, easy. What was difficult was to remain connected to the women who succeeded when she failed.

Martha came to mind, Martha as Lara envisioned her, anyway. Four attempts at insemination and no luck. First round of IVF, and off she went to the "Pregnancy After Infertility" boards, changing her handle from BBYDrms to Mommy2BeIsMe. Lara had asked her to keep in touch and update her on how her pregnancy progressed and how she settled into new motherhood.

But two paragraphs into reading Martha's birth story, as Lara soaked a tampon, she closed her browser. Lara began several emails to Martha: *I know I asked you to keep me posted. I'm sorry, but I can't . . .* Lara swallowed each letter with the backspace key, ashamed at her inability to summon happiness for a woman whom she considered a friend, someone who had been where she was, exactly. Martha had her baby. Lara had everything and nothing.

Lara remained on the TTC boards, a salty veteran of the fertility wars. Her handle was blank other than her nickname, unlike the other women who all listed a TTC start date and a shorthand list of all the methods they had tried to get pregnant. Many women referred to angels or losses. Lara refused to reduce her struggles to a batting average. Nonetheless, these women understood. Families had to be earned. Like her, they knew that women whose husbands could get them pregnant just by fucking them did not deserve their babies. The only secret she kept from the group was that, once, she'd been one of those women.

—

Lara put her coffee mug onto the kitchen counter. With her thumb, she pulled down her skirt, uncovering her left butt cheek. Thongs provided such convenience for the infertile. Hanky Panky could use that in their marketing: no unfortunate panty lines *and* easy access for hormone shots. Her right cheek was still achy and hot from the day before.

"Human pincushion," Lara said as Will loaded the thick, four-inch-long syringe—too similar to a stiletto heel—with the last injection before the day's attempt at insemination. She sucked a breath in through her teeth and held it. The sting in her lungs blunted the sting of the needle.

Will tapped the syringe, released the air from the tip. "I prefer to think of your hot ass as my personal voodoo doll," Will said. "Are you mad at anyone? Just name the target."

Lara snorted. At least he'd stopped sulking about the Saharan nature of their sex life. Before she could hold her breath again, Will pushed the needle in, deep, like they'd demonstrated at the fertility clinic, past skin and fat and into the muscle. The syringe burned in and out. When they first started the injections, he'd give her a brief, playful slap on the butt when he extracted the needle. After the first five shots, Lara gasped at the swat, her mouth registering the tenderness before her brain. For a week, the daily injection spot resembled a bee sting with the stinger lodged inside—dimpled and an angry shade of pink.

Today was the third Turkey Baster Day. The doctors at One Hope remained optimistic that it could mean the end of the injections and put the painful thirteen months of failure forever behind them. The first time, the doctors said "would." Eventually the auxiliary verb weakened to "could." When she got her period after the first try, she called Will and said, "Next time." Lara could fake flippant, then. After the second round failed, Lara texted Will from work, *Next time. What sounds good for dinner?* She knew he'd hear the telltale squeak of disappointment in her voice if she called.

As they packed their bags for work on TBD3, Lara told Will he didn't have to come to the appointment. "You've already handled your part like a champ," she said. "And it's hardly the first time."

"Of course I'll be there," he said. An afterthought: "This is about both of us." She smiled and poured out the rest of her coffee, then dragged a towel across the counter to erase the ring.

Lara plucked the car keys out of her bag and swung them around her finger. "Either way, really," she said, though his absence would be unforgivable. "I have a meeting until noon and then I'm headed to the clinic."

The gray walls and diluted gray floors of the fertility clinic, room five, were covered in bright Anne Geddes photographs of babies dressed as peonies and lions, grotesque misrepresentations of forced nature play.

Will dropped his messenger bag into one of the chairs stationed in a corner by the magazine table, cluttered with waffled *Parents* and *Newborns* magazines. He didn't remove the novel from the front flap as he always did when waiting. He didn't sit. He slid the curtain separating the examination room from the door back and forth across the curved metal rod on its plastic-coated rings. He crumpled the folded paper drape on the examination table between his fingers. When Lara took it out of his hands as she prepared to undress, he crossed the room and spun the faux-leather doctor's chair.

She piled her skirt and thong in the corner of the room and wrapped the drape around her hips. Metal squeaked. Will swung the stirrup legs out and up from the exam table, aped dancing with them. "These look like oven mitts," he said, squeezing the floral fabric covers over the feet of the stirrups. He should've waited outside, like the other times.

Normally a man of cultivated calm, Will's nervous energy channeled the beating in her chest, the breath she fought to keep steady and the fingers she willed not to tremble, at least not enough that he could see. "You know what those are for, right?" she asked. Frivolous. Was he afraid of failure, again, as she was? Or was it success that scared him, sperm meeting egg, cells dividing into a baby?

"I have some idea," he said.

"You're sure you want to watch? Plenty of seats in the waiting room." He couldn't get her pregnant; perhaps they were better off creating a child in separate rooms. Will shook his head and moved back toward the magazines. Lara's phone buzzed in her bag. Holding the paper drape around her waist with one hand, she slid the phone out of her briefcase in order to read the glowing face.

Baby blessings, AdGrl, read the email's subject line. She tapped to open the body of the message. *We're all crossing our fingers for you. Third-time charm and all that. XO. The 1 yr + TTC crew.* She allowed herself a small smile and dropped the phone back into her bag.

"Something up at work?" Will asked.

Lara paused. He knew a little about her conversations with the BabyCenter women. The messages and emails had rapidly grown deeper, more honest and personal than she had anticipated. They were friends, relationships, these women, whether she knew them in person or not. Still, she was embarrassed about how much of herself she shared with these strangers. A few of them had seemed a bit obsessed with motherhood at first. She had to play it cool with Will. "Always. It's the Zanetti account. Nothing new there."

"Do they know where you are?"

Lara waved the question away. "Of course not."

"You know," Will said, and Lara realized she was standing beside the exam table, still clutching the paper drape. "We've been waiting a while. We probably have at least a few minutes . . . maybe one more go at giving it the old college try?"

Lara flushed; her nipples stiffened to points. "Professor, they said sex *after* might help. Not before."

The doctor knocked, announcing his arrival.

Lara climbed up onto the exam table, laid the paper drape over her navel, and hiked up her shirt to her bra line. The doctor washed his hands, rinsed away their levity. Heat flushed her collarbone, climbed up her neck.

"You know the routine by now. Lara, please slide your bottom to the edge of the table and place your feet in the stirrups." She did so, feeling on display, a sensibility she'd thought lost once the attempt to get pregnant had turned medicinal, then technological. How often had she and Will recreated this same configuration, but with his body between her legs, minus the metal stirrups, fluorescent lighting, and sanitizing hand foam?

"I'm going to warm the speculum up a bit," the doctor said, holding the metal device in both gloved hands. Will stood beside her, one hand on her shoulder. The doctor slid the speculum inside her. Will's grip tightened at her sharply inhaled breath, the twisted grimace on her face. His eyebrows drew together at the sound of the doctor locking the speculum open and in place.

"Just take a few deep breaths and relax," the doctor said.

Will's exhalations were heavy and ragged, deeper than Lara's. The doctor snaked the catheter with Will's sperm into her. The procedure took only a few minutes. Afterward, Will, the doctor, and a nurse helped slide Lara into a recliner, where she would sit for the next four hours. Will returned to his office while she waited.

When the clinic released her, Lara went home and showered, dried her hair. The barrel of the iron hissed as she curled the dark strands at her jaw. She lined her eyes, stained her lips, and drank a glass of Meursalt before searching through her lingerie. Nudity was too clinical for sex. As her fingers riffled lace and satin, Lara relived the moments in the office just before the doctor had entered.

The spark with Will in the office was startling, unfamiliar, but with an echo of familiarity. Sex was scheduled and verboten on non-sanctioned days too close to the insemination procedure. Sex was something to be measured. There were now right or wrong ways or times and expected outcomes. Their shared language had fallen mute. Each doctor at the fertility clinic advised on how often or how long, which positions they should use and even where they should be doing it. Sex teased with the hope of a baby, and it had let her down. Tonight, though, she would make love to Will because they wanted each other, not because it increased the odds of insemination. She would convince him of this, too.

A distraction: what details to include in tomorrow's post about the post-insemination seduction. Certainly she'd omit the booze.

Once she wriggled into the sheer black chemise, she walked barefoot down to the kitchen to pour a second glass of wine and one for Will. When she heard his keys turn in the lock, she met him at the front door.

"Welcome home, honey," she said, hand-blown glass extended.

"I'll say," he answered. "Damn, you're gorgeous, you know that?" Lara had trained her body into a fit size eight that looked like a six. Her breasts were small, but perky and present enough to highlight the inward bite of her waist. The hormone shots had softened her ass, though, no matter how many squats and lunges she performed; the tops of her thighs dimpled, but only slightly.

"Why don't you set that down," Lara said as she slid his Tom Ford messenger bag off his shoulder. "And come and relax." She led him into the living room. He grinned at her as she turned to face him and pushed him down onto the couch.

He patted the space beside him. "Will you join me?"

She shook her head and leaned over him to loosen his tie. Shirt unbuttoned, her fingertips weightless on Will's chest, his heart rabbit-punched her palm. She caught his breath in her hand.

Lara straddled Will and wrested his shirttails from his pants. Her lips to his, he moaned. He cupped her buttocks. She winced and his hungry fingers gripped hips, pulling her against him. She unfastened his belt and unzipped his fly. His mouth was on her neck, his tongue traced her throat. The speculum was cold and sharp. She choked on antiseptic, as he pressed himself up, into her.

Chapter Seven

2007

Her beloved Fan townhome had gone under contract the first day it was listed. Most of the boxes had been opened and unpacked in their new house, but they didn't own enough to fill it. They'd bought the house for the backyard and the lovely, light-filled room steps from the master bedroom. It would make the perfect nursery. But just she and Will would inhabit the space, no baby-to-be making three. Not yet.

Lara needed some distance from the beautiful foursquare home just outside downtown Richmond with its three-quarter-acre yard, gleaming dark floorboards, and family-sized refrigerator with child-height pull-out drawers for drinks and snacks. A family needed a home; a child, a yard. Her voice echoed off the freshly painted walls of their new house, cavernous without a baby, hollow and brittle.

Despite the taped boxes piled in the entryway, Lara determined her social life required some do-it-yourself fixer-upping. First, she and Will attended a reception for a newly acquired collection at the Virginia

Museum of Fine Arts. He was quiet during the short drive from the house to the museum. As they walked from the parking garage, Lara placed her hand in his. He squeezed once and dropped his hand to his side, strode on. Perhaps the art would coax him outside of himself.

"What's got you so ruffled?" she asked Will, trying to catch up to him.

He had barely paused in front of the first two installations in the museum's mid-to-late twentieth-century gallery, normally his favorite. She'd always loved watching him interact with a piece of art; he was entirely consumed. First, he stepped as far back as possible—more than once he'd backed right into another person, dribbled drink, and mumbled apologies. Then he slowly walked closer and crouched down or sat to change perspective. After that he would inspect the work up close, mentally cataloging the details. He avoided even a glance at the title of the piece or the gallery-supplied description until he'd finished communing with the image as a whole. If a docent or volunteer started to speak with him about the work he raised a stiff finger to his lips. The rude gesture, sexy and commanding, held everything in. Only once had Lara reminded him that his manner could be off-putting. He'd answered that it was unmannerly for someone to interfere without being asked. For Will, nothing else should intrude on the primacy of first experience. For all of his lecture classes, he assigned the readings before he introduced the author, poet, or playwright.

This time, Will ignored her. Tonight his studies were quick and dismissive. He moved without comment from a Gowin gelatin-silver print of three scowling women, arms linked, one with a swollen belly, to a Lorna Simpson installation of a man fractured by Polaroid and plastic frames.

"Those women in the photograph," she said, "why so angry-faced?" She squinted, affected a cartoonish glower and mashed fists against her hips.

Will didn't turn to her before speaking. "It's some of the thesis students I'm advising. I don't seem to be getting through."

Lara relaxed her face and bumped Will gently with her elbow. "Oh, come on, they're usually pecking from your hand."

"This group is particularly in love with their own brilliance."

"Aren't we all, Will?"

"At some point a line of thought, their argument"—he paused, frowning—"becomes unworkable. They refuse to admit that occasionally you have to change course and allow room for surprise, a new thought." His hand was tight around his glass, his forehead rumpled. "Don't you ever have clients like that?"

"Every day, Will, but I wouldn't be very good at my job if I told everyone their ideas and goals were impossible. They'd find someone who'd make it happen."

"You're just as intractable as they are."

"That's why I'm so good." Lara had never been a quitter or a settler. Not when she ran for student council or completed her first triathlon, not when she had to leave New York. She wouldn't give up on motherhood, either.

The next social event in Lara's planner, a week after the art reception, was the Cap City Wine Festival. This wine festival was perennially on Lara and Will's schedule. There was one to kick off summer and this one, her favorite, to welcome fall. She'd so hoped to be pregnant by the event, planned to be.

She'd daydreamed about meeting their friends at their table, sipping sparkling water and curving her palm around her pubis, smiling coyly as she gushed about her new family and new home. Her abdomen would barely be swelling, but she imagined it would be warm.

Today there was neither swelling nor warmth from inside. Lara had failed again. Over dinner the week before the Cap City Wine Festival, Lara had pushed her salad around the plate.

"I signed up for the Richmond Marathon," she'd said, anticipating an argument. The doctor had said aggressive exercise might not be helping. They'd already invested so much in this baby.

Will's face lifted, eyes on her instead of his plate. "The one in a couple of months?" His shoulders lowered and face smoothed.

"That's the one. Care to join me? I'll have to ramp up my mileage, but it's doable."

Here it comes. She waited.

"Sounds like a great plan," he'd said as he speared a piece of steak with his fork. He'd seemed relieved, without questions.

Trying-to-conceive status: indefinitely on hiatus.

But now, facing her friends and their questions, the new house seemed laughable, trifling, a gargantuan yawn of emptiness. She consoled herself with the knowledge that she was wearing the smallest jeans since puberty, custom-cut-and-sewn premium denim. They hung, just barely, on the points of her hips. With each step, the edge of her ribbon-strap camisole fluttered against her skin; wind kissed the exposed flesh. And even with the new house purchase, they'd sold the townhouse for well more than she'd paid for it. She was skinny and fat-walleted.

"We need to do this more often," Will said.

"We haven't done anything yet, Will," she said. "Just walked from the car."

"I know. I forgot how much I love doing nothing with you."

She looked up at him and tried to really see his hair, his eyes, his smile, the translucent curl of chest hair that nipped over the edge of his collar. Why was that so hard? She'd distilled him down to the traits he would surely pass along to his child.

"Today we shall drink fragrant wine, sing songs, love women," Will said as he leaned over to plant a kiss on her neck, just below her ear. They walked up Tredegar Street toward the crowd forming, extending from the Civil War Center to the Brown's Island Bridge.

She nodded. "I'm glad Chekhov would approve."

In her free hand she swung the small glass that came with the tickets for the event. The September afternoon sun blinked through passing clouds, and a breeze blew off the James. Will walked faster than she did. Though he was taller, Lara's pace typically outstripped his longer strides. Will, Mister I'm-not much-for-a-crowd, particularly an intoxicated one, walked with purpose. He turned back to smile at her. She was pleased to be out, to be able to drink a couple of glasses of wine without any potential worry about damaging a mass of cells that would one day divide into her child. She'd been so rigorous with her vitamins, diet, sure to get enough rest, cutting back on wine. The hope that this month could be *the month* hadn't died, yet. However, she wanted more, much more, to be the pregnant woman who couldn't drink but came to the festival anyway. It pissed her off, this opportunity for carelessness.

They each flashed their tickets and a smile at the front gate to the Brown's Island Bridge, held their arms out for wristbands. The police officer even asked Lara for her driver's license. She winked at him.

The three other couples comprising their group milled around their reserved table, most with drinks in hand, scuppernong and petit verdot swirling as they gestured. Lara had organized their arrival this way. They stopped before they reached the table and bought an entire bottle of Mousseux from Veritas Vineyards. They took their seats once the catch-up conversations had concluded. She'd orchestrated the pouring of the glasses, the toasts in front of their table so that all of their friends could see her drinking. They would know better than to ask. She was excited to see everyone. Her happiness was genuine, but she would have to put a number of props in place to ensure its continuation. This wine festival was her first group outing in more than a month. She and Will went to dinner together at least every three weeks, but she felt so open and raw and exposed that it was too difficult to interact with their friends and family who had children—even their friends without children. Flooded eyes as a response to "how are you" was an awkward conversation starter. She had always been confident, heel-to-toe edging on cocky as an adult, mocking gooey, emotional women like her mother. She barely recognized this humiliating new self. *Suck it up, buttercup.*

Will poured them each a glass of the white wine. The foil was jagged. Bits of cork floated in Lara's glass. He clinked his glass against hers, the cork fragments bobbing on the surface.

She sipped; oak, butter, cork. "Where should we start?" She gestured at the white tents riffling in the wind, differentiated only by signage. "We can work on these in line."

Will shook his head. "Stay here, catch up." He pressed against her shoulder, down to the seat. "I'll go get a couple more bottles. They'll be our contribution to the table. Less waiting that way." She shrugged and raised the glass to her lips. Always the pragmatist, Will.

She offered her cheek to Karen's husband Gary, beside her. "What have you and Karen been up to?" she asked.

"The gym'll be opening right after the start of the year," he said. Lara had forgotten about Gary's new venture. She needed to check it out. She squinted to see him, even through sunglasses.

"Perfect for the New Year resolutionaries." Lara eschewed the gym for the month of January; too crowded with bodies who would stop exercising by February. "Excellent timing."

"I have options to franchise two more. But the rollout and presale have been more intense than I expected."

"I bet. But your location is perfect. Lots of parking." Shop talk, a bulwark against day care and school chatter, who was walking, talking, spelling beyond age-level nattering. "A neighborhood full of gorgeous people who work to stay gorgeous. It should be great. Congratulations!"

"Karen thought you'd be willing to help me get the word out. You know pretty much everybody."

"Give me a tour and hook me up with a free workout and I'm your girl."

"Free workouts? *I'm* your girl," a voice rasped behind her. Brian, her friend and hairdresser, planted a kiss on her scalp before he sat down next to her. He had done her hair for her wedding. She'd worn only a strapless bra and panties as he styled her.

Lara's glass was empty. Will still wasn't back. She swished water around the rim to remove the cork and sediment, scanning the crowd for Will and the wine he had promised. Brian poured some of his into her glass.

"Wine drunk isn't a good look on me," he said.

Once again Lara had more in common with Brian and the husbands in the group, anyone whose career hadn't petered out by age thirty. She could talk booze, sports, current events, politics, but was clueless about the at-the-moment Disney Channel, Nick Jr. programming.

Lara stood when she spotted her best friend. She hugged Karen hard, nose to her neck, like always, smelling the wine on her own breath.

"God, you look fabulous," Karen said. *You're getting too thin*, is what she meant.

"Doesn't she?" Will snaked an arm around her waist, heaving her into him. The wine bottles clanked as they met her rib cage.

Lara pulled away. "Thanks. Long lines?"

"You wouldn't believe. They're worse than ever," Will said.

Gary tilted two glasses at Will. "Now that you're back, fill 'er up," he said. Will slopped wine into the glass, spilling a little over the edge. He was not a man who flustered.

"I nearly dried up entirely in your absence," Lara drawled, channeling an old-timey Southern Belle in distress.

Will's cheeks were pink, his movements more animated than usual. "I'll keep your glass full," he said. He never reddened with drink. The color was usually reserved only for her, a full body blush. A naked rush of blood to the skin's surface, the color of Will's erection.

He looked over his shoulder as if he'd misplaced something, someone. "It's such a coincidence. I ran into a friend from years ago in line. We were grad assistants at the same time." He shook his head, but the small upward turn of his mouth didn't shake clean.

Anxious to catch up with Karen, Lara said, "You should've brought him over."

Will nodded. Squeezing Will's hand, Lara turned to Karen. "You, as always, are perfection embodied."

Karen had looked like Brooke Shields the day they met at college— long, wavy brown hair, a large birthmark on her neck that amplified her beauty. She had aged just as flawlessly and without enhancements. Lara hadn't pulled away from Karen on purpose. She couldn't bluff Karen. Their friendship had survived Lara's two years in Syracuse and move to Manhattan, and even her "What do you mean you're going home?" response to Karen's proud announcement that upon graduating eighth in her class from the foreign services school, she'd been offered a job at St. Catherine's. Would it survive infertility?

"Please," Karen said. "I'm aging in dog years. Gary, the kids, they're wearing me out."

Lara had told Karen when she and Will agreed to stop birth con- trol. *Be sure that's what you want, being pregnant. Because if you're not preventing it, you're asking for it,* Karen had said.

"You can't stop smiling when you say that. You love it and you know it."

After nine unwanted periods that first year, she had vented some of her hurt and frustration to Karen. *I didn't think it would be so much work,* she had told Karen.

Being a parent is work. Right now you're free to do anything you want. And I bet if you stop trying so hard and kept enjoying each other it'll happen before you know it, Karen had said.

Lara stopped complaining, except to the BabyCenter women.

"We almost didn't make it tonight. Our regular sitter canceled, and the kids will go all Von Trapp if I try to break in a new one at the last minute. Sorry, I know you hate those details."

"I don't, Karen."

"Y'all don't have to worry about any of that." Karen gestured with her wine glass between Lara and Will. "You could leave the country next weekend, and all you'd have to do is set up that out-of-office email response."

Lara ground her teeth. "No one would miss us," she said.

"That's not what I meant and you know it. You want to drink too much, take a cab home. No sitter to drive. Do it in the kitchen; no one will walk in."

"Have another, Karen," Lara teased. She and Will had had sex on the kitchen floor the night they moved in. The cold tile made her knees ache.

"Hush your mouth. You could trot off to Prague, no lunches to pack. No homework. I'm jealous."

"We've been to Prague. Last year, remember?" And to Rome and Istanbul. Her life with Will was already in re-runs, the syndicated fluff you watch before going to sleep.

"Aren't you a dark cloud tonight?" Karen said. "Let's get you another glass of wine."

The sun dipped below the river, slapping against water and bulkhead, stretching the shadows cast by the piers of the rebel-burned railroad bridge before receding. The Confederacy knew they had lost; they just burnt the bridges in spite. No one could enter. None could leave.

Lara, Karen, Gary, and the others ate and drank and talked. Mostly about the weather, the first teasing puffs of dry air, and the way the wine started out tasting pretty rotten but the more you drank, the better it got. Magic. Lara snuck a cigarette with one of their friends. Karen shook her head. Will didn't seem to notice. He had wandered away again.

A baby gurgled, close by. Lara registered the sound before she saw him. She searched wildly for Will, who would normally be sitting tensely across the table. Babies set them both on edge. He wasn't there.

Several feet away, a woman clutched Will's elbow, her fingers unmanicured, her grip tight. Will leaned toward the curly auburn hair, the undoubtedly freckled face. Lara couldn't hear them, but their expressions were intense, conversing like they were the only two people on the island. He touched her hand with his. The grad school friend. Of course he wouldn't bring her over to their table. He'd let Lara think this friend was a man. Lara splashed wine into her glass. Will didn't look her way. They were standing so close together. The woman was older than Lara, doughier, a softness in her profile, round chin, cheeks. Lara's tight ass was anchored to the chair. Will pushed hair from the woman's face, slid it behind her ear. Lara gulped as she stared, finished the glass in three swallows. She held the empty glass like a kaleidoscope, twisting the distorted view until Will and the woman were only a swirly blur of color. When she put it down, the woman would be gone, just a phantom of her imaginings. She had to be.

Something soft dragged across her shoulder. A blue-and-white crocheted bootie dangled at eye level. Lara gasped, choking on baby smell. With a loud thump, she patted her chest as though she'd sputtered on a sip of wine. Recognizing the woman holding the baby, Lara scooted her seat over and stood up. She was a former colleague who had taken maternity leave and never returned. When the woman had announced her pregnancy, Lara and Will hopeful, happy, had only been six months into their struggle.

"Hey, Melissa," Lara said.

"Lara, hi! It's so great to see you. Those jeans are to die for." Melissa slurred her words, just a little. The consonants sounded chewy.

Lara smiled at the child resting on Melissa's hip. "Who is this?"

"His name is Jacob. He's eight months old."

"He's beautiful." *But of course he is.* "Can I hold him?"

"Sure. My arm is falling asleep." *The arm holding the wine glass has gotten plenty of use.*

"Hi, Jacob," Lara cooed.

A large man, a stranger, bumped into Lara. She scowled at his thick, red cheeks.

His purple lips, teeth smiled at her. "Pardon me," he said, his accent booze-thickened. She could no longer see the water through the throng of bodies invading the space. This was no place for a baby. That's why Lara was here. Burning orange dots of cigarettes punctuated the darkening sky, waving in gestures that were wider, careless, and far more emphatic than they had been an hour before. Anything could happen to him here.

Lara murmured to Jacob and pressed his body to hers, bouncing just slightly. Babies liked bouncing. Melissa chatted away, one long run-on sentence, her arms swaying, freed of her burden.

Lara took two largish strides back, away from the table, pushed a break in the crowd. She wouldn't go far; the island was tiny. She could throw her glass and break a window, the skyline leaned so close. She closed her eyes, pressed Jacob's warm body against hers, and breathed him in. She'd show him the water, walk him to the pedestrian bridge to Belle Isle, tell him about the Civil War prison just across the river, and warn him about the rocky falls striating the James, where she'd almost drowned with Will. They looked small and smooth, but at least a handful of kayakers crashed and drowned each year. The river ran fast. It was easy to get swept away.

Melissa wasn't blabbering anymore. More like yelling. "Where are you going?" She had turned and was walking to Lara, arms straight out, fingers flexing.

"We're just walking."

"Can I have my baby back?" Melissa said as she yanked at Jacob.

"What?" Lara asked. "Oh, of course."

But she stepped back farther and her arms tightened around the baby. The heat from his rump warmed her forearm. The gathers where his diaper stuck out from the waist of the miniature cargo shorts crinkled.

Karen walked toward her. And then Gary. They were crowding her. Jacob didn't need so many adults around him and so close. He only needed her.

Her fingers wrapped around the meat of his thigh. The voices around her quieted. They'd been wine-loud and jovial. The silence closed tight. Other loud revelers continued. Her baby would feel just like this one. She had to hold on. Jacob could be hers. Some cosmic mix up could be righted in this moment if only she could keep that warm hummingbird heartbeat pressed to her chest; her antique heart lumbered. Melissa got to hold him all the time. She'd handed him off so readily and she didn't even know Lara all that well.

Hot baby breath on her neck, her cheek. Sticky fingers in her hair. Little monkey toes tickled her wrist. He wanted to be in her arms as much as she wanted to hold him. She should be his mother. She would not let go.

"Lara." Man breath in her ear now. She turned away. The smells of wine and mint smothered milk and sugar and drool. "Give him to me," Gary said.

Will never wanted a baby. Not ever. They all wanted to take this away from her, too.

She closed her eyes; a child suddenly herself, she could disappear or make all of the grown-ups disappear, leaving just her and Jacob. Gary's arms were on her arms. More veined, hairy arms reached for Jacob, whose fingers still knotted in her hair; he held on, too. A big thumb pressed into his small palm, tricking him—weren't adults always finding ways to hoodwink children into thinking they were doing what they wanted?—monkey-muscle reflex loosening his grip on her hair, then clutching the thumb of his father. Jacob was gone, lifted from her arms like her own baby, taken from her, scooped out; her arms hung.

Her baby was forever in someone else's arms, just out of reach. Like when her father had taught her to swim. "Just come to me," he'd said, and she swam furious little-kid strokes with flat-footed kicks, only to see his feet stepping back on the pool floor away from her, always farther to swim. In the pool, she eventually found the edge, the cool brick rough against her pruney fingers, or her father's arms. Now, she swam after tiny baby feet, translucent against rippling blue. Tears she hadn't noticed cooled against her nose.

Flags on the bulkhead snapped in the wind. She counted thirty brick cobblestones around her feet. Melissa and her husband hadn't waited for an apology. Lara hurled her sorry at their backs, shrinking with distance, hiding Jacob.

Karen touched her elbow. Lara laughed. Karen tilted her head, her look questioning.

Lara rolled her wet eyes. "Which one should we try next?" she asked as she picked up her tasting glass from the bench.

"I think we're done, Lar," Will said, walking toward her now. Lara linked her arm through Karen's elbow.

"We haven't tried Barboursville. And that's the only decent vineyard here, right?" Lara tugged on her friend, tried walking.

"I have a lecture to deliver tomorrow, remember? Karen, great to see you," Will said as he snatched Lara's arm from Karen. Lara stumbled as Will grasped her hand and jerked her forward. Lara turned to Karen. *A little help here?* Karen and Will looked at each other, her eyes heavy and wet, his dark and angry. *How nice, Will and Karen versus me.*

"Why don't you go find your own husband?" Lara asked.

As soon as they were seated in the cab, Will asked, "What the hell was all of that?"

Lara pretended to pass out on his shoulder. He shook her head off. "You're not asleep. I said, what was that?"

"I was just holding him, Will." The cab lurched and she slid against the door. "Melissa basically dropped him into my arms."

"You wouldn't give him back."

"Of course I did. You weren't even there." She wanted to tell him everything, to make him understand. She needed him to be on her side, but had he ever been? Who was the woman? She couldn't even ask. If he knew she knew, he'd have all of the power. What little power he didn't already have.

"How much did you have to drink?"

"Too much, clearly. Why were you being such an asshole?" A lying, possibly cheating asshole. They lurched forward as the cab stopped at a light.

"I wasn't the asshole. You looked insane."

The cab driver's reflection met Lara in the mirror. The words cut a swathe of hurt, ridged edges, snarled sutures.

"I was just holding him. I never get to hold a baby. And Melissa was drunk, too. She didn't care that I had him until Gary made such a big deal about it."

"You can even spin reality."

"I guess hormone therapy and wine don't mix."

"Whatever it was, fix it. Tonight was intolerable. I thought we were taking a break from the baby craziness."

"Maybe I'm not ready to give up yet," she said.

"I didn't sign up for this," he said.

"What's that supposed to mean? You're going to leave?" He would start over with the redhead. She'd have no husband, no baby. None of this would have a point. *No.*

"That's not what I want. All of this has taken over and I want to go back to how we were before."

The cab slowed at their driveway. She didn't tell Will it was too late. There were no off ramps left.

Despite a thunderdome rattling in her head the next morning, Lara stole out for a run before Will awoke. Running was both tactical and meditative for Lara, as well as an efficient calorie burn. The movement, the sweat would clear her head, help her body secrete the lingering alcohol that made her feel fuzzy and down. Everything looked, sounded, felt better with endorphins cruising her blood-stream. She'd have to answer for her behavior the night before, but she had some questions for Will, too. What did he want? What didn't he want? When had cracks spread across the unified front? He'd had several glasses of wine, just as she had; perhaps she was making too big of a deal of the other woman, Melissa and her baby, everything.

Someone always made an ass of herself at the wine festival. The $100 per person tickets, $1,000 for a reserved table for twelve, didn't stop well-to-do Richmonders from tying one on twice a year. Even Karen, perfectly composed, always rational Karen, admitted to vomiting in her stamped concrete driveway after the festival the year she'd had Sophie. Lara and Karen had laughed over Karen's description of trying to feign sobriety while she paid the babysitter, encouraging her to use the formal front door, to avoid the driveway.

She owed Karen an apology. She'd get right on that. Her comment about Karen having a fling with Will was certainly over-the-top but other than that, nothing else was such a terribly big deal. Wine-addled overreactions, all. She could distract Will from his questions with a blow job. Really not too much to fear there. She would have to start taking better care of him.

By the time she crossed beneath the late nineteenth-century granite arch entryway of her new neighborhood, Lara's strides lengthened and her breathing regulated. Carved into the sharply angular granite, veined white, was Bellevue.

Will had balked at the neighborhood, threatened to veto by name alone. "Who would name a development Bellevue?"

"The hospital wasn't notorious in the 1890s when this enclave was built," the perky realtor had explained. "The area used to be called Hickory Hill and was quite a significant defense post during the Civil War." Lara had wondered if the realtor would refer to it as the War of Northern Aggression as her grandfather, Beth's father, had.

Sunday jogs were paradise with fewer cars and runners even than Saturday mornings. Lara was movement and breath and thought. Her normal weekend run was seven miles, had been for years, but she'd worn in a new route length over the prior year, topping out at five miles. The swoosh of sole on concrete differed from asphalt and brick. Her calf muscles lengthened and contracted with the curvature of curb or shoulder. And her new starting point promised fresh discovery on each outing. If she could push herself for seven to eight miles this Sunday, despite a niggling hangover, her training for the marathon would be simple.

While she complained, occasionally, about her sleepy new neighborhood, she loved the variety it provided for running: wide, rounded, more suburban streets for miles; botanical garden path; or a mix with city streets and sidewalks, some heaved, some cobblestone; bridges for hill training; or all flat and fast.

Despite her early fears, the new home wasn't that far from downtown, and Will loved his new proximity to campus. This new house would be a good thing, even for the two of them. The streets were wide and dozing, newspapers undisturbed on curbs. Few of the homes had fences, their backyards blended together into one giant green space. And the styles of houses were schizophrenic: American Foursquares, like hers; bungalows; shingle styles; revivals: Colonial, Spanish, and Tudor.

The first three miles peeled away. When she ran she understood why people meditated and prayed. She could lose herself in her surroundings or cover a mile and hardly notice the distance. Training for the marathon would be fun. A challenge, certainly, but she could handle it. She hadn't added a medal to her collection in too long. Buoyed by her jog, Lara decided to ask Will if he and a few colleagues would attend a reading at the Rare Book Room, a new, independent bookseller that had opened in the arts district. It would be a favor to her arts council customers. He and the fancy U of R faculty and students would feel edgy and current but not threatened by the location. A perfect marriage of cool and intelligentsia, not unlike her and Will. The idea had some merit. Afterward, she would organize a dinner, or drinks, with her women-in-marketing group. They used to meet quarterly. When had that slipped? Once the bookstore launched, perhaps she and Will could get away somewhere, explore someplace new.

She checked her watch—ahead of pace by almost half a minute per mile. When she increased her long run distance, she'd have to remember to hold back a little, at least at first.

As Lara approached the river path, a woman jogged by her with a baby in a stroller. The baby gnawed on a rubber giraffe like a barbecue-eating contestant, stripping meat off bone. She wore socks that looked like running shoes and a baby pink Adidas track suit, Lara guessed, size six-to-nine months. The woman wore headphones.

Lara stifled a yell. *Hey, there's traffic on this street. What if something happens and you can't hear?* Instead, she turned up the volume on her own headphones and matched her pace to the beat.

At the mid-point of the canal loop, she passed a playground. A big plastic Radio Flyer wagon sat at the entrance with an overstuffed diaper bag in the middle. Sippy cups and a box of zwieback toasts hung from side pockets. A gleaming blue Cinderella bike with fat white rubber tires and blue-and-white sparkly streamers stood beside it, propped up by plastic training wheels. A green Razor scooter lay on its side. Lara ran over a sidewalk chalk drawing of a rainbow and what appeared to be tulips. Then a smiley face. Next, a peace sign. She watched her feet move through the blocks of cement sidewalk, two strides in one rectangle, one large gait over the next. She only glanced at the mother on the bench, baby breastfeeding beneath a cover in her left elbow. The woman faced the cell phone in her right hand. Flashes of skinny, skinned legs cut through Lara's periphery as a boy swung across the monkey bars. The little girl, Cinderella, dumped a bucket of dirt on her legs in the cat shit–soiled sandbox.

Lara stopped running, suddenly unable to draw a full breath. A white pickup truck slowed as it passed, honked three times. "Faster, darlin'," a voice yelled from the open window.

There was less than a mile until her turn-around point. She couldn't make it. She pivoted and walked five steps before she eased back into a jog. She did not lift her gaze from her New Balance sneakers except at intersections and crosswalks. A quick glance up, and then right, and then left, and then back down. She tried following the words to the music in her ears. She could not.

She recalled a trick she'd learned for running hills and bridges, years before, when she was training for her first distance race. To the beat of each footfall she said, "I-am-a-marathoner-one-I-am-a-marathoner-two." She could look up when she got to ten. The next time, she repeated the phrases until she got to twenty-five, then fifty, then one hundred.

A horn blared. Not a catcall this time. A Honda Civic's brakes squealed to a stop, the bumper an arm's length away. She waved her hand, all wide palm and spread fingers, mouthed *I'm sorry* to the blanched man in the driver's seat. If she died on this road, Lara would be nothing more than a blurb in the newspaper, a cautionary tale for runners with iPods. To Will, she would be only photographs, a polished, one-dimensional brunette, designer labels on hangers, unopened shoeboxes. Like her father, Will would live forever, or at least as long as his students. Both men had published countless scholarly papers—her father, three books of poetry. Satisfied customers would not mourn her; their files would line the desk of one of her protégés, a seamless transition. No one would inherit her savings, like she never existed. She kept running.

By a final count of 350 I-am-a-marathoners, Lara was back in front of her house. She hinged over, wheezing, feeling as if she'd outrun something, holding onto the railing beside the steps. She lifted her left foot to the top step, her leg straight before her so that it looked like she was stretching her hamstring. Her quads always came first, but she knew she couldn't balance on one foot. Not yet.

She switched legs. Caught her breath. Her headphones were too loud; the bass pounded static. She popped the buds from her ears. They dangled and scraped the brick steps as she stretched, each lyric distinct.

The front door groaned as Will opened it. "Mornin', Mrs. Pontellier," he said, shirtless and wearing only loose cotton pajama pants, hair splayed. "You're quite the escape artist."

Lara hinged upright. "Hey," she said. With her left arm on the railing, she grabbed the top of her right foot in her right hand and strained until the heel of her shoe dug into her butt.

Will pushed his glasses up the bridge of his nose. "Have you been crying?"

Her eyes had stung for so long she'd stopped noticing. "Stupid sunscreen." She rolled her eyes. "Waterproof, my ass."

He laughed and stepped back just far enough for her to enter. "How was your run?"

"My heathen run was great, thanks. Just what the doctor ordered."

"I missed you this morning." His voice was low.

She slid past him and wiggled her ass as she pulled the door closed, husband close. Lara had to convince him that she was fine, her normal self, that they were fine. *I'm fine.*

Chapter Eight

Her behavior at the wine festival still stung, even four months later. Despite having spent two years trying to conceive, all Lara wanted was to be pregnant. This time, after her first attempt at In Vitro Fertilization, she was—for approximately six weeks. It took the body so long to get the message that she wasn't.

Even the Roman shades, muting the sunlight in her bedroom to a warm glow, mocked her. When she and Will had toured the home, arrogantly signed the offer letter, Lara had imagined slow mornings in bed, a baby swaddled beside her, or better, suckling, feeding. Instead of baby powder, the damp, metallic musk of blood and uterine tissue and pad stunk between her legs.

The nurses and doctors called it a "procedure"—the dilation of her cervix to remove the dead baby that refused to miscarry all the way. Lara had wanted to wait it out, expel the baby on her own. What if they were wrong? But after ten days, the doctors' fears of infection trumped her wishes. The nurses tried to soothe with semantics: it was an abortion, just like her first.

But this procedure was so loathsome, she needed to re-brand the D&C, some kind of I-never-wanted-this type of name.

The morning after her procedure, Will brought breakfast up to her on a wooden tray. The smell of burnt coffee, along with toast and eggs, wafted ahead of him up the stairs. Her pregnant bloodhound nose was sharp, even without any child or placenta left inside her. How could she feel so pregnant and scraped clean at the same time? The news on the TV blurred with tears. She tried to blink them away before he stepped into the bedroom.

"Are you hungry?" he asked. Will was showered, shaved, and dressed, his movements quick.

"A little. Thanks. I'll definitely take some coffee." He set the tray down beside her—as predicted, scrambled eggs with Havarti and red peppers and whole-wheat toast with a tell-tale glisten of butter. She pushed the eggs to the side of the plate. He'd poured orange juice into a crystal highball glass. It was the same breakfast he'd prepared for her after they'd made love for the first time.

Beside the plate was an envelope, below two purple hydrangeas cut from the front flowerbed. She opened the envelope and slid out the thick cardstock, recognizing the stationery she bought for him when he'd successfully defended his thesis. A masculine script font in deep navy, embossed *William James, PhD.*

You're all the family I need, W.

The gesture bruised. For so long she would've said the same thing. She gulped the hot coffee. The tears she'd tried to hold back forced their way out. Why was he so calm? Why the romantic gesture? She could hear her mother, in the year after her father died, wantonly needy in sadness: "Sit with me. Don't leave." Will would recoil from such a demand just as she did as a child, then an adult. To ask would be too needy. He'd know how much she needed him to grieve with her. He had to.

She raised her wet eyes to his and didn't hide. *Don't make me ask.*

"I'll give you some space," Will said. He turned away. "Just call me if you need anything."

"Are you leaving?" She nibbled the toast.

He peeked his head into the bathroom and pushed an errant hair from his forehead. "I need to head into the office; I have a call at eleven."

"Why are you being so cryptic?"

"The timing is terrible, I'm sorry. It's a phone interview for a visiting professorship in Paris."

No wonder he's so perky. She would trade the coffee for a screwdriver. "Paris?"

"It wouldn't be until next summer, but think about it: Paris." She looked down at her lap, tears plopped onto the sheet. "I could stay if you really needed me to," he said. Lara hated Will for Paris, among other things.

Lara's father's eyes watched her from a photo behind fingerprint-smudged glass on the windowsill he had to himself. Beth touched the frame whenever she finished washing dishes.

Lara, Beth, and Bea were gathered in Beth's kitchen, and Lara knew she had to tell them about her baby-making failure. Lara had expected that baby talk would be a language she could speak with her mother and sister, common ground. She could hear the easy back and forth they'd establish over soiled diapers, sleepless nights, and each new milestone, however minute. But now, Lara couldn't find words to say that she did not know if she could have one. Two plus years of failed fertility treatments clogged her mouth like sand.

The gray-white refrigerator hummed loud. When Lara opened the door to find the half-and-half, a flurry of papers, secured by magnets and tape, waved. She could barely find the creamer. Two shelves were stacked two levels high with bottles of Lipton Iced Tea.

"I won two cases of those," Beth said, gesturing to the tea. "It's delicious."

Bea's nostrils flared.

Lara didn't comment on her mother's burgeoning stores of sweepstakes giveaways. Her mailbox hung open each day, jammed full with mail from all the lists she'd subscribed to. After Lara's father died and Beth's house had emptied again, she'd started playing contests online. Beth had found web page after web page of sweepstakes, and every time Lara visited, she noticed at least three new items. Beth had won perfume from *Elle* magazine, a gym membership, and printer toner for a year. And her new favorite cooler was red and white, with the Budweiser logo on the top and all four sides. Her mother never drank beer.

Lara had to move three logoed notepads off the wraparound counter to make space enough for the quart of half-and-half.

"Sorry," Beth said. "You know how forgetful I can be. Always nice to have some spare paper for my lists."

The refrigerator, the kitchen as a whole, had always been busy with papers, announcements, clutter. Beth wasn't one to throw anything away. A pad with emergency phone numbers, still including Lara's father's doctor, hung above the water and ice dispenser. The boys' artwork from preschool through elementary, each school picture from kindergarten through the second and fourth grades fluttered. Beth even had pictures of Karen's kids on her fridge. Lara had made the newspaper for one event or another almost quarterly, but the only picture of her was from Ted Jr.'s wedding, when she'd danced with him.

Lara opened the cabinet to find coffee mugs. None of the mugs matched. Each one advertised a different prescription drug. Lara selected a Latisse eyelash enhancing mug for Bea, a Dexatrim mug for Beth, and Cialis for herself. After pouring cups of coffee, Lara, Bea, and her mother left the kitchen.

Beth said, "Your face says this is a living room couch conversation, not kitchen chair talk."

Lara removed the red, white, and black Marlboro fleece throw from the cream-colored couch. "Really, Mom? He died of cancer, you know."

"You don't have to smoke to get those. You just have to be over eighteen and sign up. Feel how soft it is, and it didn't cost anything!"

Bea sighed. "So, what's going on, Lara?"

Lara tasted tears before she began to speak. "Will and I have been trying to have a baby for a long time, and we can't," was all she could say.

Bea blinked fast but sipped her coffee silently. Beth tugged on a lock of her hair, wound it around her finger. "Honey, that's hard," she said.

Her mother sounded like she was reading from a textbook when they spoke, even in person. Lara envied the easy relationship all her siblings had with their mother. Without their shared physical traits, Lara would question her maternity. When she spoke, Lara inevitably wounded Beth. But her silence dug a gulf, too.

"It is. Thanks, Mom." Why was it so hard to speak to Beth? Why did it always feel so forced?

"You know I had two miscarriages," Beth said.

Lara sat, stunned silent. Her mother had been pregnant for the entirety of Lara's youth. As the oldest of four children, her mother's fecundity had ashamed Lara. She was four years older than her younger sister and ten years older than her twin brothers. She saw the way men's eyes had pulled at their sockets when they looked at her mother's rounding belly, the saliva they would lick away from the corners of their mouths as they took in her swollen breasts. Lara wasn't an idiot: she knew where babies came from. Her parents were having sex, quite a lot. And seeing a footprint press against the equator of her mother's girth was creepy.

"Between you and Bea, and one after the boys."

Lara vaguely remembered the summer that her mother was sick all of the time, often too tired to get out of bed, swampy with tears. "That pill is just too hard on her," a neighbor had remarked, casserole in hand. "Solves one problem, causes too many others."

Lara turned up her palms before her mother. "I didn't know."

"You never told us any of this," Bea said.

"Hardly something we used to talk about, especially with a child. And I ended up with plenty as you've so loved to point out, Jo." Beth's eyes watered.

Next would come the oily mascara spider lashes. Lara would buy her some waterproof mascara the next time she went to the drugstore.

"Sometimes it's out of our hands," Beth said.

"But at least you had one baby before." Lara's voice faded, choked on the idea of *one* baby. Her baby.

"S'true. But it's not going to happen overnight at your age."

Lara nodded. "You're right, Mom." She studied the design on the rug, the busy toile wallpaper, counted the pattern repeats. Beth's voice was a distant hum. She was a nodding head. Lara didn't have to listen to know what she was saying. *Slow down, work less, eat more. Be patient.*

Bea had shifted in her seat while Lara and Beth spoke but remained silent. Once they had finished, Bea said, "I can't keep up with you. Let's see, 'Anyone can get pregnant. You need a license to drive a car, but not become a mother.'" Bea's face was calm, the corners of her mouth upturned.

"I'm sorry," Lara said, trying to keep from shouting. "I shouldn't have said that." Bea help up her hand. Beth spectated, as though seated at a tennis match.

Bea shook her head and fluffed her hair, an impersonation of Lara, apparently. "'There's a big world to explore as an adult. Life constricts when you decide to reproduce.'"

"Bea, stop." Lara ground her teeth. Bea was taking her words out of context. Lara hadn't known. How could she have known? *Respond.*

Master's Degree. Forty Under Forty. Practically her own firm. Her life's work would sound so shallow.

"'Maybe you'd still be married if you hadn't had kids so fast,'" Bea repeated Lara's own damning words again. Lara squinched her eyes closed.

"Will worships the ground you walk on. What do you have to complain about?"

Lara jumped off of the couch and stood over her sister, her eyes pooling, fists clenched. "Stop! I shouldn't have been so harsh." Her voice shook. "You have no idea what it's like between us right now." She walked to the window, the grass and trees beyond the glass blurred.

Bea's hand rested on her shoulder. Lara hadn't heard her cross the room. "I'm sure this is so hard for you, Lara. I don't mean to take away from that. It's just . . . it never seemed like you wanted kids. You never mentioned any of this until now."

Lara shrugged. She could only cry.

Chapter Nine

2008

Every woman on the TTC 2+Yrs board knew Lara was scheduled for her second round of IVF in July. They also knew better than to ask how it went or if she thought she was pregnant. They were a small, tight-knit circle with all too much experience saying farewell to their infertile sisters who either got pregnant or finally gave up. They had splintered off from the main TTC board when so many women had appeared to be getting pregnant so quickly, even in less than a year, and they knew more about Lara than anyone. Who else could understand the necessity of deep, preparatory breaths to mask the grimace before your welted butt made contact with any surface? Or the sadness or the anger or the walleyed, fun house, tunnel vision that reduced daily life to a macabre baby-winning carnival? Who else could understand the contortions, pain, and experiments each woman would gladly undergo to graduate from the TTC to the PG boards? The constancy of their group provided solidarity, yes, but it was scary, too. Lara felt like a castaway on the island of misfit women—hopeless and pathetic for not accepting her childlessness. Each member of the group told Lara to "hang in there" because "it's going to happen" and "this could be the time." She looked up their messages whenever she felt low or if she felt crampy and certain that once again she had failed.

When day fourteen post-IVF arrived and she hadn't started her period or even spotted, she carried her Clear Blue Easy two-pack into the bathroom. She debated waiting until evening, until Will had come home, when they could read the results together. But she couldn't.

She would need hours to reassemble herself when the test inevitably came up "not pregnant." She would need to write a list, for at least the hundredth time, of all the reasons her life was perfect, of all the reasons she didn't need a baby to be happy. She would need time to convince herself of this lie and to not hate Will when he suggested that they give up on making a baby. Testing alone, again, she could feel sadness and rage and frustration without being studiously observed. Then maybe she'd be strong enough to make quitting her idea.

With her bladder full, she opened both test sticks and used them one right after the other. "I'm used to this," she said instead of counting. "It's okay if it's negative." Her hands were shaky. She placed the sticks flat on the floor, face down, and walked down to the kitchen where she set the timer on the microwave. *No going up there until it beeps.*

When would she call babymaking quits? She'd been trying to get pregnant for nearly four years. She had tried Chinese lunar calendar charts; vaginal mucus monitoring; basal temperature plotting; a pillow tilting the sacrum up during intercourse; a macrobiotic diet; reduced caffeine intake; lowered alcohol consumption (just in case); Clomid (nine months); acupressure; Follistim injections (six months); intrauterine insemination (three times); acupuncture; a doctor-mandated ten-pound weight gain; Lupron injections (six months); egg harvesting (round one); and IVF. Each was followed by the Two-Week Wait, and inevitably: bloodstains, cramping, grief.

Next came six more months of Lupron injections, egg harvesting (round two), and a second try at IVF. She had been reduced to medical procedures, injections, and hormone levels. The need for a child had cost her more than $250,000. And then the psychological costs— how it distracted her from work, taxed her marriage. When would her efforts be enough?

The microwave beeped. She made herself walk, not run, up the stairs. *It's going to be okay if it's negative. It's going to be okay. And if it's negative, I'm done.*

Lara sat criss-cross applesauce on the floor and gently flipped the test sticks over. Side-by-side, the two test sticks had identical result screens: *pregnant.* Big Fat Positive. She'd seen nothing but "not pregnant" every month since her miscarriage after IVF round one, seven months of no after three years of no. Her breath hitched. A thrill circuited through her, giddy and terrified at the same time. She wasn't sure she could survive another loss, the dashing of her every hope. Her hands cupped her abdomen unbidden.

"Hi, baby," she whispered. *Please, please, please.*

There would be no self-protecting. She leaned back against the bathroom wall, closed her eyes, and sat with her hands where a belly might grow. Warm, grateful tears broke over her cheeks and slid down her neck.

She needed to tell Will in person when he came home, so she would wait. But she needed to tell someone, someone who she wouldn't run into later and have to explain a miscarriage. The only women who could understand were her friends in the TTC group. Yet how to do it? As long as it had taken, her pregnancy seemed sudden when it came time to tell the women. First, Lara realized she hadn't expected the procedure to work. More importantly, she knew their fragility, that dark-edged hope for your friend that turned spiteful when she got what she wanted, what they all wanted. Hadn't a part of her hoped that the women who'd announced their pregnancies and moved on would miscarry and then delivered the self-flagellation that followed when some of the women reappeared, demoted from the pregnancy message boards?

She spent hours typing and editing her announcement post. She couldn't remember any message more fraught than this. She had to get it right.

```
TO: 2+YRS TTC Ladies
FROM: AdGrl
SUBJECT: None
I can't believe what I'm typing. I think I'd stopped
hoping I would get here. I had a BFP on 7/31! Follow-
up blood draws scheduled for 8/15 and 8/21. Beta at
56, hoping to at least double by 8/15. Can I hang out
here until I hear the heartbeat? U know my history.
I can hardly believe it. If this is possible for me,
it's possible for all of us. Thank u for ur friendship
and support. I wouldn't have survived w/o u. Can't
wait to read ur posts saying the same good news.


TO: AdGrl
FROM: BByDrms
SUBJECT: Hooray!
Go on and graduate already, u lucky biatch. J/K! Hang
around as long as u want.


TO: AdGrl
FROM: WWHOPE
SUBJECT: Prayers answered
U give hope to us all. Can't wait to join u on PG
After Infertility boards!
```

—

She'd never wanted to hug a stranger until that moment. She got high—better than a run, nicotine, or sex—from sharing the news, from her friends' excitement. Will wouldn't be home for an hour. An olive branch, she'd call Bea and swear her to secrecy.

"Hello, Lara?" Bea sounded like she was in a tunnel. "I'm so glad you called. I'm sorry for everything I said. I shouldn't have."

"It's fine. Really," Lara said, pacing around her bedroom. "Everything is great." She was going to enjoy this moment. She'd put herself through so much just to get this far.

"Really?" Lara understood Bea's skepticism. She was rarely the first to forgive.

"I'm glad to hear it. And again, it wasn't cool for me to kick you while you were down."

"Forget about it. You owed me a few, anyway. Bea, I'm pregnant."

"Yahoo! When did you find out?"

"Just today, so it's early. And I need you to promise not to say anything, especially to Beth."

"See, you were worried for no reason."

Lara opened her mouth to argue, to give Bea the myriad sources of her worry, but she stopped herself. "Will you keep it quiet?"

"Of course. What did Will say?"

"He'll be home in a little bit. I'm going to tell him then."

"Thanks so much for telling me. And buckle up, big sis. You're taking the ride of your life. And don't worry, with the next one, you'll be so busy that you won't even know you're pregnant."

"I'm sure this will be it for us, Bea. Another four years of trying and I'll be forty-two. But thanks. Your excitement means a lot to me."

Lara hung up smiling. Her sister had no idea what the last years had been like for her, but she could forgive Bea's ignorance now. She rinsed off the pregnancy test sticks and put them in a gift bag topped with bright tissue paper in preparation of Will's arrival. Surely he would remember that today would be the day she was supposed to test.

At 5:30 p.m. Lara heard Will before he opened the front door. He was arguing with someone on his cell phone. "We're going to lose good teachers if this keeps up," he grumbled as he walked in. He was scowling. He didn't immediately put down his bag or shrug off his coat as usual. Instead he walked around with the bag slung over his shoulder, intent on finishing his conversation.

She gingerly slid the strap of his bag off of his shoulders and smiled at him. He gave her a silent kiss on the cheek before continuing, "No one wants to be forever mired in Comp 101. I want to go on record as being opposed to this."

Back in the kitchen she spruced up the tissue paper, two pink sheets and two blue sheets, that stuck out of the gift bag. Once she heard him hang up she counted to fifty before leaving the kitchen. *He'll remember*.

"Hey, honey," she said, walking into the family room, bag behind her back.

He shook his head. "Hi. Sorry about that." He moved over so she could sit down.

"That's okay." She handed him the bag. "Surprise."

He looked from the bag in his hands to her and back. He swallowed. "What's this for?"

So what if he doesn't remember what today was. Obviously he's had a rough day. It was fun to draw out the reveal, anyway. "It worked," she said, effervescent. He squinted at her. "Just open it." For someone so brilliant, he could be a real ass.

He dumped the bag into his lap, the test sticks clacking against each other and landing in the small mound of tissue paper on his thighs. Both result screens: *pregnant*.

"Oh my God." He pulled his fingers through his hair. "It's been two weeks. Whoa."

The longest two weeks of her life, but who was counting? "Yes. It's still early, but it worked, Will. Both tests said pregnant right away." She clasped his hands and watched as he shaped and weighed his words.

"That's wonderful, honey. I know you were so anxious. And so was I."

She nodded, grinning.

"It's great news. I do think it's safer, though, for us not to get too attached at this point."

He was right, of course, as if attachment were a choice. Clearly the miscarriages, the waiting, the raised and dashed expectations had cost him, too. "You're probably right. But this is really good."

He stood and straightened his pant legs before collecting the tissue paper and jamming it back into the bag. "So exciting, Lar. But let's not tell anyone just yet, okay?"

She hesitated. "Sure. Of course." Tugging at the raffia gift bag handle in his hand, she asked, "But you're happy, right?" The question didn't sound like one she should have to verbalize.

A light kiss on her forehead. "Of course I am."

Being a solo rider on this coaster would be lonely. Thankfully she had the women on the message boards. At least they got her.

After the early ultrasounds to confirm implantation, the presence of the gestational sac, and the fetal poles, Lara asked the doctor to put off her first real prenatal appointment, the heartbeat appointment, until the beginning of her ninth week so there would be no confusion. Either there'd be a heartbeat or there wouldn't. No prolonged, fruitless search. She'd already researched a company that rented fetal Dopplers so she would not have to go weeks or more without hearing the baby. The heartbeat would reassure her. It had to.

The morning of the heartbeat check, Lara flipped through a magazine on the counter without reading a word. Already she'd taken a walk, watered the front flowerbeds, answered twelve emails, and re-recorded her work voicemail message to reflect the two hours she expected to be out of the office. Two hours remained before her appointment. She showered, dried her hair, ate breakfast.

"There's an interesting article above the fold, section two," Will said, though he usually took the paper with him to read in his office after she'd finished in the morning. He was still in his pajamas.

Two slips of computer paper slid out from between the front and home sections. Lara caught them mid-flutter, before they landed on the kitchen tile. Will's handwriting on the top corner of page one: *All shall be well, Will. P.S. Science says so.*

The headline: *Spontaneous Abortion/Miscarriage Unlikely After Eight Weeks Gestational Age.* He'd printed a WebMD article for her.

"I can tell you're nervous, Lar. Everything's going to be fine." How could he be so confident, take for granted they would get what they wanted?

He'd put a jinx in her hand. "That doesn't mean it's impossible, just less likely."

"One thing I can do, Lara, is read, thank you."

Static and goo. Lara's pinched breath.

And then, hoofbeats on sand, galloping through churned tide foam.

A hiss of breath, released.

A rim of tears broke on Will's eyelids. Blood throbbed through Lara's temples, tapped across her eyes. The baby's heartbeat a jailbreak tempo, but at least for now this baby, this wondrous echo, was staying put. She pictured a moth butting against a light, frustrated and entranced.

"We've never made it this far," she said breathlessly to no one in particular.

The doctor smiled and nodded. "Everything sounds good. One hundred forty-eight beats per minute or so."

Lara closed her eyes. Listened.

Will squeezed her hand, then shook it. "We did it, Mama." His smile cut wide across his face.

Her throat squeezed. *We still have so far to go.* Will considered this pregnancy, their baby, a done deal.

As they walked to their cars after, Will said, "You've worked so hard, been through so much, Lar." She smiled at him and shrugged her shoulders. "You should take a minute to enjoy."

"The client won't wait! That was really something, though, wasn't it?" Her smile felt tight as she spoke, but she knew it was there.

The lusty heartbeat inside her eased Lara's worry. Each Wednesday night after work, she and Will sat together and listened to the baby's heartbeat through the rented Doppler. As soon as Will turned on the shower in the morning, Lara grabbed a tube of aloe vera gel from beneath the magazines and notebooks in her bedside table, squirted it on her belly, and listened. Her own heart beat fast as she kept an eye on the bathroom door. The Doppler had come with three bottles of gel, supposedly enough for six months of use. Lara used those first tubes in just over a month. The women on BabyCenter.com also recommended baby oil, even KY Jelly, as budget-friendly alternatives.

She barely had any morning sickness. Yes, she was moody, but that had started when she began the course of fertility drugs. The nausea would reassure. It was also a rite of passage, a currency among pregnant women. A club that, up until now, had excluded her.

She had several appointments during each month of her pregnancy, rather than the standard monthly check-ups. Part of her wondered if the doctors and nurses were just saving themselves from the high-risk woman's constant neuroses in the forms of frequent calls and emails—the worry about every symptom, or worse for Lara, the occasional normalcy of a lack of symptoms.

On her fifth visit, as always, Lara stepped up onto the scale. This time she did not study the nurse's hand, tarnished rings on each finger, as it slid the weight tracker in front of her nose. She looked up at the poster of a sad-eyed woman in a hospital gown. Beneath the woman, the poster read, "The number one side effect of childbirth is depression."

No infertile woman ever said that. *Try four years of wondering if you'd ever even give birth. Spoiled bitches.*

"Got it," Soleith, the nurse, said, pressing something round into Lara's palm. "You can step down. I need you to collect some urine for me."

Soleith was Lara's favorite nurse. She worked Tuesday through Thursday, and Lara scheduled her appointments as often as possible on those days. Soleith could stick a vein on the first try and she had the perfect balance of been-there-done-that-nothing-shocks-me in her dark brown eyes, a tenderness in her hands, and meticulously short, squared-off fingernails. When her hand patted Lara, it transferred power and calm, never a "There, there." More of an "I've got you. I feel you. Don't panic, but you've earned your worries."

"So, you're going to be one of those fly pregnant ladies," Soleith said to Lara after she provided the urine sample. Soleith laid out a fresh paper drape on the examination table, folds crisp, corners sharp.

"If you say so," Lara said.

"Still wearing your sexy panties," Soleith said with a laugh. Lara had worn thongs or tiny boy shorts ever since she was in charge of buying her own underwear. The double butt created by a thick seam in a brief or bikini flattered no one. Those women had given up.

Lara shrugged.

"With the discharge and soupy mess that starts brewing down there, a lot of women find increased coverage to be more comfortable." A nurse who saw vaginas all day and still called it "down there" was a keeper.

"Yeah, well, I'm not there yet," Lara said.

"No, girl, I guess not." Soleith shook her head. "Get comfortable. Doctor will be in soon."

The next morning, Lara turned the ignition in her car and slid the gear into reverse. As she applied her foot to the brake pedal, her inner thighs went cold. Her thong was damp.

"Oh, no. Please no."

Will was still inside the house. He would wonder why she went back in. She never forgot anything. Lara looked over both shoulders and in her rearview mirror. Nobody on the sidewalk. No passing cars. She hiked up her black pencil skirt, shimmying in the driver's seat so that she wouldn't strain the slit in the back that was already high enough. The waistline slipped up, just beneath her bra. The purple mesh of her thong with its pink scalloped trim formed a dark triangle between her legs. She looked over both shoulders and in the mirror again, then at the front door in case Will was exiting. She hooked her fingers into her underwear and pulled it away from her skin. She braced for blood.

She was not bleeding.

A thin strip of beige goo clung to the miniscule piece of cotton lining her crotch. She exhaled. Her inhale was painful relief, stinging like the first gasp after she'd fallen from a tree after climbing too high, ignoring Beth's warnings, flashing her underwear beneath her skirt, and landed hard, vision black; that first impossible breath.

Lara slid her skirt back into place, checked the mirror, this time for her reflection. *Stick with me, kid. Anything you want, it's yours.*

She checked her underwear four times that day, thankful for her hectic schedule, knowing that without work she would've spent all day in the bathroom. At her desk, Lara checked off the Google analytics for her clients, documenting trends in website traffic, customer posts, and referrals. Afterwards, Lara crossed off days and then weeks in her calendar, confident that as each passed she would not be so afraid of losing her baby.

But a new fear always sprang up, another test awaited: beta levels, chromosomes, neck folds. "After that, I'll relax," she told herself, Will, everyone. She had not counted on the amount of time it took for the results to return.

She then told herself that once she could feel the baby moving inside of her, she would calm down. She would learn the baby's rhythms. They could communicate that way.

When she called her mother to confide her fears, Beth said, "If you're worried now, just wait until after that baby is born." *Thanks for the reassurance, Mom.*

By the tenth week of her pregnancy, Lara learned how to mask her anxiety. Beth had never learned to contain her crazy. It spread from her like a virus. Lara wouldn't repeat her mother's mistakes. She had asked several people, doctors included, if it was normal. *All pregnant women worry*, she was told. The world became a scary, dangerous place when you realized you were bringing someone new into it. Worry about her baby's well-being coupled with a militant approach to nutrition were the only ways Lara knew how to mother this fetus. If this kiddo was willing to hang in there and grow, anxiety was a bargain.

Only Kathy poked fun at Lara's pregnancy neuroses, particularly her exacting diet. If they weren't taking clients to lunch, Kathy and Lara either ordered into the office or went out to eat together on weekdays. "Here we go," Kathy said, as Lara was about to order lunch at their favorite French cafe. The waiter chuckled.

"Enough with you, Kath," Lara said. Then, to the waiter, "I'd like the nicoise salad, please. But may I have chicken instead of the tuna, no anchovies, and please ask them to hard cook the eggs."

"It was hard enough to cut out the wine when I was pregnant," Kathy said with a laugh. "Sounds like the rules have gotten even stricter."

"You're not kidding. It's only nine months, right?"

—

The day that One Hope Fertility Center confirmed Lara's pregnancy, Will gave her a gift, a pink Polar watch with a heart rate monitor and a copy of *Runner's World Guide to Running and Pregnancy*. Possibly Will was terrified she'd balloon up. She read the book but never wore the monitor. She'd stopped jogging when instructed just before the implantation procedure and hadn't restarted. If it was bad for the baby then, when would it be safe and why? She had asked her doctor, but was unsatisfied by the assurance that there was nothing to "contraindicate" running at this stage of pregnancy.

Instead, Lara swam almost every day. That was the hour she felt closest to the child inside her. In the earliest days of her pregnancy she swam so that she could be alone with her joy, her surprise, and worry. Visions of people blurred and waved whenever someone walked onto the pool deck, but they were reduced to color and movement. And it was quiet. She imagined the sounds she heard in the water were similar to the sounds her baby would hear—the world muffled through amniotic fluid.

When she first started menstruating Beth had told her that being in water stops your flow, keeps it in equilibrium, at least temporarily. It couldn't happen in the pool. Lara felt sure she wouldn't miscarry underwater.

Her echoing heartbeat in her ears, and her body moving through water. A slight turn of her face as she broke the surface, a robust slurp of air before slipping back underwater. Lara closed her eyes for half of each pool length. She lengthened her stroke, but slowed her movements, thinking with each smooth reach of what it would be like to feel her baby's form beneath her fingertips, the way she and her baby would learn each other by touch, like reading Braille. She wondered if the slow kicks, the gentle turns at each end, were lulling her baby to sleep. She told her baby that she felt as though she were swimming through honey. That this slowness was sweet. They didn't have to rush. *I love you already.*

Beginning in her twelfth week, the end of her first trimester, Lara asked Will to photograph her in profile. She held a sheet of printer paper with a calligraphic twelve beside her bare belly. She loved the juxtaposition between the thick, bold, black numbers and her new softening.

"You look exactly the same," he said.

"I won't for long. I want to remember all of this," she said. "If you're going to be such a pain in the ass I can call Chuck from next door over to do this next month."

"Who are you?" he asked, then held the camera to his eye. "Now, smile."

Each month she stood in the backyard and posed beside the cherry tree seedling they'd planted the spring they moved in. Each month Will clucked his annoyance at the ritual.

"You're going to hate these pictures," he said. "You never keep ones that make you look fat." She knew he was wrong. She loved posing for the photographs. She could relive every wonderful moment of this pregnancy someday.

The evening Lara began her thirteenth week of pregnancy, she put her hand on Will's shoulder, leaned close to his neck, and said, low, "I could use some help getting to sleep tonight," as she had done countless times throughout their marriage. Will would usually snap *The Oxford American* closed, lay it beside him on the table, fold in the arms of his glasses, place them on top of the journal, stand and rub his hands together like an excited child. There was some comfort in the predictability of their sex life.

But, no.

Now he patted her hand, closed his fingers around hers, where they traced his ear, and held them, chastely.

Will was quiet, thoughtful, but ran hot. Lara couldn't always untangle the threads of his mind but she could flush his flesh, make it rise with her fingertips, mouth. For most of their life together, Will had sought her, a bumped foot against her toes, pointy in Blahnik.

She tried not to be angry. But she was hot for him, again, finally. She hadn't been game for sex during the first trimester. In the early weeks, she had been relieved not to have to turn him down. His extra time in the shower each morning gave her a few more minutes alone with her baby's heartbeat.

Was this new reticence payback for the fertility treatments, life created in a lab, or was Will still worried that he'd hurt the baby somehow? Will had rebuffed her. Would he prefer his buxom grad student friend, the woman Lara had seen at the wine festival? Auburn curls in Will's fingers instead of her dark strands; she couldn't wrangle her imagination.

Tonight, she stepped up her game, made her movements, her intentions overt, bawdy.

"Maybe not tonight," he said. "We should have asked about it today. Let's run it by your doctor at the next appointment."

"She told me it was fine."

"But what if I hurt it," he said, his face down.

Wow, delusions of grandeur.

"The next appointment isn't for two weeks." *Two more weeks.*

"We'll make sure then." Her lips, this time on his ear, teasing glances of tongue. Will tilted his neck away.

With each raised stake in the fertility games, from timing to pills to injections to pills-and-injections to egg harvesting, Will had always deferred to Lara. "She's the boss," he'd say. Or, "I want what Lara wants."

His lack of interest and investment pissed her off. In every instance, though, she'd gotten the answer she wanted. She didn't complain, to him. She'd only posted once to see "if any other DHs don't seem to care if you get pregnant." The women on the boards reassured her that spouses tried to be considerate of how much pressure they might be applying, and "aren't you glad he isn't fighting you over the cost?" She'd laughed, then typed, "Wanted to check that he had a pulse."

She budgeted for and scheduled the myriad fertility treatments and doctor's appointments and marked them on the calendar in her planner, never using a red pen or tab—too like blood, too fate-tempting. She carved a line through every completed meeting, exercise class, luncheon.

Two weeks later (after her doctor's laugh and then to Will: "No, your penis won't touch the baby"), she made sex a regular part of her marriage again. Even if routine sex was as inorganic as their methods for getting pregnant, it had to be better than nothing. Forced or not, his body in hers felt good. She never circled Wednesdays, but that was their night. Work each day; prenatal appointments every other week, then weekly; belly photos; scheduled sex.

Check, check, check.

Chapter Ten

Lara loved her swelling belly, the blue web of veins that crisscrossed her body. Their darkening reflected new purpose and importance. This baby would be someone she could tell her stories to; she could pluck her accomplishments off the shelf and they'd sparkle. This child would be the nexus of all of the choices she'd made up until now—the way she forced herself to be independent of her family, building a career, traveling, and then marrying Will after knowing plenty of suitable and attractive men and finding them wanting. His pull on her was stronger than anything she had ever known and her pregnancy fulfilled that promise. She could stop waiting for life to make sense.

By week fifteen, Lara stood sideways, pressed against the ice-colored walls of what would become the nursery. With a silver paint pen she traced her silhouette, starting at her clavicle, over her breasts and the growing arc of her stomach.

"It's a bit grotesque," Will said, when he noticed. "A fantasized chalk outline."

"I think it's gorgeous," she said. This life was changing her from the inside out, and she could capture the transformation, magic. This line without words was the most beautiful she'd ever known.

Every two weeks, she traced the changing curves of her body on the wall. The pictures were for preservation, to show the baby someday. This staggered, one-dimensional topography was for Lara. The lines looked like waves one day, a sensual top lip another day, birds in flight. A new coat of paint would cover them, anyway.

"Your eleven o'clock is here." Her JE, Jason's voice crackled from the speakerphone, along with the scratch of cotton. He sat there, she knew, nervously rolling and unrolling his shirtsleeves. Jason's arms—and most of his body, presumably—were covered in elaborate tattoos. Neither she nor Kathy had asked him to cover them, but he did for every meeting. Lara enjoyed her tiny part in the ruse, though. She liked watching him fool everyone.

"*Our* eleven o'clock." Delegation disagreed with Lara; relying on one of the junior employees took twice as long than if she did the work herself, and the product met almost half of her expectations. Still, she was trying her best. "Review their names, show them into the conference room, and I'll be right in. Don't forget the flash drive."

"Loaded and ready, Lara."

At Jason's age, her teeth had clanged against bit and bridle as her seniors, though not necessarily superiors, held her back. Now, she needed him to be ready.

This proposal to Shades of Light wasn't Jason's first; the store was a significant customer with six mid-Atlantic area showrooms and an international customer base. Luckily, Tom, the owner, had been a client forever and was one of the nicest guys Lara knew.

Before she closed her planner and shoved it in a desk drawer, she tapped her finger once on the blue star she'd drawn on the following Monday: seven days until her next ultrasound. The normal pregnant girls on the boards nicknamed it the "Big U/S", the day they'd learn whether to paint their nurseries pink or blue, the viability and health of their babies a minor concern. She would be twenty weeks pregnant.

Time to shift gears.

In the conference room, Jason, Tom, and his team sat on both sides of the long table. Jason had remembered the remote and laser pointer; he'd set them at Lara's place at the head. Everyone stood at her arrival. Tom, in waxed khakis and hiking boots, the same he wore duck hunting, gave her a kiss on the cheek.

"Let's dispense with the formalities, shall we, and show you what you've paid for," Lara said. Jason dimmed the recessed lights as Lara sat. "You're on, Jason."

He cleared his throat and began.

Lara gasped. There was a scrape inside her, but by something yielding, curved, not at all like a kick or a jab. Not a gas bubble, either. She fought the urge to lay her hands on her stomach, slowly curving outward, that she'd been trying to conceal with empire waist dresses, baggier cardigans and tunics like the one she wore today, and the deep indigo jeans that still fit—with an elastic band holding the top button together. Everyone in the office knew about her pregnancy by now, but she didn't want clients thinking her unprofessional. She kept her hands on the conference table, occupied them with her pen and notebook, advanced the slides.

"Everything all right?" Tom, seated next to her, leaned in. He tucked an errant strand behind his ear. The man was born to have long hair.

She nodded quickly and tried to contain her smile. "Yes, excuse me." Heat prickled up her neck and jawline. Before he straightened up, Tom winked at her.

Had her client figured it out? Lara didn't care. *Do it again, guppy.* Nothing. Jason was wrapping up the PowerPoint presentation. The instant he finished, the heads of her clients would swivel to her as they asked questions about the campaign.

"Nice presentation, Jason," Tom said. "I like the concept, but I have some questions about implementation and how we make this work with our current branding."

Even Jason turned to Lara. The question was a softball, inevitable when modernizing a well-known, successful company.

"Of course," Lara answered. "Jason and I have pored over all of the Shades branding, the catalogs, the website, most of which we've worked on together. And we can implement seamlessly, and significantly manage costs—" Another scrape. She stopped talking mid-sentence. She'd never fumbled a proposal. Expecting shame or frustration, she bit back a giggle. She tried to rediscover her drive, the significance of this campaign's success, but Lara just wanted to be alone to enjoy this fluid movement inside of her. The meeting was suddenly an intrusion.

"Jason, why don't you bring Tom up to speed on our discussions, particularly the colors and font work?" she said. "You have a solid grasp on how we will integrate. Hell, you wrote most of it." As much as she wanted to, she still couldn't walk out of the room. Lara allowed one hand to fall to her thigh.

"You sure you're all right?" Tom's voice was concerned, moist in her ear.

"Never better."

She was ready to stand still. She wanted to slow down her life and watch for a while, the way she edited TV commercials: freezing the movements of the actors so that she could immerse herself in the details, the curve of a woman's elbow or her cheek, the angle of the lighting, the point of a shoe. She was that happy. Getting pregnant, she realized, was the first finish line that meant something, and for years she'd only been able to glimpse that future at the top of the hill, blurry and shimmering with distance. Before her pregnancy, each race was a step to another race, longer or faster than the one before. Work had progressed the same way. To stop moving forward professionally was the last step before falling behind your competition.

The fears and anxiety over the baby's health and viability had clouded the earliest months of her pregnancy. She'd wanted to fast forward in between a blood draw and a test result. She'd learned time and again not to get too attached to the lines and words on a pregnancy test—all they meant was that the baby-growing hormones were present and a speck of baby, too, might be growing.

But the day her baby's body spoke to her, Lara knew forty weeks, half of them already behind her, were too short. She envied elephants, who gestated up to two years. Even giraffes grew their young over fourteen months. She'd reached the good part, after so much effort, and for the first time she could remember, Lara didn't need to rush anything.

That night, after her Shades of Light meeting and the baby's first palpable movements, Will didn't believe her when she told him. "Wishful thinking, I'm afraid. That kid's not even a pound yet."

She frowned at him but was happy she didn't have to share. These sensations were hers alone, just a little secret between baby and mother. To Lara, it underscored the primacy of the mother-child relationship. Who better could there be to parent this child than the woman who felt its first gesture, and understood?

Through her first two trimesters, Lara checked her weekly gestational updates like a zealot, awaiting a sign each Monday morning before starting anything else. But lately she found herself remembering to check only on a Wednesday or Thursday. Then one week, she forgot entirely. She no longer checked and rechecked her deadlines. Her recurring dream of arriving at a college class for the first time on final exam day stopped.

Instead, she immersed herself in the signs of her baby. Her baby liked chocolate and electronica. After turning up the volume on the stereo, Lara stretched out on the couch, eyes closed, as her baby bumped around inside her. No meditation had soothed her this way, nor any yoga. The baby's head felt large, smooth, and round. The hands rat-tat-tatted small, gentle strikes. But the baby's kicks—perhaps she would birth a swimmer. This fetus had a strong, natural flutter kick. The nights that the baby rolled and bounced from side-to-side, Lara envisioned plump white skin, strengthening muscle in the kick-turns being performed against the walls of her uterus.

Grow strong, little love.

In her twenty-third week, Lara and Will were propped on pillows, side-by-side in bed, the first time Will felt the baby's movements.

She shook his hand free of the newest issue of *Orion* and pressed it low on her belly.

"What are you doing?" he asked, eyes still on the magazine. The baby turned; Will's eyes snapped open. He looked younger to her than ever.

"This is really happening, isn't it?" he asked.

"You're just figuring that out now?"

She smiled as he dropped the magazine and placed both palms against her tight skin; the baby rolled again. His jaw loosened.

"Does it hurt?" The question struck Lara as childlike.

"No," she said, eyes closed, never wanting it to stop. Never ever.

"You're so calm. It's . . . quite strange."

"I just feel good. Enormous, but good."

"Perhaps motherhood suits you after all."

It suited Lara just fine, perfectly.

Arms out, the baby in her rounding belly led Lara forward; she became a blissful sleepwalker. She could smell motherhood. The scent was sweet, like dried milk on flesh, warm skin on skin. She could taste the welling up of happiness—it was salty. She felt sated. Uncomfortable, sure. Moody, sometimes. But her body had never been so useful. Once she felt the baby move, every nudge was a promise. A tease. She opened to the magic of it all. Her hair and nails grew thicker, strong and glossy. She dreamed in color and remembered her dreams in the morning. The universe had breathed a secret inside of her. She could see the intricate design behind it. Excitement and hope quickened her blood. This baby had already changed her, and would make Will new.

Though she loved work, this new life that prepared to unfurl before her reduced everything else by comparison. Suddenly, she didn't see a place for a career in the life, the vocation that she had envisioned down to each excruciating detail for so long. This would be her only shot at motherhood.

By the time Will casually asked, "What are you going to do about work?" Lara already had her answer. She had worked so hard, given everything for this baby. She was going to enjoy the time she had with it.

"I'd like to stay home, at least for the first couple of years."

"Can we afford that?"

"Of course we can. We're in a good place financially." She added, for levity, "At least we won't be paying for fertility treatments." The realization that this might be her only child pressed urgency into Lara's every decision. "I've never wanted anything more than this."

"Good childcare is certainly expensive," Will said.

"Do you want to see our bank statements, investments, retirement accounts? I can pull it all up for you."

Will wrinkled his nose, waved her request away. He paused before speaking. "What I should have said is, you've worked really hard."

"I get it. Money talk is repugnant to you," she said. "So base. You certainly didn't fight the move into this house. You seem pretty comfortable."

"Money, all this"—Will gestured around him at the high ceilings, Bryght furniture, sleek lithographs on the walls—"has never driven me."

"You're right. A one-bedroom apartment, dust, books for furniture, schlepping to the Laundromat . . . I've never romanticized that," Lara said. "This kid is going to be little only once. I deserve to take a few years off."

"Have you thought this all the way through?"

"There are plenty of obvious places I can trim the budget. The housekeeper for one, that's a huge expense and I'll be home all of the time and can handle that. The gardening, too. And there will be way fewer lunches out. I've put a lot of thought into this."

"I just think we should talk it out."

"You keep talking. I'll keep doing."

Will sighed and rolled his eyes. "I asked a simple question. Your behavior is childish."

"You've said my income is obscene. Now it won't be. I've earned the chance to enjoy this."

"Of course you have. But quit your job? You love your job." Why was he fighting her? He'd been so blasé about all of it. Will didn't get to decide this.

"I've hardly had a choice. One of us had to make some money."

"Clearly you've decided what you're doing. I misread this as a conversation." He opened the book in his lap.

She walked over and closed it. "Do you want to take charge of raising this child? Trade doctor for Mr. Mom?"

Without answering, Will stood and walked out of the room.

She called after him, "I've already given Kathy my notice."

Kathy said she wasn't just disappointed that Lara wasn't going back to work after giving birth, she was shocked. Just like Will. They couldn't understand her choices, but Karen would, even if Lara had some heavy apologizing to do. Following the wine festival dust-up, Lara had emailed Karen four times asking to meet for lunch. She'd received no reply. She backed off for a few more months. When she had called to tell Karen she was pregnant, she was greeted by voicemail.

"Big news," she'd said, trying to ignore the sting. "Call me back."

Karen phoned within fifteen minutes.

"I'm pregnant, Kar. Almost thirteen weeks!"

"You're going to be a mom, Lara. How wonderful."

Lara still hadn't seen Karen. They had scheduled lunch three times. Twice, Karen's kids were home sick, and once Lara had to reschedule. She could do without the other friends she'd pushed away, but she couldn't live without Karen. And now, blatantly pregnant, she missed her. Karen was her best friend, and she had kids.

"I'll come to you," Lara told her in an email.

Karen's house was kid heaven. She had transformed the all-weather side porch into a playroom worthy of a magazine. Where once Karen had had a bar and operated a keg-o-rater with her husband's home-brewed beer, red and blue bins bulged with polyester dress-up gowns and emerald Mardi Gras bead necklaces. The floor, formerly hardwood, was now a soft, liquid-repellant, gymnastic quality mat that ran corner to corner. Thomas the Tank Engine wove through a miniature town atop a train table.

Sophie and Gabriel, Karen's kids, had their backs to Lara and Karen, vertebrae tensing, releasing as they manipulated their toys. Sophie was almost seven, Gabe five.

"Look at you, Lara, like a snake that swallowed a rat," Karen said.

Lara smiled.

"I thought you'd die before you had to wear a double-digit size."

Lara cupped her hands beneath her belly. "Ha ha. I'm eating all kinds of words these days, Kar."

Karen turned her attention to the children. "Y'all get an hour of tube time while Aunt Lara and I catch up. It's Little Bear or nothing. No changing the channel, Sophie, you hear?"

"Yes, Mama," two light voices answered in unison. Karen shook her head, sighed, as she pulled the child-proofed French doors closed.

Karen poured two glasses of raspberry lemonade and they sat at the small round table in her kitchen. Lara had to stretch her arm wide to set her glass on the table; she couldn't slide her chair in, her belly was so large.

Lara apologized for her crazy behavior at the wine festival. "I was a monster. The hormones, too much wine. I held that baby. I lost it, Karen." She shredded the paper napkin in her hands.

"I'm sorry, too. I had no idea. Why didn't you tell me what was going on?"

Lara shook her head. "I wanted to be able to handle it, whether I could get pregnant or not. It was humiliating."

"And I have the opposite problem." Karen glanced at her lap. "I get pregnant by mood lighting."

"Shut your mouth. Again?"

Karen blushed. "Would you save me your newborn clothes? I—I thought we were done."

"That's great, Karen! They can play."

"Easy, tiger, they'll be at least eight months apart. I haven't told the kids yet. I'm still coming around to . . . starting over again. I survived two infancies, two toddlers. I don't know if I can do it again." The skin beneath Karen's eyes was darker than Lara had ever seen it. Karen had always reminded her of the Energizer Bunny, but she looked spent.

"Why are you trying to scare me?" Lara asked. Lara had survived the last four years: the outrageous expenses, the shots, the D&C. She couldn't wait for her infant, her toddler. No, Karen had to be wrong, or at least exaggerating.

"I'm not. It's just stuff that I wished someone had told me before I had my first, that's all," Karen said.

"It is amazing though, right?"

"Sure." Karen toyed with the napkin beneath her drink. "There are so many moments that take my breath away, even now. What I wasn't expecting was how hard it is. I thought Sophie would give something back to me. Stupid, right? You're basically a food source and a diaper changer for the first few months. I wasn't prepared for that."

"Yeah, things are about to change, that's for sure." *Finally.* "Nothing will ever be the same." Lara traced her fingers over her stomach, imagining a little finger inside mirroring the movement. "I can't wait."

"You have no idea. I know you've heard it all, but make sure to get as much rest as you can now and baby yourself a little while you have the time. Before you have to check the shower door for moisture to know for sure if you've bathed that day."

"I never knew what a pessimist you were." Children had come too easily for Karen. "Where was all of this before? You were like Mother Earth to Sophie."

"Just being honest. I think I might have done better the first time around if I'd heard someone admit how tough it can be. I was afraid to talk about it, like I was doing something wrong."

Tough? How hard is changing diapers and rocking someone to sleep? Tough was facing a future that never changed, where she and Will would have the same conversations over decades. Tough was never getting the chance to be who her father was to her. "If you think being a mother is so awful, why are you having another one?"

"As if you ever wanted to listen. You don't want to listen now." Karen pushed her chair away from the table so hard the spindle legs squeaked on the tile. "Jesus Christ, Lara. Listen to yourself. Why does everything have to be a battle?"

"I thought you would be happy for me," Lara said. She had worked too hard, sacrificed too much not to be happy.

"I am. I'm sorry I didn't tell you what you wanted to hear. I need to go check on the kids."

Silently, Lara dropped an invitation onto the tabletop—a Chekhov-themed birthday party for Will in their backyard the following week: *Celebrate* The Darling *Will As He Turns Forty-Four. Come dressed as your favorite Russian.*

Karen did not RSVP.

Chapter Eleven

Will set the newly assembled crib upright and surveyed his construction. He ran his hand over the smooth, rounded rail. No hard corners in this crib; it was a gentle oval. "You don't want to find out the gender?" he asked Lara. "Your planner has color-coded tabs and extends for two years."

Turning her back to him, she continued placing books on the small shelves in the nursery: *Goodnight Moon*, *Pat the Bunny*, *Poetry for Children*.

"Yes, I'm a planner. It's just that we've known everything—the moment and location where the baby was conceived. How many eggs were harvested, the number of sperm injected."

He cut the plastic from the mattress. She gathered the freshly washed organic cotton crib sheets made to fit the unconventional mattress shape and walked over to Will and the crib.

"Does anyone not find out these days?"

Lara handed him a gathered edge of the sheet and he stretched it across the mattress. "If you really want to know ahead of time, we can find out. But wouldn't this be a wonderful surprise? The only surprise left."

"I don't want to ruin the mystery." He lifted the mattress up and set it in the crib, then wheeled the crib away from the wall. Lara tied the breathable bumper to the crib slats as Will placed the step ladder against the wall.

"We just have to ask the tech not to say and to avoid any close-ups of the genitals. You know, no money shots."

"You are so crass," he said with a laugh and shook his head. "As ever, you're fully in command." He held up a simple sage-green mobile over his head. "Is this where you want it hung?"

She nodded. "What do you want, Will?"

"You mean a boy or a girl?"

"Anything, Will. Just tell me what you want." Had he always been so listless? Would he always be?

"You know I couldn't care less about some legacy, a boy child to carry on the name and all of that." He screwed the hook into the ceiling.

Lara hardly had to be reminded of his lack of interest. But she was less bothered by it now. She no longer needed him to care as much; she didn't want him micromanaging her mothering. She had her child, would see him or her soon. She smoothed out the sheet and folded a crocheted blanket from Beth at the foot of the crib.

"Well, what names do you like?" Lara asked.

"I haven't given that much thought yet. We still have almost two months left, and won't it be hard to select a name without knowing the baby's sex?"

"I have an idea. It'd work either way, boy or girl. It's literary, too. I really hope you love it." She opened the closet and pulled out a framed uppercase A and showed it to him.

"Are you holding out on me? Just tell me it isn't one of those wacko celebrity baby names."

"Auden." The name whispered through her lips like prayer.

"That's a big name."

"Just give it some thought, will you?"

"It's beautiful, Lara." He bent over and kissed the swell of their baby, then stood and put his arms around her.

"That's a relief. There was no way I was going for Anton or Antonia." She relaxed into his arms.

"So, in that secret heart of hearts of yours, what are you really hoping for? I promise not to tell a soul."

"I don't care, Will. I really don't. Just a healthy, happy human." She meant it. "Ten fingers, ten toes."

"Everyone says that. And you always have an opinion. On everything." It truly didn't matter to Lara, a mama's boy or a mama's girl. Initially she'd hoped for twins, one of each, in her fantasies. But she would be more than grateful for either. Her dream baby was alternately girl and boy. The genitals weren't her focus. It was the creamy skin, the nose, the wrists and ankles so chubby it looked like rubber bands had been wound around them. She saw herself gazing down at a baby cradled in one arm; a toddler looping an arm around her thigh, giving her a painting—a Thanksgiving turkey made from his own handprint. A tutu-clad tiny ballerina shyly bowing on stage. Youthful fingers flipping the tassel of a mortar board from the left to the right. A youngish man who looked like Will standing at the end of a long aisle. Yards of creamy silk dupioni or lace slipping through her fingers and the svelte arms of her daughter.

"Mother of the bride, mother of the groom, either one works for me."

"Whoa. Fast forward, huh? I've heard it goes fast. Hopefully not that fast. Think how old we'll be!"

They would age and the baby would grow. A healthy, happy baby for a healthy, happy mother. At first, her days with the baby would be all dreamy naps and nursing and quiet walks while the baby met the world. There would be no deadlines, no demanding customers, none of the nonsense that had filled her hours for so many years. No longer did happiness hide just around the corner, beyond her fingertips. The hands linked beneath her belly would gently dab drool from a round, drippy chin. Her daydreams were composed of chubby hands wrapped around thick crayons; Lara re-learning the words to "The Itsy-Bitsy Spider." She pictured a checkerboard mouth as teeth came in and then eventually started falling out. She and the baby would listen to story time at the library, paint with their fingers and feet at the children's art classes at the museum. Auden would be her best, most constant companion, combining the highlights of Lara and Will. Lara and Auden would watch the stars twinkle alive at night and the sun awake at dawn. Never had anything felt so right.

The weight in her belly had shape, was sturdy, solid, and alive. She couldn't wait to experience her baby in the world, and yes, she couldn't wait for the adorable baby clothes.

"The nursery looks great, Lar."

"Perfect," she said. "Will you sign this, please?" Lara fetched a few pieces of paper from the changing table.

"No rest for the weary," he said. "What is it?"

"My birth plan. Just a list of things I'd like to have happen when I go into labor."

"It's four pages long."

"Ha ha, I'm thorough. That's nothing new. I've been working on this for the last month." She sat down in the rocking chair.

Will pinched the bridge of his nose as he read:

Birth Plan Worksheet

NAME: Lara Jennings James

ATTENDANTS

I'd like the following people to be present during labor and/ or birth:

Partner: Will James

Doctor: Yes

Midwife: Yes, if on call

Labor and Delivery Nurse: Yes

*No residents or students should attend the birth.

HOSPITAL ADMISSION & PROCEDURES

- I'd like the option of returning home if I'm not in active labor.

Once I'm admitted, I'd like:

- my partner to be allowed to stay with me at all times.
- to try to stay hydrated by drinking clear fluids instead of having an IV.
- to walk and move around as I choose.

OTHER INTERVENTIONS

As long as the baby and I are doing fine, I'd like to:

- be allowed to progress free of stringent time limits and have my labor augmented only if necessary.

LABOR PROPS

If available, I'd like to try a:

- birthing stool.
- birthing chair.
- squatting bar.

I'd like to bring the following equipment with me:

- exercise ball

PAIN RELIEF

I'd like to try the following pain-management techniques:

- acupressure
- bath/shower
- breathing techniques/distraction
- hot/cold therapy
- massage
- Please don't offer me pain medication, even if I ask for it.

If I decide I want medicinal pain relief, I'd prefer:
- I don't want medication.

PUSHING
When it's time to push, I'd like to:
- do so instinctively.
- be allowed to progress free of stringent time limits as long as my baby and I are doing fine.

I'd like to try the following positions for pushing (and birth):
- semi-reclining
- side-lying position
- squatting
- hands and knees
- whatever feels right at the time

VAGINAL BIRTH
During delivery, I'd like:
- Will to stay up by my shoulders. No mirror, please.

After birth, I'd like:
- to hold my baby right away, putting off any procedures that aren't urgent.
- to breastfeed as soon as possible.

- to not get oxytocin (Pitocin) after I deliver the placenta unless it's necessary.
- my partner to cut the umbilical cord.

CESAREAN SECTION

If I have a cesarean section, I'd like:

- my partner present at all times during the operation.
- the screen lowered a bit so I can see my baby being delivered.
- the baby to be given to my partner as soon as s/he's dried.
- to breastfeed my baby in the recovery room.

CORD BLOOD BANKING

I'm planning to:

- bank cord blood privately.

POSTPARTUM

After delivery, I'd like:

- all newborn procedures to take place in my presence.
- my partner to stay with the baby at all times if I can't be there.
- to stay in a private room.
- to have a cot provided for my partner.
- twenty-four-hour rooming-in with my baby.

FEEDING ISSUES

I plan to:

- breastfeed exclusively.

Do not offer my baby:

- formula.

- sugar water.
- a pacifier.

CIRCUMCISION

If my baby's a boy:

- I want him to be circumcised at the hospital.

DISCHARGE

I'd like to:

- be discharged from the hospital with my baby as soon as possible.

"Thorough is one word for it," Will said when he finished reading. "It's very detailed."

"If you want, I could take out that part about you being at my shoulders, but I thought you'd appreciate not having to watch anything you can't unsee. I figured we'd like to have sex at some point after this kid is born."

"That part is fine with me." He gave her the thumbs-up sign. "Why the formality, though? Signatures. Certainly this plan isn't legally binding."

"No, but I really want to get started on the right foot, you know? And I want the doctors to know we're on the same page here." She rocked faster.

"From what I've heard from Karen of your days in Georgetown, you're not the girl to turn down drugs when offered." He flipped through the pages again.

"Shut up, Will." Playful. "I just want to do it right. Feel every-thing, live it. This birth has been such a long time coming. And this could be our only child. Do you want to add anything?"

"No. But why rule anything out? What is it your mom said the other day? 'Birth is just a day. A life is long.' Something like that."

Certainly birth was one day, the most important day of her life. And she could visualize every moment, a calm room with just Will, her obstetrician and the nurse. Her body transitioning and moving her child into the world. A gooey, perfect baby, still vernix-coated from her womb, placed against her chest. "You're taking advice from Beth now?"

He looped his signature onto the page, just beneath Lara's.

With less than three weeks before her due date, Lara draped the one-piece sleeper over the hard expanse of her belly. One foot of the tiny garment rested on her belly button, which stuck out hard like a fresh tree stump. There was a baby inside her, of course, but she couldn't imagine that the life inside her would need clothes, would actually wear this cotton sleeper. Her baby's first outfit, the exciting going-home garment, the one she'd dress the baby in before leaving the hospital for home, was simple: white cotton, soft but light, with white powder-coated snaps down the middle and the inside of one leg. On the chest, a tiny duck, yellow fluff body and orange beak, was embroidered. Two small duck appliques were stitched, one on each foot.

Will's mother had sent a long, gauzy white dress with a note explaining that the gown was appropriate for both newborn boys and girls. It didn't look comfortable to Lara, and she wanted her baby's start to life to be all comfort and warmth. She folded the sleeper, unfolded and refolded, weaving the fabric legs through her fingers.

It was impossibly itty-bitty. Once folded, the arms and legs of the garment tucked into a neat square. Perhaps she'd bought it too small. She couldn't use a cloth that scant to wash her face. She'd bought the sleeper before her thirty-fifth week checkup. She hadn't even been looking for it. And it was the only zero-to-three month size left. At the ultrasound, the baby had measured over five pounds ("Perfect," said the tech). Neither too small, nor too big. Still, she'd waited two more weeks to even wash the sleeper in preparation. She didn't want to rush.

Yes, she was hot. Yes, her lower back burned and her hips felt like they were coming unhinged, but she wanted her baby fully cooked and ready for life on the outside. For now she didn't have to share the baby, not with anyone. Only she knew the baby's rhythms: the quiet naps and the kickboxing rounds and gymnastics demonstrations.

In the hospital bag Lara packed, she included two other pairs of soft T-shirts, no diapers—the hospital would take care of those—and a onesie. She packed a special breast-feeding nightgown for herself—*as few pictures in a hospital gown as possible, please*—and a crocheted white and yellow blanket, a perfect match for her little duck. Karen had made it for her. She'd left it with Lara's receptionist. The note, in Karen's loopy cursive: *I love you. And I'll love this new little you, too. I'm so excited for all of you.*

Initially the baby's earliest movements in her had felt finned, and as the baby grew, she'd thought of her little duck, palmate feet padding and scraping, swimming.

She tossed in a deck of cards to play with Will and a hard copy of her birth plan. She'd already emailed it to her obstetrician, but wanted to have a copy for the labor and delivery nurse and the midwife. She wrapped her headphones around her MP3 player and tossed it into the bag. She zipped up her toiletry bag and unwrapped a fresh tube of ChapStick. She folded her own going-home dress—a gorgeous, flowered caftan and leggings, along with a black nursing bra. She didn't need much. She'd only be in the hospital for seventy-two hours.

"Sure you're not forgetting anything?" Will teased. "You know the hospital is less than twenty minutes away."

She poked him in the ribs.

Suddenly, Will's hand cupped her breast. Lara bit her lip, tasted the Perrier Jouet they'd shared while she packed. Since the beginning of the week, she'd had to peel off her bra as it clung to her skin with the sticky beginnings of breast milk. He licked his palm, then slid Lara's

pants off. He hooked his thumbs into the awful cotton maternity panties as if touching the side seams of a silk g-string and tugged them off.
On his knees, he kissed the curve of her ass. His hair tickled the underside of her massive belly, his hands gentle behind her knees, then up
the inside of her thighs, opening her. The surprise of his tongue against
and then inside her was like doing it blindfolded. She sighed, swayed
with pleasure.

"Oh."

He stopped, looking at up at her, his cheek against her distended
navel.

"It's good. Don't stop." She couldn't remember the last time it had
felt this good.

He led her to the bed and eased her onto the mattress. At first
tentatively, his body explored the new heft of her. A lone, guttural moan
escaped Lara and her head rolled back to rest against his chest as he
moved in slow, gentle pulses.

Will's breath sped and he moaned again, her body responding
to his. He had one hand in her hair now as he thrust in and out. She
panted, mouth open as heat moved in waves through her. Cresting.
Building. Rising. His forearms tensed at her hips. His thighs strained
behind, beneath hers.

The heat spread outside her. Hot liquid slid out, on, between their
flesh. Will slowed. She'd heard about women urinating during sex, like
shitting on the delivery table, too hideous to be real.

"Oh, my God," she said, chuckling. She clenched around him.
Fluid kept running.

Will moaned and thrust harder. "Oh, shit." His pre-ejaculatory
prayer. He shuddered.

She tapped his thigh. "Will!"

She moved forward, he slid out of her. "What?"

She gestured down. More liquid coursed out, hot between her
thighs, sticking to her hair, his legs to her legs. Will was pale, jaw loose.

She lifted herself off of the bed and slipped on the fluid splattering her feet. His arm steadied her.

She looked up from the puddle forming at her feet. "I'm not peeing," she said.

"Go time?" he asked, naked, flaccid, and beaming.

Chapter Twelve

Sharp implements glinted on a shiny tray: thin, hard, and steel cold. On the surgical table, Lara could turn her head far enough to see the razored edges before she felt the yoke of the oxygen mask. The smooth crescent on the scalpel surely would be bloodied first.

"We're going to start the incision," said one doctor. His glasses, above the blue gauze curtain bisecting her body, reflected two of Lara as he picked up a gleaming knife from the tray he slid out of sight.

Will's mouth opened and shut. Opened again: "I just want everyone happy and healthy," he said, with a squeeze of Lara's hand. "Happy and healthy," he repeated, his voice high, adolescent. His grip tight, her fingers wriggled to make room.

A cool, electric line spread across her abdomen, like an ice cube sliding across her skin on the other side of the blue screen. Will turned the color of a slug and looked down at her, his face back on their side of the screen. His chin dropped. His eyes followed to his feet, which moved in a strange, small box step.

Her baby wasn't supposed to be born here. Not this way. Sound bounced from the shiny floors of the operating room to the white walls. Figures in blue scrubs, caps, protective glasses, indistinguishable, scuttled around the room, sent the midwife away. Outlined hopes—perineum oiling and stretching, yoga, breathing exercises, use of an exercise ball, animalistic birthing postures, no epidural, natural, slow conscientious childbirth—dashed. Now folded in Will's pocket, the concise, bulleted text of her birth plan was smeared and finger-printed.

Lara wheezed, punched deep in the stomach, organs pushed to her sides. Vomit churned up her throat. The doctor's head could be in there; her ribs were splayed so wide, wishbones from a Thanksgiving turkey, broken in a rush. The wheeled tray squeaked behind the blue shroud that bisected her body.

Lara whipped her head back into position, wild beneath the mask that was there to comfort her, calm her, provide the oxygenated blood her heart could not circulate fast enough to send down to the baby, barely alive inside of her. The air from the mask was tinny and dried out her mouth. Her lips cracked but didn't bleed. The mask didn't hurt but it was the only one of many tethers on her body that she could feel. Even Will's hand on hers was uncertain, he squeezed so tight. Only the inside edge of her right thumb had any sensation. Lara felt contact when his fingers crossed that part of her hand. She sensed the beginning of fingertip-sized bruises around the knee that Will had gripped while she'd attempted to push.

Even with the bumping, the beeping, the hum of fluorescent lights, the shuffling of feet on sterile linoleum, the absence of sound keened. Silence brought her into this room, gurney wheels squeaking, movement a blur of light and ceiling tiles overhead. The reliable *beep beep beep* of her unborn baby's heartbeat on the monitor had been her companion these many hours of labor. It was only into the twentieth minute of her second hour of pushing that the *beep beep beep* had stretched out into a *beep . . . beep . . . beep*, taffying, meeting her own heart rate and then dying out for seconds at a time. Only her pulse had remained, amplified by the speaker, beeping faster and faster as though she could beat for them both. A fall and a rise. With each contraction and the collapsed-forward, dizzying push that accompanied it, Lara's belly had changed shape: billowing and rounded to start, angular and off-center the next moment.

The doctor: "We need to deliver this baby."

"Yes," Lara had said, the words tear-stained and weary, her thighs shaking. "Of course," she said, "whatever you have to do." The words tumbled easily from her tired lips. They had been her mantra all along: Anything to get pregnant with this baby; anything to keep this baby from running red and clumpy and cold down the inside of her thighs; anything to bring this baby to term; anything to make this baby live.

Her midsection fell, a gaping slackness.

"It's a girl!" a voice proclaimed, but no one lowered the screen.

How many organs had they removed? She remembered the fetal pig she had dissected in high school. The stiff body, leathery with form-aldehyde, had collapsed when she removed the heart. Its eyes, her eyes, glassy and rubbery. Open.

"I can't see," Lara said into what she realized was a room silent with a dozen people holding their breath.

Silence. Sucking, syphoning. Plastic, squeezing in and out. Gurgling. But no crying. Will nodded at someone Lara couldn't see and then pulled the drape aside. Lara saw the baby. Her daughter. *My daughter.* A pulsing cord, beating still, attached the child to Lara, now a mother. The infant was bruise-colored; mottled white clumps dappled her skin.

A cry meant life. Blood thumped in Lara's ears. A cry would signify a successful end to this long journey. In the silence, sustained so long it trussed her throat, Lara saw the sweat beading below Will's sideburns, betraying the tight smile he meant to look hopeful. He didn't look at her. A heart rate monitor still beeped the speeding, scared call-to-arms of Lara's heart. She tried to live for two, but that didn't work with the baby outside of her. The second person didn't know how to breathe, or live. Lara held her breath beneath the oxygen mask, bargaining.

You breathe, little one, then I will. First you, now. Listen to your mother.

The tips of Will's fingers turned white in her hand. He didn't speak. He looked surprised, paralyzed, ineffectual. The stiff metal table pressed cold against her back.

The nurse plunged a blue suctioning bulb back into the baby's mouth, the color and size of a raisin. The infant lips closed around it, wrinkled. A shockingly pink tongue emerged, rolling the bulb out.

The raisin lips spread into an *o*.

"MWAAAH! RWAAA!"

The baby's eyes were swollen shut, but the mouth opened wide, gulping the oxygen it just discovered and screamed again. Lara had never heard anything like it. No sound had ever given her such relief and sharp-stick pleasure.

"RAAAAAAH! MWAAAAAAH!" The cries echoed.

"Little drama queen," Lara said as she sobbed.

Will's grip on Lara's hand eased. Lara's eyelids were speckled, egg shells, that drooped like a shade over her vision of her daughter, now in Will's arms. The spots swelled, stained the white, then blotted it out.

She passed out to the symphony of her daughter's screams.

When Lara awoke, she was no longer hair-netted and draped or in the operating room. Her legs were mechanically propped up above her heart on a pneumatic bed in a recovery room. Feet belong on the floor. Hers had been up in the air for what felt like days. There was a baby in her arms, *her* baby.

The past day or days had been a fugue of exhaustion and manic bliss. Raw nipples clamped between the nails of the lactation consultant. The warm wet of her daughter's mouth soothed. Phone calls, phone in Will's hand but her own voice: "I never knew . . . She's perfect . . . I'm so in love."

Every sign and grunt was a revelation. Her baby's face relaxed from swollen birth fist to human.

Lara unswaddled Auden. She wanted to lick the warm, drumbelly skin of her baby, the red wrinkles in her arm pits, the long, long arms. When the nurses watched, she reswaddled her. White cotton diaper against ruddy, lanugo-hairy skin was an addiction. She gently tugged on the baby's toes, stretched her legs out, just to watch the knees bend, curl the feet back into her core, *little monkey*.

None of it mattered, the hell it had been to bring this baby into the world. It was all worthwhile. Even stretched out, Lara's body, her throat, was too narrow to release the skin-too-tight sensation that she experienced holding her child. Was this mother's love? The emotion was too much for her lips, too much for the vague symbols of language to organize, categorize. She could explore the wrinkles of her daughter, wait for the flash of open eye forever. The baby's beauty was painful straight on, like a god's.

The click-click of her pain medication. Swimming sleep.

Seventy-two hours after Auden was born, the flower arrangements in the room stank, needing fresh water. The balloon bouquets drooped. Will moved around beside her bed. In his arms he cradled a crocheted white, pink, and blue cap and a tightly wrapped white blanket with stiff blue and pink stripes. No flesh peeked out to differentiate it from the waxy rubber dolls used for practice in the newborn parenting classes. If not for her emergency C-section, Lara would have been home already. Only seventy-two hours before, she'd been pregnant. She had been a mother for nearly three whole days.

Lara tasted blood; the hospital air dried her out. When she swallowed, her mouth was one large canker sore that she bit into and released. Pain pushed against numbness. Her fingers and hands were swollen from the fluids she had been given, her feet, too. No part of her was as elastic as she had expected. Her body both a before and an after.

Will smiled. "I just can't bring myself to put her down," he said. Lara smiled back. Her lips cracked. Will stood beside her. Lara's vision was filmy. He was an actor on stage holding another woman's baby. "How are you, Lar? Both my girls gave me such a scare."

"Good, I think," she said, her voice raspy. *Your girls?* "So thirsty." Each syllable struck a matchstick on the flint of her throat.

The blanket in Will's arms moved, then began to mewl. The sound connected to the base of Lara's throat. Each cry grappled and rent Lara's viscera.

A nurse shuffled in. "Good, Mom, you're awake. It's time to try and feed her again."

Lara studied the nurse as she lifted the quivering and grunting blanket and hat from Will's arms.

"Which side do you want to try first? We need to get your milk established." The nurse gestured to the plastic hospital port-a-crib with a neon yellow sign with black block print: No FORMULA. MOTHER'S MILK ONLY. Lara recognized her handwriting.

She nodded, remembered herself at the class learning how to cup her breast in her hand, tease rubber lips with her nipple. The memory was more concrete than the swollen, wrinkled flesh the nurse lowered toward her. Lara pulled at the string of her gown to release her breast. Every movement stung, her skin stretched tight like parchment over knife-edged bones. Lara sucked in air through her teeth so she would not cry out. She accepted the bundle from the nurse.

"Isn't she beautiful, Lar?" Will's voice was dreamy, wistful.

The face was all mouth, stretched wide, gums alarmingly purple, toothless but tooth-shaped. The force of the child's cries lived in those gums; even her lips drew far away from them. Teeth would have been less menacing in their uniformity. C-section babies were supposed to look perfect.

Lara's hand shook as the baby cried and she tried to bring her breast to her daughter's mouth. Each cry stuck straight pins into her eyes. Finally extending her nipple into the baby's mouth, the angry gums closed around Lara's skin. The baby gnawed, did not suck. Still crying.

"You need to relax, Mom," the nurse said. Sweat pooled beneath Lara's breasts. "You won't have much milk for a couple of days. Some babies are more patient than others."

As the days passed, Lara found she didn't like looking at her baby. She watched her daughter's eyes race and flutter beneath translucent, veiny eyelids, heard her newborn breath catch and hitch as she slept, but all Lara could do was cry. Tears were appropriate. "I can't believe she's here," Lara said.

Her body couldn't contain the love, the ache she felt for this child. The ferocity of her love for the purple skin beneath the scale-thin fingernails, for the lips that pursed, parted, rested for only a second, was the most exquisite agony. Even so, in her arms the baby was too close. Lara would be more comfortable, could love her better, from a distance.

The light through the blinds modulated from white slivers of sun to milky gray, dull black. Time passed beyond the windows, walked down the hall outside Lara's room. When the shift changed, the nurses scrubbed one name off the dry-erase board and replaced it with another. Some nurses wrote in cursive, with curly *y*s, others in angular block print. Lara memorized the spectrum of faces on the pain chart on the wall: the have-a-nice-day smiley face to the tomato-red circle with the mouth of a jack-o-lantern. She learned the rhythm of the *drip-drip-drip* of the antibiotic solution into her IV, clicked the button to up her pain medication.

Will held Auden. He liked it. He talked to her, cooed and clucked, formed words and sounds Lara had not known existed. *Hold me, Will. Not her. Pick me.*

One morning, her last in the hospital, Lara remembered Karen's advice: *You won't want to do it, but ask the nurse to take the baby to the nursery so you can sleep. It's really your last chance.* She had just attempted to nurse, and Auden was sleeping. It was now or never, even if her friend had only been half-right. Her last chance.

"Excuse me," she said to the nurse, surprised at what it took to summon her voice. This nurse took three steps to get from the open door to Lara's bed. Julie, the last shift nurse, needed to take four.

"Yes?"

"Well, I was wondering if maybe you could take her to the nursery." The nurse did not speak or move toward Auden. "It's just that I'm still so tired from the delivery that I thought it might help me sleep. And she's just eaten, so . . ." Lara stammered and her voice faded.

"I guess I could do that. The moms are just always so desperate to keep the babies right there with them." The woman paused, seemingly to emphasize her point.

Will stood there, silent, his eyes pinging from woman to woman. Couldn't he see she needed him to stick up for her? She needed rest.

"She'll be fine in here," Lara said. Her breath was a defeated sigh. When would she fall asleep?

Sleep, sleep. Will dozed in his fold-out chair, lips parted, breathing slow and even. He was so *goddamned* relaxed, so content to hold Auden, burp her, rock her. He didn't want Lara.

"I know you hate to pump," he said the last night in the hospital, "but I love getting to feed her." Lara glared at him, but her eyes filled, muddying her anger. "I—I'm sorry. I didn't mean . . ." He waved away whatever he didn't mean, his wedding band glinting in fluorescent light. Chastened, he thought he'd hurt her.

She was envious of Will and the joy he found. Her newborn daughter made her edgy, not completed. She knew how she was supposed to look to the doctors, the nurses and Will, in love and over the moon. Catapulted and flung and reeling, yes. Serene, no. The still unseeing eyes of her daughter followed nothing. The strange, sinister sounds of her stuttered, irregular breathing made Lara jumpy. *Must her cart be so close to my bed?*

The regular squeeze and release of the blood pressure cuff on her arm, the monitor's beeping comforted. The mechanical monotony faded into hospital life; the tightening and beeping were predictable, safe.

With Auden in the bin beside her or in her arms, Lara gawked at her, waiting, wondering what to do. The fear that she would never figure it out filled her belly. She wanted to feel it again, the recognition, the pinprick of love. Maybe it was the medicine that swam between her and Auden. Perhaps they could dial it back. Mother love is instant, instinctive, eternal.

It should've happened by now.

She lay in her bed bleeding through pad after pad, gored, and tried to sleep.

Five days after Auden was born, she and Lara were released from the hospital. Lara held a tightly swaddled Auden while Will pushed her wheelchair through the wheeze of the automatic doors. Fresh air for the first time in five days. She turned her face up to the sun like a dog as Will pushed her to the curb. Beth carried the loaner breast pump, Lara's antibiotics, pain pills, and the spiral-bound notebook she used as her breast-feeding log.

At the curb, a nurse helped Lara up out of the wheelchair and to the car. It took Will less time to secure Auden into her car seat than Lara needed to lower herself into the backseat. Her bottom was bruised and sore from her attempts to push, and sitting so upright sent a whine of pain from her incision that reached her temples, fingertips, and groaned up and down her spine. The pain had a color, white: antiseptic, blank, and ruthless.

Lara couldn't imagine sitting up front where she couldn't see the baby. Auden had so rarely been out of arm's reach since she was born. Auden whimpered. The crochet cap slipped down her furrowed forehead. Lara thrummed her fingertips on her daughter's legs, pulled in so tight, trying to calm them both. Traffic was hectic and dangerous. Each time Will braked, the seatbelt dug into her incision. The pain made her dizzy. She was afraid she would throw up, so she closed her eyes as soon as Auden did, matching her breath to the shallow rising and falling beneath her fingers.

"It'll all be so much better once we get home," Beth said from the front.

Nothing could be worse than this car ride. "Mmm hmm," Lara said.

Bea waved to them from the driveway as they pulled in. Once parked, Will and Beth fussed over the baby and all of the items they had accumulated in the hospital. Bags barely opened. A novel untouched. The magazines Lara had flipped through, uncomprehending, during the hazy hospital stay.

"You're here," Lara said as Bea helped her from the car.

"But how?" Lara asked. Bea had driven for over an hour and arranged for her boys to spend the school night in Lynchburg (something Lara couldn't remember her ever doing before).

"I wish I could be here more." Her sister's presence put Lara at ease. Bea was so capable, so calm.

"Take it slow." Bea lifted Lara's arm over her shoulder. "Put your weight on me. It's like you've been to war, isn't it?"

Lara's vision rippled. She nodded.

"Let's get you inside and try to make you comfortable."

Lara could only take steps half of her normal stride. Her midsection and lower back were gummy. She labored to stay upright.

Lara could hear Auden fussing when she walked through the door. It was good to be home, among familiar smells and fabrics and floors that hadn't been shined to a squeak. The air inside wasn't stale; Bea must have opened the windows before they arrived. A small wicker basket was tucked beside Lara's favorite leather arm chair. In it, Lara found a portable changing pad, diapers, baby wipes, and diaper rash ointment.

Bea smiled. "Battle stations," she said. "I put one in here, obviously, and one in the kitchen and upstairs in your room. You never know when you'll need to make a change. And you're not going to feel like doing any more walking than necessary."

The basket was lined in brushed twill and blended perfectly into the room. Lara's nostrils twitched and her cheeks tightened in that about-to-cry-again way. "Thanks, Bea. That's so thoughtful." When Bea's boys were born, Lara had sent two gigantic stuffed animals from FAO Schwartz: one a lion and the other an elephant. Beautiful, but useless.

"Of course! I wish I could do more, but sometimes it's the little things that keep you sane." She had also recovered the Boppy nursing pillow so that it would match downstairs. On all of Lara's prebaby to-do lists, she'd never included either of these. She could feel herself starting to blubber. She had never cried so much in her life, and always with an audience now. Mortifying.

Bea eased her down into the leather arm chair in the den and propped Lara's feet up on an ottoman. "You know so much more about this than me," Lara said. Panic bubbled. How could the hospital have allowed her to bring this fragile animal home unsupervised? And Bea would have to leave soon. Her limbs were leaden. She'd never been so worn out.

"Tell me someone else heard that," Bea said, smiling and wrinkling her nose. "You'll get the hang of it. No one has a clue at first. I'll go grab you some water." As Bea walked out of the room, in came Beth and an unhappy Auden. Beth clucked and tried to quiet her.

"This is your home, Auden," Beth chattered. Her slippers shooshed against the wood floors. Auden wasn't listening; she at least wasn't quieting down. "This is the family room." Lara's breasts hardened. They felt rocky in her hands, like a bad boob job. "And this, this is your Mommy," Beth said. "I think she's getting hungry, Mommy."

Lara shook her head at how ridiculous her mother sounded and unhooked the flap from her nursing tank top. Milk, thin and gray-white beaded on her nipple. "Thanks, Mom. Give her to me, and I'll feed her."

"Really, you should rest." *Is that why you started pacing around in here with her crying? So I could rest?*

"I'll take a nap after. I can't sleep when I hear her crying."

Chapter Thirteen

Seven days old

Each seat in the pediatricians' waiting room was full. Women sat, arms wrapped around their babies. Mothers. Hands gently swiped sweaty curls from foreheads. Cheeks burned red with fever.

"The new ones go straight into the exam rooms," a woman in Spongebob Squarepants scrubs said, shooing Will and Lara away. "You don't want any of what's flying around out there." Influenza on the chairs, Coxsackie virus on the magazines, *Streptococcus*. A cold could kill Auden, just pneumonia under a pseudonym. But in the sick-check area, maybe Lara could catch the love these women radiated for their children. Auden needed only her first well-check.

Lara's entire body groaned with the redirection, the additional steps. Will carried Auden, asleep and still in her Peg Perego infant carrier, the padded handle crooked in his curved elbow. The sleeves of his Oxford shirt were rolled up to the elbows, but the creases in his summer weight wool trousers were as crisp as when Lara had picked them up from the dry cleaner. His sport coat hung on the back of the driver's seat of his car where it would remain clean until he left for work. With his other hand on Lara's back, he guided her. Her kidneys ached from the weight of his palm.

"I'll catch up," she said, motioning for him to get Auden into the room. Will slowed.

As she pushed open the Crayola-red door, Serena, the nurse, said, "Mom, I need her undressed to her diaper so we can get a weight. Just wrap her up once she's undressed and I'll be back."

Lara bent over Auden's carrier, now lying on the crinkled paper lining the navy faux-leather table. She winced as she opened the harness clasp.

"I'll get that," Will said. "Sit down."

Bracing with her hands on the chair's arms, Lara lowered herself, hoping she wouldn't have to get up for a while. Little hurt more than standing up. On her second day home from the hospital, Lara had cut her pain medication dosage in half, convinced she was having a reaction and that once her head cleared, everything would be better. A haze of pain had replaced the twilit narcotic glow.

Will lifted Auden, still sleeping, from the car seat and laid her on the table. He took off her socks and unsnapped her long-sleeved onesie. Lara suspected he thought she hadn't put enough clothing on Auden to leave the house.

"It's almost eighty outside already," Lara had said, stuffing two extra Pampers, a pacifier, and a burp cloth into her diaper bag. He didn't argue but had slipped a hospital-issued crocheted hat onto Auden's head before they walked out the door.

In the exam room, Will kept Auden's hat on and shook out the receiving blanket to wrap her back up. "I'll hold her," Lara said. *I'm the mom.* "You can just lay the blanket over her."

"Sure," he said and handed Auden off. He draped the blanket over her, tucking and re-tucking the fabric around her feet and hands, trying to cover her neck.

Auden's drying umbilical cord, thin and blue-black like a smashed fingernail, scratched against Lara's T-shirt, catching a thread. Lara followed the Noah's ark wallpaper border around and around the room. Pairs of baby animals paraded to the arks. Each corner had an ark, four in one tiny room.

With a quick knock, Serena opened the door. "You're seeing Dr. Wohlleben today, correct?"

"Yes," Lara answered. She'd interviewed doctors at the three main pediatric groups in town, checked off the box on her to-do list at exactly thirty-five weeks pregnant, according perfectly to the recommendations of her many baby books.

Dr. Wohlleben was female, young, and an outspoken proponent of breast-feeding, precisely aligned with the mother Lara had believed she would be. Lara's memory of the doctor was far clearer from the interviews several weeks before than the hazy hospital visit the day Auden was born. The doctor had two young children herself and said she chose pediatrics because she loved kids. Also, a group practice provided her ample time with her own children: a smart professional who put her children first. She didn't dress like a dowdy doctor, either, Lara recalled. She'd complimented Lara on her earrings when they'd met. Surely she could instruct Lara on how the loving was done.

"Great," Serena said. "She'll be in soon. We'll rotate some of your other well checks over the next few weeks so you can meet the rest of the doctors in the practice." Lara nodded, but she was going to love Dr. Jenn Wohlleben.

"Take off baby's hat, please, Mom, so I can get a weight and length," Serena said.

Lara smirked at Will as she took off Auden's hat, running her hand over the nearly bald scalp, resisting the urge to pick off the scales of cradle cap and tiny remnants of lanugo.

"Dad, you can follow me. Mom, we'll be right back," said Serena as she lifted Auden out of Lara's arms. They walked out of the door. The scale squeaked. Then Will's voice, echoey, from the hallway. "She's still below her birth weight?"

Back in the room, Serena refastened Auden's diaper on the exam table. "Still dry, Mom." She steadied Auden with one hand on her belly and with the other she pushed the pile of baby clothes out of her way. "Dr. Wohlleben will be right in," Serena said as she walked out the door.

The door hadn't fully closed when it opened again. When Lara first interviewed Dr. Wohlleben, she had appreciated the doctor's slim figure and the obvious care she took with her body. She had runner's calves, like Lara, and a heavy fringe of blunt-cut bangs that must have demanded frequent maintenance as they hit just below her well-arched eyebrows.

But this woman couldn't be the doctor she had interviewed; she was wholly inappropriate, dressed for a burlesque. Dr. Wohlleben's sexy, bias-cut skirt, sleek, silk blouse—top two buttons open—peep-toed and freshly pedicured feet beneath her lab coat, and spindly heels shamed Lara.

She refused to wear maternity clothes; their stretched-out slackness made her feel emptied out. Her stomach billowed, still airy and doughy, no longer tight with purpose and life. But she only weighed fifteen pounds more than her pre-pregnancy self. If she relented and kept wearing the maternity clothes, she'd be the mother who gave in and never lost the rest of the weight. So she went with yoga pants and a black T-shirt. At least she endured the pain and breathlessness of tying the laces of her running shoes instead of sliding on the flip-flops that sat at the ready beside her bed. Still, Lara covered one foot with the other.

Wohlleben shook Will's hand first, presumably because he stood at her arrival, her fingers slim, bright eggplant at the tips. He introduced himself.

"It's so nice to see dads come on these visits," she said. Will smiled, taking the good dad mantle out for a spin. "You can call me Dr. Jennifer."

"She's quite a sleepy baby, isn't she?" Dr. Wohlleben asked.

Lara hadn't looked forward to sleepless nights with a nocturnal infant, but she'd expected it. All parents wear their exhaustion like a merit badge. But Auden's lethargy had been the topic of one of Lara's few calls to her mother.

Beth had chuckled into the phone before remonstrating, "You never wake a sleeping baby."

"Yes, we've wondered about that," Lara said. Will stood, his chin between his thumb and index finger, waiting for a response from Dr. Jennifer.

"And her color is a little yellow. I'd like to check her for jaundice."

"Like what the sailors used to get?" Will asked, the professor now.

Dr. Wohlleben laughed, frilly. She tipped her chin back and touched her throat. "The same thing, largely. Is she nursing well?" Will dropped his hand from below his chin to his side. Both he and the doctor turned to look at Lara, noses angled down.

Lara reached into the diaper bag for her breastfeeding log, proof. "I've been trying to wake her and feed her every four hours. Sometimes she feeds well. Other times she's so sleepy and disinterested." She waited for Will to agree. Nothing.

"She should feed every two hours or on demand when she's awake. Especially with her slow weight gain. You're pumping to increase your supply, correct?"

"Yes, particularly after the bad feedings when she doesn't eat much," Lara answered. She was averaging three times a day.

"Let's shoot for after every feeding," said Dr. Wohlleben. Will nodded.

"Feeding her takes so long," Lara said, words flung like spit. "I wake her. She eats a few minutes, sleeps, we wake her again. It can take forty-five minutes to drain one breast." She had to tilt her chin up to address Will and the doctor.

"Right now it's all about you two. She needs to eat and eat often. Pumping is critical for a lazy eater and low milk supply. Little else should matter right now."

"Yes, doctor." The words soured like a *yes, ma'am.*

"How are you doing, Mom? I know those tired, weepy eyes very well."

Dammit. I'm not weepy. At least I wasn't until this lecture.

"She's doing great," Will answered cheerfully, slinging an arm across Lara's shoulder. He remained standing.

"Sleepy babies can sleep their lives away. Head down to the lab and get that jaundice test. You can redress her, just leave one foot bare."

Lara carried Auden down the hallway to the lab. Hand-painted fish, each with a single glittering scale, swam the walls. Doctors' offices always went over the top on cheery décor. She counted each square in the hallway as she proceeded gingerly, her footfalls slow and silent, knowing that she'd have to walk back down this hallway to leave. She could count down each painful remaining step.

Once they reached the lab, Dr. Wohlleben bent her lithe body around the doorframe and spoke to the technician. "Bilirubin check." To Will and Lara she said, "Don't worry, we'll wake up your sleepy girl." Then she turned back into the hallway, a rustle of silk against her lab coat and the *click-clack* of heels as she walked away.

"Mom, please hold her arms against your chest, as well as her other foot," the tech explained, swabbing Auden's heel with an alcohol wipe. Lara laughed aloud. She had wondered how they were going to find a vein in her tiny elbow; of course they'd use her foot.

Lara curled her baby into a ball. Auden's bare foot in the tech's blue-gloved hand looked impossibly fragile and so small. Her skin was see-through; the only sign that her tiny foot was not a doll's were the whiskered veins that ran just beneath the Saran-wrap skin. How had Lara missed the yellowish tint to the translucent peach of her daughter's skin?

The blue glove clutched Auden's miniature heel. Auden's toes curled up tight. Her heel turned red, then purple. The tech pricked her heel. Auden was silent at first, until the tech started squeezing to force the shockingly red droplets that beaded on Auden's skin into a short blue straw. Lara wanted to slap the woman's hand away. Auden wailed. She kept trying to pull her leg back in. A cord pulled tight, the tension between Auden's foot and the tech's rigid grasp.

Finally, the tech stopped squeezing and pressed a cotton ball over the puncture. Then she applied a brown Band-Aid that wrapped the length of Auden's foot. "Smallest one we have," the tech said before telling her to remove it as soon as the bleeding stopped so that Auden couldn't remove it, try to swallow it, and choke.

"We should have the results tomorrow. Here's your form for checkout." The hand waved a paper in front of Lara.

After the appointment, Will dropped Lara and Auden at home and returned to campus. They were both exhausted. Auden's eyelids drooped and opened. Each time she closed her eyes they stayed shut longer, veins purple beneath the light. Nurse, put Auden down for a nap, then pump. That would be the order of Lara's afternoon. And on and on.

Auden latched on immediately, but only suckled for several moments before her breathing slowed, her mouth slackened then dropped Lara's nipple. Auden's pink lips damp and parted. "I can't blame you, kiddo," Lara said. "I'm beat, too." *Maybe we can both get a rest.*

She swaddled Auden and placed her on her back in the padded Moses basket she kept downstairs. The pediatrician said it could be helpful to keep Auden close when she pumped—"get those feel-good hormones going that make the milk flow." And it would save her a painful trip upstairs. She noted the lackluster feeding in her log with an asterisk followed by "so worn out by check-up." Below the space for time at each breast she drew a new line for "oz pumped" so she could record how much milk she extracted after each feeding.

The pump was still plugged in from early in the morning. She assembled the freshly sanitized parts, screwed on two new storage bottles. Since she was the only person home, Lara took off her shirt and pressed the conical shields onto both breasts—at least the pump was hands-free and could drain both breasts at once. Funny how important form once seemed. Lara was all function. She pretended that the mechanical whir of the pump motor was the sound of a neighbor mowing the grass outside, a hum she might learn to ignore. Closing her eyes and lolling her neck back into the chair, Lara closed her eyes and breathed through the pinching and stretching of her once sexy nipples. Visualizing rivers and waterfalls, liquid abundance, drip by drip her milk splashed against the bottom of the bottle. As much as she loathed the breast pump, the rhythmic whine, the cord and tubing leashing her to one spot, perhaps she was getting the hang of it. Small puddles of milk were forming. She closed her eyes again, counted her breaths.

The doorbell rang. She tensed. Lara was topless; she would ignore the door. Karen wasn't visiting until later in the week. Whoever this was could wait. Relaxing her hands, she conjured the water imagery again. The doorbell rang again. No more milk sputtered out. The dry squeak of skin against plastic. Auden flinched in the basket.

A woman's voice: "Oh, maybe we should just knock instead of using the bell."

Auden's eyes opened sleepily. *Damn it*. Lara snapped the pump off and pulled the shields from her breasts with a wet smack, red circles where the cones adhered to her breasts. Auden squirmed. Lara was furious and exhausted and resentful. She had to look awful. But if she could stop the ringing, Auden might not fully wake.

"Coming," she said quietly as she tugged her shirt over her head, plunged her arms through the holes. She walked to the door hoping Auden would fall back asleep, knowing there was zero chance she would. Two immaculately dressed neighbors greeted her as she opened the door, one with a foil-covered 9 x 13 casserole dish extended before her.

"Lasagna," the younger woman said. Her coral lip gloss coordinated with the slim cardigan she wore, her teeth a brilliant bleached white as she smiled. "You can heat it up for dinner tonight or stick it right in the freezer." Her wrists were so delicate as she handed Lara the casserole dish.

"Thank you," Lara whispered, standing in the doorway, desperately trying to remember the women's names. "That's so thoughtful, Virginia." They were smile-and-wave as you keep driving acquaintances, not the roll-down-the-window-and-idle type.

The older woman straightened the skirt of her tennis dress, starched white pleats against golden thighs without a vein in sight. "We just couldn't wait any longer to meet your new little one," she said, peeking past Lara into the entryway. "I hope this isn't a bad time."

"Barbara, right?" Lara asked. "Please forgive me. What they say about mommy brain is true."

"Barb. And of course. We won't stay but a minute."

"Auden's a little cranky after her check-up this morning." The women each moved up one step. Lara backed up, opening the door.

Barb walked past her and took the casserole out of Lara's hands. "I'll run this back to the kitchen for you," and she headed expertly in the right direction.

Auden was awake in the basket, sucking on her fist.

"Oh, she's darling," Virginia said.

"Precious," Barbara echoed, slipping back into the room. "We came with an agenda," Barb said with a conspiratorial glance at Virginia. "I'd love to host a little luncheon for you and Auden. Introduce you both to the neighbors."

Virginia was crouched over Auden's basket, cooing at her. "That's so generous, Barb," Lara said. Auden's face was pink, her sucking insistent. "Can I think about it and get back to you?"

"I don't plan on taking no for an answer," she said, sweetly. "We'll do it sooner than later, before she's on a schedule and all of that."

Auden's knuckle was purpling where she sucked so hard. She frowned and grunted, then the unmistakable gassy poop, loud as Lara fumbled for an argument.

Virginia laughed a glassine tinkle. "We both know what that means! Thank you for letting us see her. She's just darling."

Lara lifted Auden out of the basket.

"I'll drop a copy of the invitation in your mailbox. Just take a look at it and let me know what you think! We'll let ourselves out."

Lara wondered if Auden could learn to shit on cue.

The following day, Will came home in the late morning for the first time in their marriage. From upstairs, Lara heard him struggle to open the door. He hummed as he walked into the house. "Ladies of the house," he said, his voice quiet but theatrical. "I say, lullay, my girls."

Lara rose silently from the rocking chair and laid a swaddled, dozing Auden in her crib, eyes closed, mouth silent, lips kissing the air. She re-clipped her nursing bra, lifting her breasts an inch higher, closer to where they belonged. She closed the nursery door and dragged fingers through unbrushed hair.

"Will?" Ruffling noises, Scotch tape squeaked in the kitchen.

"I'll be right there. Sit and relax a minute."

Lara sank into the living room chair. Will's footsteps approached from the kitchen, slow.

A light kiss on her neck. "I come bearing gifts," Will said. "I couldn't figure out what to get you."

She didn't need to ask Will to remember her, make her feel special. She smiled, eyes closed, imagining. Lara would never ask for a push present, such a gross misrepresentation of labor, a reduction of birth to input-output. She hadn't pushed Auden into the world, anyway.

Lara's largest jewelry account, MacPuryear and Banks, had loved her campaign for post-birth mother gifts: *She gave you your one-of-a-kind. Thank her by taking her breath away.* In the ad, the Photoshopped baby's eyes matched the gem's sparkle. Year-round sales increased. Babies are born every day, not just on the high holy jewelry days of Valentine's, Christmas, and Mother's Day.

A cool glass pressed against her palm. "First this," he said. She opened her eyes to a glass of water with sliced cucumbers and sprigs of mint floating in suspension among the ice cubes.

"Mmm, grown-up water. Thanks, Will."

"You're welcome. I didn't know that nursing mothers needed to consume eighty to one hundred ounces of water a day."

"You've been reading up."

Two gifts sat on the coffee table beside him, a small box with tissue paper sails pointed up and a larger, rectangular box wrapped in birthday paper from the hall closet.

"Sorry," he said. "There's been so much baby wrap in the trash from gifts, but we don't own any."

"Stop," she said with a smile. He never wrapped gifts; so wasteful, an invented industry to support consumerism. These presents, though, he'd dressed up. "This is a wonderful surprise."

"Start with the bigger one. That's for you and Auddie. The smaller one is just for you." He handed her the box—inside, metal clinked metal, the present heavy in her unhealed lap. She tore apart the paper. The box read *Medela Infant Scale. Hospital Grade.* She smoothed her fingers over the hermetically sealed tape. The cardboard reeked of that pediatrician, Wohlleben. *Cunt.*

"A baby scale?" Lipstick on the collar would've been classier.

"You've been worried about whether or not she's getting enough to eat. Now you can weigh her before and after each feeding to know exactly."

"I guess that will cut down on some of the wonder . . . thanks." The next gift would redeem him.

"I'll put it together before I head back," he said.

"No rush, really, Will." Nursing log, growth charts, head measurements, length records. In her professional life, Lara had spoken in metrics, craved and manipulated them, made the data work for her. But with Auden's erratic growth, her trouble keeping enough milk down, a dossier built against Lara. "But thank you."

He didn't immediately pick up the smaller gift, building the suspense. A locket, maybe, where she could keep a picture of Will and Auden or even a first lock of her hair or her first lost tooth. Earrings, a pen. When she had unpacked what remained of her work office at home, she'd arranged her Mont Blanc pens first. She had four: college graduation, grad school, first "real" job, Forty Under Forty Business Award.

With two fingers, Will dangled the bag before her. He coughed. "This one may need some explanation."

The bag rattled when she took it from him. Not jewelry, then. She pulled out a pill box with a bright green *Herbal Rx* label. "Pills, Will? How very Hunter S. Thompson."

"It's fenugreek, an herb that increases breast milk production."

"Ah."

Still seething about the fenugreek and infant scale, Lara watched the clock ahead of Karen's planned afternoon visit. She couldn't wait to tell Karen what an ass Will had been. Though she'd said she'd arrive by two, Lara knew Karen was incapable of being any less than fifteen minutes late. At two-thirty, Karen walked through the front door carrying a large, wrapped rectangle. Auden continued nursing under Lara's T-shirt. Lara stood as Karen set the package down on the coffee table and wrapped her free arm around her friend.

"God, it's good to see you," Lara said.

Though perfectly round in the middle, Karen was frail. "I can't believe it's taken me so long to get over here. First Sophie had some crud while you were in the hospital and then Gabe. I had to make sure we were out of quarantine."

They sat on the couch. "It's okay, Kar. Really. This place has been Grand Central Station. I want to rip the doorbell out of the wall."

"Contact with the outside can be so good. But I know what you mean, visits can be a real pain at first. So disruptive."

Karen looked as worn out as Lara had ever seen her. Lara would wait, tell her about Will in a little bit. "How are you, Kar?"

"This pregnancy has been the hardest and I'm only halfway through. It seems kind of cruel." Lara knew Karen's morning sickness had lasted more than sixteen weeks. "Gabe says he wants to stay the baby. And Sophie has been acting out in school." Karen rested her head in her hand. Lara touched her knee and she rallied. "But I'm not here for all of that. Open your present!"

Lara switched Auden to the other breast and reached out to tear the wrapping paper. "I was so lucky." Lara had felt so hale while pregnant, so useful. And Auden had been so happy, so quiet inside. But Karen couldn't wait to be as empty as Lara, a baby in her arms. Karen was more than late spring pale. She was January gray; even her birthmark appeared faded. Even so, Karen had painted a lovely barnwood sign to hang from the front door: PLEASE DON'T RING THE BELL. BABY SLEEPING.

"It's so perfect, Karen. Thank you." Her friend had known to protect her from the world. It was okay that she couldn't pour out her grief and worry. She didn't need Karen to promise her she would make a good mom.

"I'm always here for you, Lar. I know it doesn't seem that way right now. I should be here all of the time."

Lara couldn't remember another time when Karen had actually needed her. "Oh, shut up. Your problems have distracted me for five minutes. I've forgotten that I'm half naked and that everything hurts."

"I should be giving pep talks."

"You've done more than that. You've made me a beautiful 'keep out' sign. What could be better than that?"

"I couldn't stand people showing up unannounced. There's really no good time the first few weeks."

"Finally, someone who understands! And if only this sign would work on Beth."

"Good luck with that. I know she's driving you crazy, so I'll wait to hear from you, okay?"

"Yes. And you get some rest. Take care of yourself."

"You know how impossible that is now," Karen said, winking. "You really are putting her first, Lara."

"Well, she's a benevolent dictator most of the time."

Chapter Fourteen

Ten days old

The real crying started on day ten, six days after Lara and Auden came home from the hospital, four days after Will went back to work and Lara didn't. Auden lay swaddled in the pale wicker Moses basket nestled against the arm of the leather sofa where Lara sat folding laundry. The first noise from the Moses basket was a mewl. By the time the half-folded, rose-colored blanket landed in Lara's lap, the sound swelled, tugged at her belly button and the smile-shaped incision in her abdomen. Auden's eyes were closed, lids loose and fluttering, purple veins visible, her mouth opened wide.

The clock on the cable box said 2:15 p.m. Auden had nursed only an hour before; Lara's breastfeeding diary, open on the walnut coffee table, noted the time of her last feeding, the length at each breast, which breast Auden started on, and where she finished. Lara searched the notebook for answers.

Lara jiggled the Moses basket with one hand; with the other she ran her fingers over the seam of the blanket. Auden's face changed but her eyes stayed shut. Her eyebrows, sparse and light, pulled in and down, aging her. Shriveled lips sucked together. Even the soft roundness of her cheeks angled and planed. Her lips darkened, more purple than pink. Deep white lines curved around her lips as they opened to cry. Botox for babies could be the mommy business of the future. Auden's hands coiled into fists, the backs of her hands turned white. Eyes squeezed closed, Auden opened her mouth and screamed.

"Shh, shh, shh," Lara whispered. She jiggled the basket harder.

Auden pulled her legs tight against her chest, howled and thrashed at the tight swaddle; the polka dot receiving blanket slid apart. Lara picked her up, shh-ing and clucking and swaying, feet bare on the cool wooden planks. She pressed Auden to her chest, the baby's belly tight and hard, eased her palm behind the soft skull. Lara patted the tiny back, working for a burp, but none came. Auden's legs lengthened for an instant, long, slim feet flexing and releasing. Auden's head moved beneath Lara's hand. Her cheek, then lips grazed Lara's clavicle, then up and over her shoulder. The baby's head pressed back against Lara's hand as it tipped up next to her ear before screaming again. The sound was a high-pitched metallic keening, a demonic chainsaw revving. She gently placed her thumb in Auden's mouth; "Nature's pacifier," the lactation consultant in the hospital had called it. Auden drove it out with her tongue.

She must be hungry. Lara fumbled, one-handed, with her nursing bra, nipples pricked and strained. She placed Auden beneath her T-shirt, offering her breast. Auden's head turned away from the nipple cupped in the perfect *c* of Lara's hand. Lara tried the other side, with the same result. Auden cried louder, so she lifted the baby away from her breasts and out from under her T-shirt. Lara's breasts tightened with milk, unused, her nipples achy and cold as milk leaked through her shirt, the cotton sticky and chilly. Auden's eyes stretched open wide and stared flatly at Lara's. The clock blinked 2:22 p.m.

Lara slipped Auden into the sling and then turned to the Internet, Googling how to soothe a crying baby. Search results provided remedies for calming fussy babies. No one would mistake this yowling for a fuss. She danced with Auden. Flipped through the pages of *What to Expect When You're Expecting* with one hand. She bounced gently on an exercise ball with Auden in the sling. Then in her arms. She went back to the Internet, to the newborn chat rooms, recognizing three women's handles. No help. All of the babies of the women with whom she had shared infertility and then pregnancy were blessings of incandescent happiness, perfect darling sons (DS) and dear daughters (DD) to complete, contented Stay at Home Moms (SAHMs). No one else searched for the UPS return label.

Lara shushed. She hummed and rocked on her feet and in a chair, paced, turned the lights down. Lara paced from room to room to room. Auden cried at the cool blue paint of the now-family room, contorted face reflected in the glass covering the oversized black-and-white photographs framed on the walls. Auden's face superimposed over her father's face, a blurry crossbreed. Her eyes, his eyes. Small. Alive.

Her cries ricocheted off the antique map-print wallpaper in the office, off the garden greens and yellows of the nursery. She screamed downstairs, screamed while Lara climbed the stairs, and screamed while Lara walked back and forth the length of the upstairs hallway.

When Auden accepted her breast, Lara nursed until her raw nipples cracked, scabs crumbling, sticking to Auden's lips and cheeks. Auden cried. Lara changed her diaper: clean bottom. Inspected her infant toes for hairs knotted around them: no hair. She checked Auden's temperature: no fever.

Auden cried.

Lara swaddled the baby, just like the nurses at the hospital demonstrated. *Sleep, baby, sleep.* Still, Auden cried. Lara laid Auden in the crib, rubbed the baby's stomach, and closed her own eyes, swaying with exhaustion. She picked Auden up. The baby, eyes closed, fingers in fists, channeled all of her energy into crying. *Careful, girlie, your eyelids could stick like that.*

So she could change out of her stretched and stained T-shirt, Lara laid Auden, crying still, in the center of her king-sized bed, the baby's arms fluttering out, translucent palms and fingers splayed, startled by the motion as she sank into the down comforter. As soon as she put the baby down, out of her arms, the tightness around Lara's throat slackened, but guilt prickled the base of her jaw. Lara threw two pillows on either end of the bed, in case Auden mastered rolling over in the time it took her to grab a tank top out of the closet.

The outfit Lara had hung on the back of her closet door—a loose sundress and scarf to hide the residual plumpness around her armpits and where her bra straps bit into her shoulder—required that she shave, which required a shower. No chance of that. Her two makeup bags, monogrammed for her honeymoon, squatted zipped and lumpy on her bathroom counter. Will had never seen her disassembled at the end of a day, but hopefully she'd accomplish a swipe of mascara and a sweep of gloss later.

She ran to and from the closet, shoving her neck and one arm through the mouth of the top and tugging it over her stomach. A small treat not to smell like her own sour milk. She'd put on some nicer shorts, a skirt maybe, once Auden calmed down. She pulled the hanger with the dress off of the closet door and shoved it back on the rod. Her culled gallery of a wardrobe hung silent, a second skin for a different life, an elegant *fuck you.*

Auden's purple mouth stretched wide with each howl before contracting into a wrinkly *o.* With each breath, her navy eyes eased open, taking in the revolutions of the ceiling fan before closing again into thin lines, delicate eyelashes wet and clumped. Forehead trenched with creases, Auden balled her fists up against her ears, the skin of her fish scale fingernails purple, edged in white. *This kid is her own mood ring. Purple is bad.*

Lara lay down beside Auden and gestured at the ceiling fan. "Look, Auddie. See?" She propped Auden against her knees, but still she cried. *Maybe this house is too quiet for her.* With Auden against her knees, Lara mock cried.

"Wah!" Lara blurted out, a taunting child. "Wah!"

Auden's eyes blinked open wide. The lines dissolved on her face, an Etch A Sketch shaken clean, her daughter's face newborn again, with fewer traces of the ancient rage she'd channeled.

"You like that?" Lara asked. "Wah!"

Auden's eyes blinked, blue with a pinprick of black at the center. Lara laughed an insane laugh. Both of their bodies shook. Auden was quiet for five minutes. Lara laughed until she coughed, desperate to prolong the calm.

By 4:30 p.m., the cries stained the cotton of Lara's tank top, yellowing the underarms and the seam above her breasts and burrowing into her skin like smoke. Lara tasted it on her tongue, dry and rough. Bitter. Old office coffee, no milk, no sugar, burnt on the bottom of the glass carafe. The smooth plaster walls held Auden's cries. The wooden slats of the floorboards vibrated the sound back into the soles of Lara's feet. Her cuticles itched; she picked at them. The crying scratched a way back out.

"Hey there, baby girl," Lara said in her best attempt at a singsong chirp. "I think we need a change of scenery."

Barefoot, Lara passed the wicker basket beside the door that contained a pair of her running shoes and two pairs of flip-flops, his and hers, and carried Auden into the front yard. Lara liked the heat of the brick walkway on her feet and then the cool of the grass. Hot and smooth, then cool and textured. She stepped from paver to grass to brick paver one foot at a time. She fanned her fingers out over Auden's crying face, diffusing the bright sun.

"Shh, baby," she said. "Feel the sun. And the wind." She closed her eyes.

The cry chased Lara to a memory of the fort of blankets and pillows she'd constructed as a child between her big-girl bed and Bea's toddler bed. She had hidden with a floppy-necked giraffe and *The Phantom Tollbooth* when her mother's face had spread too wide and loose with a wild, frightening sadness Lara didn't understand. Her mother's messy crying and worrying cornered Lara's father in his study. When the wooden doors to his office did not soundproof him, he gathered his fishing gear and left. One morning, he'd slid open the wool door flap to Lara's fort and said, "Let's go to the river."

Just Lara and her father fishing on the James River. No mother looking for her nine-year-old help, no little sister or twin brothers. He asked her to unsnap the green canvas fishing bag, didn't rush her fingers as they pulled at the bronze snaps. She spread out the flannel blanket at the top on the clearest square of ground at the river's edge, only the slight veining of oak tree roots as they vanished into the dirt. She lifted out the three plastic tackle boxes, laying them side by side on the blanket.

"Only open the first one, Lara. S'all we need in there."

She unlatched the plastic lip closure with her thumbs, careful not to disturb the contents of the twelve sectioned squares. All but one compartment held metal—shiny hooks, dull weights, clippers and clamps. One held two red and white bobbers, just for her. Her father tugged the filament line tight on her small spinning rod.

"Hand me one of the bobbers and the smallest weight." She did. He dropped the weight into his pocket before sliding the bobber up the line. "Carefully now, give me one of the little gold hooks."

She asked him *are you sure* with her eyes. He nodded. She grabbed a hook by the stem, held it between her thumb and index finger. No way would she stick herself. He tied a knot through the eye and attached the weight to hang below. The hook dangled, glistening.

"Are you going to bait your own hook?" he asked. "The fish can tell." She nodded and grabbed the plastic baggie containing the worms and topsoil she had dug from the garden that morning, her fingernails still rimmed with dirt crescents.

She opened the bag and pulled out a worm. The worm wriggled in her fingertips. "How do I?"

"Bring it here," he said, lowering the rod tip. She stood, the worm limp between her fingers. "Don't crush it. The hook needs to go through twice. No free lunch for the fish today." Taking the hook in her left hand, she pressed the worm's tail onto the barb of the hook. *Pop.* The worm shrank in her grip. Her fingers shook. "And one more time," he said. Refusing to disappoint the proud eyes, she poked the hook through the thick-necked part of the worm. A louder pop. The worm oozed onto her hand.

"You've earned your fish now," he said and rested his arm on her shoulder. "Let's cast your line and see how we do. Just lean there a bit, lower your hook, but keep an eye on it." He pressed the rod into her hand. "Just hold it over the break in the spartina and push the release button." The worm dropped. Another pop, this time the water. When the bobber splashed, he said, "Finger off the button. And take two cranks on the reel."

"Like this?"

"Perfect. Now we wait."

She would have waited all day if it meant not baiting another hook. The grass tickled her sandaled feet.

"Look," her dad said, gesturing across the finger of river to the opposite bank. A blue heron balanced on one spindly leg. Lara mimicked its posture, wobbled and straightened. She didn't see the bobber dip below the surface of the water. The rod bounced against her hand. The heron took off. The bobber flashed red. Then back under. Red top, then white bottom. Under again. The line pulled taut, snared her belly.

"Dad?"

"You've got a bite. Turn the handle once. Slowly."

As she turned the handle of the reel, the pull strengthened. She could feel the hook, buried deep.

"He's shaking his head, trying to spit the hook. You're doing great. One more slow turn. Gently."

The tugging, slight as it was, hurt a little. The hook in her tummy ran up her side and connected her arm to the nylon line to the fish with the worm and hook stuck in its mouth. *Spit the hook, fish. Free the worm.* She wanted to snip the line off with the brass clippers in the tackle box. She wanted to turn and turn and turn the handle and pop the fish out of the water.

Someone spoke. Not her father's dream voice, but old, craggy syllables: "That little one sounds hungry!"

A golden retriever pulled a middle-aged couple wearing matching khaki shorts up the steps from the sidewalk to Lara's home. She didn't recognize them, but everything looked different in the sunlight. She wouldn't ask their names. They'd stolen her best minute. She hated them. The man gestured with his thumb at Lara's open mailbox as he passed, multicolored papers and envelopes and the glossy corners of magazines stuck out of its mouth.

Auden bawled.

"I was saying, that sounds like an awfully hungry cry to me," the woman beneath the brimmed hat said. "So urgent."

"Maybe," Lara said. *Idiot.* Lara shifted her weight side-to-side. Patted Auden's back. *Because I wouldn't have tried to feed her to get her to shut up.*

"Your first, right?" the woman asked with a condescending tilt of her head.

Lara nodded but stepped back. Her hip bumped into the wrought iron railing beside the steps up to the front door. "Yes. Excuse me. I think we'd better be going back inside." Her hand on the doorknob felt the vibrations from the grandfather clock just inside, chiming five o'clock.

—

He was late. A squalling, hot animal coiled in her arms; Auden wearing only a diaper. A cave baby.

The red, flashing numbers of the cable box, the scripted Roman numerals on the grandfather clock, the white digits of her cell phone, the bottom left corner of her computer screen, or the blue window of the microwave clock—none of them reminded Lara it was time for Will to come home. Even with the heaviest traffic, Will always stepped through the front door before the globe-trotting Food Network chef completed his culinary adventures and the credits scrolled up the screen.

When Will had returned from his first day back at the university after Auden's birth, he'd kept his voice low when they spoke, forcing her to turn down the television volume so they wouldn't compete. Today, Lara had muted the television volume hours before the end of Will's day. No more sound layered over sound over sound. The white chef's coat was what she wanted, the bleached-for-TV-smile, company at the close of the day.

Breasts sagging beneath an unfastened nursing bra, Lara stood in the hallway, both the TV and front door visible, holding an angry Auden like a football. Lara's eyelashes were too light without mascara, her lips dry and unvarnished.

Where was he? What happened? She'd already done this for so many hours. She needed dinner. She needed a shower. She needed a drink. She needed her arms to herself. Lara's breathing was limited to her throat, her lungs corseted in panic.

Finally, a splash of headlights. The car engine cooling. Footsteps on concrete driveway. Silence as he cut across the grass—he used to walk on the sidewalk to their walkway to preserve the lawn—a skipped step up the entryway. Thumb latch depressed. His sandals dribbled into the house before the rest of him. Silty toe and left hand, pushed the door open, wedding band glinting.

He stumbled over a bag of kitchen trash, a gory mix of salsa and diapers and wipes sprawled inside the door, then smoothed a grimace into a smile. "Hi, girls," Will said. He had a suntan, rakishly mussed hair, and a hint of stubble to mark the trials of his day. Where French cuffs should have been rolled up, his arm was a ratty T-shirt sleeve. Instead of trousers, he wore mildew-scented shorts.

"You were on the river?" Lara asked. *Asshole.*

"Yeah, only a few people appeared for office hours, so . . ." *So, he's trying to ignore the crying.* Put a good face on it. But he hadn't even come from work. He'd left them here together.

He wound his wedding band around his ring finger and then reached out his arms. Unlike hers, they were curved to cradle, elbows in *v*s to support the baby's head and body.

"Wait, should I shower first?" he asked.

Lara held the baby out to him without a word.

His eyes moved from Lara's face to her feet, polish-chipped, nails untidy. "Should I ask how today was?" His Adam's apple pulsed. His quiet voice rebelled against the noisy baby in his arms.

"Different," she said. "Long."

Chapter Fifteen

Twelve days old

You're being absurd, she told herself, *too much like Beth.*

But Lara craved a scene, a violent shattering of Will's polite atten-tiveness toward the baby. She sat with her knees folded beneath her on the leather couch. She flipped idly through the *Parents* magazine she never subscribed to, a free trial for new parents. A baby on every page. Airbrushed and smiling. She flipped the pages so quickly that the images morphed like early cartoons. *This is what I get to read. I live this.*

Will unfastened Auden's wet diaper, balled it up, and threw it in the trash can. A clean organic cotton gown was draped on the arm of the sofa beside him. He cupped his large hands lightly around her tiny skull, reverent and gentle. He inhaled audibly, then rubbed the baby's arms starting at Auden's shoulders, like in the baby massage book they'd received. He circled her umbilicus. The attention he lavished was unset-tling, like a seduction. He used to study Lara that way. After stroking the length of Auden's thighs, he flexed the baby's feet with the pad of his thumb. He used to massage Lara's feet when she draped them in his lap. The massage always evolved into more.

"Isn't she getting cold?" Lara asked.

He turned to her, startled by her presence. "Come here, beautiful girl," Will cooed as he lifted Auden from the changing pad, fresh and powdered, and dressed her in the gown. At the edge of his T-shirt sleeves, Will's biceps curved into taut semicircles when he held Auden. Lara had told him she'd read that speaking to an infant in real, human language, even just simply explaining what you're doing, boosted childhood verbal skills. She blamed herself for his endless babbling since Auden's birth.

"Wet's make you a wittle burrito baby," he said as he spread a receiving blanket across the couch cushion beside Lara. He smoothed it twice with his free hand before laying Auden onto it.

The words didn't rankle Lara so much as the tone of voice he used. Will ranted endlessly about his students' sloppy grammar in the emails he received from them. He refused to use any abbreviations even via text. But this timbre was new. The day she met him, Lara had ached to roll naked in the gravel of his voice. This note was softer, a stream smoothing over rocks. He'd saved this voice for his daughter. What else had she stolen?

The cordless phone on the coffee table rang. He answered, keeping one hand on Auden's belly to prevent a fall off the couch. Lara stared down at the magazine, unseeing, unable to ignore the conversation occurring beside her.

"She changes every day," Will said into the phone as he reached down to pick Auden up, the motion fluid and practiced. He continued, "Sometimes she looks different between when I leave in the morning and get home at night." He swayed around the living room, Auden cradled in his elbow, the phone between his chin and shoulder. Auden's eyelids were low, only the bottom whites of her eyes visible between thick lashes. She could be so good for him sometimes. It was maddening.

He paused to listen to the voice on the other end of the line. "I know. Crazy. Who knew you could love someone so much. She's only a couple of weeks old and I can't imagine my life without her."

Another long pause.

"Lara? She's a trouper. Keeping this monkey fed and clean is a full-time gig."

She was a mess. She smiled at Will anyway. Her husband was a better person and a better parent than she. He was smitten with his daughter. What more could she ask, the jealous shrew?

Will laid Auden in the middle of the receiving blanket again beside Lara, though there were six other rooms in the house. In mid-conversation, he pressed Auden's arms next to her sides and tucked one corner of the blanket tightly around the baby's left arm and under her bottom.

Lara pulled her toes farther beneath her, away from the baby being swaddled and Will's caring hands on her body.

Lara knew every emotion she was supposed to feel, though no matter how hard she tried, she couldn't conjure them. She could try them on but she couldn't leave the store. She could put on an acceptable show, but if she stretched her false smile too wide she risked tipping the tears over the rims of her eyelids.

Recalibrate your thinking, said the note from Beth. *A mother's work never appears on the balance sheet. You're doing better than you think. Love, Mom.* The note was stuck to a book purportedly validating the stay-at-home choice. Its genre? Christian lifestyle. *Wonderful.*

The Amazon smile on the box the book arrived in had teased Lara. She thought it was the gripe water she ordered for Auden's crying or the heated wrap that promised to "soothe painful infant tummy troubles!" or the white noise machine. Maybe she'd ordered those items from Drugstore.com. No telling. So many boxes had arrived; she couldn't keep up. She set them in her office until she had time to go through them.

She read the epigraph on the first page: "'Each morning, I frame the day by listing and prioritizing what I need to accomplish. Then I tackle the important chores first, seeing the unimportant for the distractions they are.'—Barry Burrow, *Women Trading Work for Home*."

Lara picked up the planner that held days of blank pages, the days of Auden's life. Each day, she had scribbled down small goals including: shower, laundry, nurse six to eight times, pump four to six times, call a friend, go for a walk, buy groceries. At the end of the day, defeated, Lara would only cross off two or three items at best. Another list of targets she couldn't strike. A blog she'd read had encouraged new mothers to focus on what they've accomplished each day, in place of lofty to-dos—a *Done List*:

A hand plunged into soapy water so hot it tears at the dry unhealed flesh, so hot the skin emerges scalding though dripping. Raw. Tight. Red. Hand dropped back in, groping for the rest of the pieces of the breast pump and bottles, blind fingertips scraping against the stainless steel tub, water heating the metal that was usually so cool.

Clock on the microwave said 8:15. Breakfast plates washed. Stacked in rows. Largest to smallest. His coffee poured out. Ceramic mug slid onto the rung, in place in the dishwasher.

Walked to the laundry room. Sprayed stain treatment on soiled baby clothes and burp cloths and blankets. Pretended that yellow blobs were something charming, not shit or vomit, the baby's insides, outside. The baby that was once inside her is now outside. Her eight pounds had crushed Lara earlier in the day, but Auden was sleeping now.

Then back to the kitchen—twelve medium steps, sixteen small. Set the timer on the microwave to allow the stain treatment to set, rub into the stain with fingers, nails thin and ridged.

Once, seeing the manicurist had been a chore, one more appointment on the calendar. Enforced sitting and talking about nothing or not talking. No one dependent. The only responsibility was to pay the woman and tip her. *Make sure to use the cuticle oil,* Natalia had said, *tsk-tsk. I can tell when you don't, like flossing.* Lara could peel her cuticles off in strips now. They wouldn't stop at the nail bed. The skin would keep pulling, the length of her thumb, across the knuckles—those were cracked and ready to split away—to the joint of her hand, yanking hair now, down the back of her palm, wrist, up her forearm, elbow over her shoulder and across clavicle, climbing her neck, cutting a raw swath across cheek, ending at the hairline, leave a long striation of pulsing, unprotected flesh. A pile of her, stripped to reveal ivory patches of skull, wrinkled on the floor.

She pulled the misshapen blue sponge from the edge of the sink to nuke away the bacteria. Mr. Coffee's square face said 8:26 a.m. On the microwave door she met her reflection: face, skin still intact. Studied her hand, no tear. The microwave beeped, sponge clean. She reached in. Soap bubbles hissed from its pores. Water steamed and scalded. She dropped the sponge into the sink, tweezed it out, worked it back and forth over the pot from last night's dinner. No amount of soaking would rip the rice from the bottom. She picked the grains with her fingers. Dishpan hands? There's a soap for that: it was green and smelled like aloe.

She piled the clean cookware, evidence of a day's accomplishment. The dishcloth in her hand squeaked dry pots. She stacked the plates in the cupboards. Wash, rinse, dirty, repeat. Every item in the kitchen should be the gray color of the water in the sink with all of the washing. The timer dinged as she dried the last bowl, porcelain cool in her hands.

8:50 a.m. Laundry time. She balled up the wet dish towel and stepped back from the sink, crushed the hot wet in her fist. So much water on the floor. The drips puddled. Her toes, a scalded red. She closed the cupboard doors slowly so they did not slap or bang. She eased everything closed now: drawers, doors, toilet seats—afraid to flush, the water in the pipes might wake the baby.

She left the water on the floor and walked into the laundry room, throwing the green towel into the wicker basket, which was overflowing again. She sat on the floor beside the basket, divided the laundry on either side of her, lights and darks. The rhythm was predictable and steady. The spray-and-washed garments soaked her palms, chemicals nipping at the cracks. Hands streaked dry against the fabric on her thighs.

A good mom is a clean mom. Whites first. They needed the hottest water and the longest cycle. She picked up the mound from the floor and heaped it back into the basket so she didn't lose anything on the way to the washer. *We make white what we dirty the most*—sheets, underwear, diapers, onesies, toilet paper. The fabrics sagged with pre-treater. Stains. Even if they remained discolored, they'd have been washed. Nothing bad remained but a blot, a reminder. No place for stained laundry on the done list; it wouldn't be done right. If she kept moving, kept cleaning and organizing, she wouldn't have to stop and think. Idle hands, standing still, invited the itching fear, hair in her throat, that there was no escape. She could strangle the tiny clothes, twist and pull and stretch them between her fingers, all in the name of clean.

She kicked over the spray-and-wash bottle and tried to slide it out of the way with her toe but sent it farther underfoot. Lara slipped, lost her balance, and rocked forward against the washing machine, the wicker basket knocking against her so hard her ears gonged. When she caught her breath, she heard crying. *That's not new crying, unless Auden impaled herself on a crib slat. How long has that been going on?*

She dumped the laundry into the mouth of the machine and turned the buzzing handle to whitest whites, highest heat. As she walked to the stairs up to the nursery, the grandfather clock chimed 9:15.

At least eight hours to kill before Will came home.

"What is the matter with you?" Lara asked as she picked the crying baby up and out of the crib. *Maybe that's the answer: the doctors, they've missed something.* She put her back down. "Auden, I need two hands in the name of science."

She skipped steps on the way down to her office, Googling inconsolable crying, high-pitched. Hundreds of results lit up. She couldn't stop reading. Extreme jaundice. Liver failure. Mitochondrial disease. Metabolic disorders. Countless genetic disorders. Death in infancy. She only stopped reading because she had to pee.

Auden was quiet.

Oh, my God. She ran back up the stairs, certain she would find Auden with a grotesquely swollen brain, tissue bulging from her eyes, like the child who could not metabolize amino acids without medication that she'd read about online. Even if you heard the warning sign—the keening, strangled cry—you were too late. Retardation was immediate, death quickly behind.

She's asleep. Just asleep. Lara waited for the choking cry, the mushroom-cloud skull. Like an auditory afterimage, words, images of sick, dying babies, singed into her retina long after she closed her eyes.

Lara took the baby monitor into the backyard with her. Will had checked, double-checked, to make sure it worked, demonstrated to Lara the limits of its range. She sympathized with dogs in yards surrounded by invisible electric fences.

She was close enough to save her daughter, just outside. Lara was afraid to leave the house, but she had memorized the veins of cracking plaster in the corners of her bedroom. She could navigate the entire upstairs blindfolded. The left side of the third stair from the top creaked. The second spindle of the banister rattled. Lara had spent more time in her home in the weeks since Auden's birth than she had in the previous two years combined. She needed some air.

Natural light could be bright enough to make her blink, squint even. She enjoyed the compression of contracting pupils. Bright light startled Auden, though, so the interior remained permanently at boudoir setting.

Will and Lara had bought their home for the backyard no one else could see. On evenings and weekends they'd reclaimed their three-quarters of an acre, choked then by overgrowth. They built a raised deck of sustainable Ipe with a door into the kitchen. Lara had arranged a high-top table with two chairs on one end and two lounge chairs separated by one round table, the perfect size for a bottle of wine and two glasses. Their hands would touch as they reached for glasses, fingertips lingering for a moment together. Even on the most humid Richmond summer day, the backyard had a breeze. Crows chattered in the trees. Squirrels dropped acorns and gumballs into the leaves.

She glanced at her watch, sat down on the lounger, then stood back up and walked over to the exterior outlet where she'd plugged in the monitor. Turned the volume dial up and down to make sure it worked. Nothing came from the monitor except the white noise of faint static. Only the breeze carried an echo of a cry.

Oh God, she's in there dying, and this is on the wrong channel, and I can't hear her. She took a deep breath. *Stop worrying. You're being crazy. She's sleeping. Trust the monitor. Enjoy the moment of peace. It's all you've wanted all day, right?*

Lara couldn't help herself. She opened the door and stuck her head in to listen. Silence. She counted to ten. Then fifteen. Silence. She shook her head and stepped back outside, easing the door closed behind her. She flopped down on the lounger, exhausted and relieved. Her eyes closed to the warm sun, the hum of lawnmowers in neighboring yards.

She slept.

"*R-R-R-R-R-R-RAAHHHHHHHH! R-R-R-R-R-R-RAAH-HHHHHH!*" shrieked the monitor.

Lara's eyes blinked open as the lights on the monitor crescendoed, arcing green to yellow to orange and red, each light larger in circumference than the last.

—

At 6:30, the sweep of headlights and the crunch of tires on gravel as Will's car pulled into their driveway marked Lara as a survivor of one more day.

She couldn't indulge the fantasies of what would happen if he didn't come home. If a truck jackknifed, snarling traffic on I-95, or if there was construction on the Powhite. How would she face the hours of darkness?

In the hour before he came home, she'd refolded the portable changing pad, placed it in the shiny rectangular diaper caddy on the shelf in the living room, straightened the diapers, snapped the lid tight on the tube of A&D ointment, wiped off the smeared goo on the outside. She'd carried Auden upstairs and held her, yowling, in one arm as she swept Kleenex across her own sweaty armpits, changed into fresh clothes, applied mascara and lip gloss while Auden cried in her ear and again, reflected in the bathroom mirror. In the nursery, she fastened each powder-coated snap of flowered, footed pajamas onto Auden's hot, flailing body. Lara had bundled Auden into the sling across her chest, tidied the kitchen and family room.

When she heard his car, Lara wrapped Auden up and brought her out onto the front steps. Lara held Auden's fist in her hand and waved the tiny infant arm at Will.

"Welcome home, Daddy!" Lara called, mimicking a child's voice. Will pecked her on the cheek as he scooped Auden from her arms.

"Hi, beautiful girl," he cooed as he stepped past Lara into the house. He slumped one shoulder over to allow his briefcase to slide to the floor. His eyes never strayed from Auden. "What did you and Mommy do today?"

Lara snorted. "Seven wet diapers. Three poops. Some vomit." Lara sniffed, certain crust had dried in her hair. "Then we mastered cold fusion."

"Is it as bad as all that?" he asked, still in baby talk to Auden.

"Auden and I could both use some adult conversation."

"What do you want to talk about?"

But she had nothing to talk about but tears and anxiety, diapers and baths (which Auden hated) and how much milk she'd been able to pump. Or the two hundred dollars in online purchases—special swaddling blankets, soothing lavender sachets, a lamb that replicated the sound of the mother's heartbeat through amniotic fluid.

Will perused the nursing log, which now included Auden's weight, daily, since the baby scale had taken up residence in the nursery. She held his eyes. He waited to hear what she had to say.

She couldn't tell him how she felt; she couldn't tell anyone. Pediatricians and even her ob-gyn probably had a hot phone, dialed straight to child services. No one would leave a child with a mother like her. Her mouth opened then closed, dumb.

"I ran into Kathy today," he said.

"Really?"

"Yeah. I had a lunch at the Bistro." Will raised his voice over Auden's cries but he stood still. No pacing. He didn't pat her back or change position. Lara rocked back and forth, her go-to move when Auden started crying, unable to remember how to stand without a baby in her arms. "Looks like she was there with a client. She says hi. Says she wants to meet Auddie. Hopes you guys can have lunch soon."

Tears welled. The only time Auden ever napped was late morning. She cried so much as it was, Lara needed that rest. "Lunch at the Bistro. How good that sounds." There was no way Lara would let Kathy see her like this. She reached for Auden. "It's time for her to eat."

"Do you want to nurse and tell me if I need to supplement?"

"It's hardly a matter of want."

He brought her a small glass of wine, slid the nursing stool beneath her feet. The baby's cries, any baby's cries, summoned a surge of milk to her nipples. They pinched and then cooled as the milk released. But so often, only those few early droplets dribbled out. The milk pooled inside her, pressing against the underside of skin, stretching the milk ducts, refusing to emerge. Auden latched to Lara's breasts endlessly, even when her nipples were fleshy pacifiers, drained and slack from the previous feeding.

"How about you burp her while I pump?" she said. It was always worse when there were other eyes and ears.

While Lara assembled the breast pump, Will unbuttoned his shirt and took it off. *Must be nice having spit-up-free clothing.* On the highest setting, the pump extracted a splattering of milk. Her sore breasts wheezed with every pull, stretching, purpling her distended nipples. Will slid his hand up Auden's back until he cupped her neck, chin resting between index finger and thumb. He sat there, gently thumping her back, surprised when each pat did not garner a burp.

"Do you have to let her neck loll to one side like that? She's flopping all over the place."

He stopped clapping her back. "She must not need to burp."

"Yes she does. Keep trying." Auden's face contorted. She pulled her legs into her trunk, stretched them out, curled them back in. She growled her sinister baby growl. "She needs to burp. That's what all this means."

Will laid her back into his bicep. Her growling turned into a whimper. She balled and opened her fists. She spit up thin, yellow-white milk, more than Lara had been able to pump. Because Auden was reclined it splattered all over her face.

"I expected things to be easier once you got home. Not worse." Titrated doses of the poisonous sadness and fear released. *He's an adult; he can handle it.*

"I'm sorry," he mumbled, wiping himself, then Auden.

Lara clicked off the power to the breast pump. Her nipples stuck to the cups. She pulled up her bra and tugged her T-shirt down. "Just give her to me."

"Lara, I'm sorry. Why don't you go take a bath or something? Have some time to yourself."

"Can I trust you alone with her?"

He sighed, but didn't answer.

She wanted to stop criticizing him but she couldn't. It was the only way to get his attention. "Look, even if you're the one holding her, I can still hear her crying."

Chapter Sixteen

Fourteen days old

Before the 11:15 jaundice recheck appointment, Lara raced to the car twenty minutes later than planned. Auden cried at the click of the harness. Not only did she have to hear her daughter's cries on the drive, people on the sidewalk of her neighborhood stopped and turned their heads when she passed. Even with all of the windows rolled up, the Volvo couldn't contain Auden's screams. The bass in her old Saab would have drowned her out, but Volvo's high safety ratings apparently included hearing protection. That stereo couldn't touch Auden's volume. Mouths dropped open; eyes sought Lara's with concern and disdain. Twenty-five miles per hour was an onerous speed restriction with a screaming child in the back. She stopped turning her head to see their expressions.

Even facing forward, Lara could see her daughter screaming. Before Auden was born, Will had secured a mirror onto the headrest for the back passenger seat, above the black-and-white geometric print fabric that promised to entertain the newborn eyes and mind (a *Parents Magazine* Best Buy). Lara had asked him to do it—what if a blanket fell over her face or if she choked?

If this child stopped breathing: quiet. *Maybe a blanket would muffle her.*

The day Will secured the base for the car seat and then the print and mirror, Lara had envisioned day trips to the beach, visits to her sister and friends. What a joke. Sweaty hair stuck to her forehead and the backs of her ears as she turned into the parking lot of the pediatricians' office, only six miles from her house. A fifteen-minute trip, twenty with any traffic, rattled, left her panicked and jittery.

"You'll be seeing Dr. Johnson today," the nurse said as they entered room three, a baby-circus-animal theme. Dr. Wohlleben was dead to Lara after her collusion with Will. She'd asked to see a different pediatrician in the practice for Auden's follow-up.

Five minutes after Auden was weighed and measured ("Up almost half a pound! Way to go, Mom!") Dr. Johnson opened the door. Auden squirmed and fussed but not half so loud as in the car. The doctor, Lara's height, wore shiny loafers—the sensible flats pleasing—a linen blazer, and twill pants. Her hair was gray and cut into an angular bob.

Dr. Johnson swooped to Auden. "Well, hello there, wittle one." Lara frowned as the *l*s morphed into *w*s and *th* became *d*. The pre-Auden Will would have lost it. But he, too, now spoke the bizarre tongue. "I'm Doctor Kat, Auden. How are you today?" She never looked at Lara.

Lara waited a moment to speak. "Hello, doctor," she began, awkward, the only person speaking like a grown-up. "We're here for a bilirubin and weight check."

"Ah, yes, the bilirubin"—in baby talk. It could be a speech impediment. But, no, Lara had seen her at the gym. She'd spoken normally. "You're supposed to be a sleepy baby. That's what your little chart says."

"Sleepiness doesn't seem to be a problem anymore."

"That's good. And you're sure growing, growing."

"She's been crying. A lot the last few days. So much more than before. I'm not sure what's going on. I looked up jaundice, and . . ." Her throat slammed closed on her voice.

"Say, 'oh Mommy, stop. Babies cry, and I'm just a crybaby.'"

Lara stepped closer, peeked her head between the doctor and baby to force the woman to make eye contact with her. "You don't think it's the jaundice, then?"

"Say 'no, Mommy, my *wevels* are nowhere near that high.'"

"So, doctor, what should I do?"

Dr. Johnson raised her chin and met Lara's eyes through her glasses. The look was rude, as though Lara had interrupted an intimate conversation. "She needs another heel stick. Assuming her levels have dropped by at least half, we're on the right track." Her consonants were crisp and dismissive, adult. Right track. Lara was dizzy. Where had they hidden these clowns?

"Head back down to the lab."

Standing barefoot and braless in her pantry, Lara scanned the ingredient lists on everything she had purchased before finding a suitable snack. There had to be a cause for Auden's crying.

The pediatrician's first question was, "What are you eating, Mom? Caffeine agitates, dairy constipates, and leafy greens make babies gassy."

Encouraged by her doctor to forego first dairy and then wheat for at least three weeks before slowly adding foods back into her diet, Lara knew every scientific alias for milk.

Onions had been ruled out early, along with all things cruciferous and seeded. Bananas and peanut butter were all she had left. She couldn't even spread them on bread as most breads were pumped with dairy proteins, whey hiding itself in the paragraph-long ingredient catalog. But then she read an article that postulated a link between nursing mothers' consumption of peanuts and a child's likelihood of developing an anaphylactic peanut allergy later in life. So, bananas it was. She was blazing a trail ahead of Auden, eating her own version of baby food, one squishy, bland food at a time. She didn't have to chew the bananas. They mushed around tongue, against molars.

As she swallowed the last of another banana, her third of the day, Auden's cry crackled through the monitor. *I haven't seen her in hours. Shouldn't I be excited to see her? If she'd actually wake up happy just once . . .* Tired from the check-up, Auden had slept well since one, and it was almost three. Lara poured a glass of water. Her dry lips cracked when they met the rim of the glass.

She carried the glass upstairs to the nursery. Auden whimpered until Lara picked her up. She laid Auden on the changing table and pulled apart the tabs securing her diaper. Her skin was peach and plump; her diaper was dry. Lara's heart sped. Her neck prickled. *Asshole. This kid hasn't peed in over four hours. And I'm whining about no coffee and bland food.*

"Come here, baby, let's get you fed," she said. "What are you trying to do to me?"

The baby nursed happily. Auden reached one hand up and wrapped her fingers around the corner of Lara's T-shirt, as if memorizing the fabric. As her milk let down, Lara's neck loosened, and she lolled back into the rocking chair, drowsy. Auden's face and her pink pursed mouth were the perfection of human design: the curves of an infant's lips made to meet the breast. Drops of filmy, white-gray milk pulsed in the corner with each suck and swallow. Auden's eyes drowsed, but one dark blue iris met Lara's eyes.

"Hey, baby." The words were breath and prayer. Lara's eyes filled. Her chest was tight and hot. Auden blinked but fixed her gaze on Lara. *Maybe we'll make it yet, kiddo.*

Lifting Auden up to burp shattered the peace. Auden writhed, furrowed her forehead, clamped her eyes shut. She vomited Lara's milk, splattering her neck and cleavage. Perhaps Auden was allergic to her, on the level of pheromones, deep and innate, but not Lara's fault, just like the way Bea's face pocked with rash and hives after a bite of strawberry.

At four, Lara tugged Auden's arms through the sleeves of the flowered bishop dress her mother-in-law had given her. She'd never seen any reason for a newborn to be in starched cotton, but Lara knew how her host Virginia Beckley would look, that each of her daughters would have an enormous pastel bow in her hair, a monogrammed dress.

Virginia lived one street over from Lara, three large houses away from her parents, the retired Dr. and Mrs. Montgomery, and across the street from her in-laws, the retired Dr. and Mrs. Beckley. The neighborhood was her own family compound. Virginia hosted every welcome-to-the-neighborhood luncheon. As weekday affairs, Lara had missed every one. Each Christmas, Virginia organized the neighborhood pot-luck dinner. Lara contributed holiday spirits—wine, booze. She hated the labeling and retrieving of cookware and plates, identified by Sharpie scrawl or ill-adhering Post-It notes.

Virginia's youngest child was under a year old but Virginia always appeared well-rested. The skin on her face was plump, the half-moons between her eyes peach, not gray like Lara's. Auden needed to make up for Lara's appearance. Virginia typically dressed to match her children. The color theme for their clothing was either determined by or extended to Virginia's toe and fingernail polish.

"Tea?" Will had asked the night before. "With all of her kids there?"

"It's not like Auden is going to be rolling around on the floor with them. I'll hold her or keep her in the stroller."

She barely knew Virginia, but was desperate to speak to another adult when the sun was up. Lara couldn't understand how Virginia could even have someone over to her home with so many young children, but Virginia had three daughters; who better to reassure Lara that she was normal and that childed life got better?

"Just be careful," Will had said. "That's a lot of exposure. You'll never forgive yourself if she gets sick."

Walking into Virginia's home felt like stepping into the pages of a magazine spawned by *Southern Living* and *Town & Country*. Where Lara's interior was cool, shiny, and Scandinavian, Virginia's home was covered in white bead board, sumptuous window coverings, and so many accent pillows. To the left from the entryway, pocket doors opened to the kitchen. Beside the square kitchen table sat a miniature table for the children, a replica, with four tiny matching chairs.

"I'm so excited you're on maternity leave now," Virginia said as she led Lara down the hallway to the living room. The burp cloth on Virginia's shoulders matched her fuchsia and white twinset. Her twill trousers hung flat. The baby in her arms was disproportionately long against the petite mother.

"Actually, I—" *Change the subject.* Large frames filled the walls of the hallway, pastel portraits of Virginia's two older daughters. A sepia-washed photo captured a man's arm, ring finger retouched in gold, with the newborn in only a white cotton diaper cover held from his hand to his forearm. "These are lovely."

"I so rarely get to know the working moms very well," Virginia said as she waved her hand in a *please sit.* Her gold charm bracelet sparkled in the sunlight through the windows. *This woman has time for accessories.* "Our schedules are just so different."

"I'm not going back to work." Lara sat down too quickly. Her incision burned.

This wasn't maternity leave. This was her life now. Nothing would ever be the same again. She had laid out her plan so confidently only weeks before, trained her own replacement.

"Really?" Virginia's matte eyes widened with pleasure. Lara sat up straighter. This woman, at least, thought she'd done one thing right.

"No. I've never been able to do anything part-time, so—" Lara tasted tears and stopped talking.

"And, I mean really, there is nothing more important than being a good mom to a child," Virginia said. "Nothing else compares."

The crunch of leaves under Lara's feet, iron-cold white breaths, on the Central Park canal path. The sound of her father's voice. An impossible deal made possible. Nights that stretched to infinity because there was no need to wake the next morning. The 10,000-foot airplane ding, takeoff. How was she supposed to forget, reduce these memories, pretend her past wasn't better than her present? The future and on and on and on was a locked closet, no lights. She was the mom. Bang on the door all you want, no one's coming to let you out.

They talked interior decorating and sleep training and when to introduce solid food.

"I grew up in this house," Virginia said. "Since Mother and Daddy downsized, I've been making it my own."

Even with her own father dying, when Lara left New York, she'd never looked at homes in Gloucester or Williamsburg. Living too close to her childhood home, to Beth, was like the view from a sharp, eroded bulkhead. Lean too far in looking for your own reflection and you'd teeter over.

Virginia's hand was gripping, tightly, two versions of beige floor tiles when Auden gave a howl and started rooting around, her bird mouth seeking Lara's breast. There was violence in Virginia's fingertips, flesh pressed ruby between cuticles and the tile samples.

Lara plumbed the inside of her Petunia Picklebottom diaper bag for the aptly-named Hooter Hider. "Excuse me," Lara said. "I apologize."

"I don't miss those days! I'll give you a second to get situated," Virginia said and walked out of the room.

Lara looped the strap over her head, around her neck. Only Auden's feet showed. Sweat beaded on Lara's nose as Auden tried to latch and suck. *Slow, deep breaths*, Lara reminded herself. Once she relaxed, Virginia came back.

She tucked a pink box into Lara's diaper bag, patted it. "They're some petal nursing pads. I just loved them. So discreet, you won't even know they're there."

Lara's face burned.

"It's great that you're able to nurse. I couldn't make it more than two months with Hayden." Virginia nodded toward her oldest daughter. "We just weren't compatible, I guess," Virginia said with a laugh and a wave of her manicured hand.

"You seem like such a natural," Lara said, feeling like she'd broken the surface of the water, had something to swim toward. "This is so much harder than I ever imagined."

Virginia's face tilted, concern covering like concealer. "Isn't that the truth? Mothering is not for the faint of heart."

"And the car! This kid screams so much I wanted to leave her on the corner of Patterson and Malvern today."

Virginia's eyes were flat.

"Just to teach her a lesson, kind of a you-stop-yelling-or-I'll-pull-over."

Strained silence from Virginia.

"I was kidding," she said. *Mostly*.

"There are certainly tough days." Virginia bounced her baby on her knee, flattened its bib against her chest. "But I just can't wait for mine to wake up in the morning. I almost want to go in and get them."

Lara couldn't imagine ever feeling that way. "Maybe when we get into a sleep routine," she attempted.

"Take it from me, they are so wonderful at this stage. They grow up so quickly. I wish I hadn't rushed it."

The tea tasted of failure, too long steeped.

—

The morning's visit with Virginia did not result in Auden napping, as she had hoped, so Lara spent the afternoon with Auden strapped in a sling across her chest. With at least twenty minutes before Will got home, Lara pulled the desk chair away from her computer and rolled the purple exercise ball into its place. She had mastered bouncing while typing. She picked up her favorite Mont Blanc from the vase beside her desktop and drummed it against the wooden desk with her left hand. She clicked on her bookmarks with her right. First she opened the BabyCenter Birth Club page, the zero-to-three monthers. More like zero to life. She recognized all of the handles, though each had been altered slightly from their pregnant monikers. StorkHope became StorkHopeDlvrd. TwnMMY2B was now Mommy2X.

Hi, Mamas, Lara typed, her handle still AdGrl. Before posting, she changed the greeting to *Hi, Ladies*.

After only seconds, the two women who had given birth closest to Lara messaged back.

Mommy2X: *Hiya! Been looking 4 yr birth story. How r u?*

StorkHopeDlvrd: *Welcome 2 the mommyhood. You've been so quiet. U ok?*

Auden slept quietly. Lara bounced. Stillness hurt too much. She typed back: *C-section. I'm fine. Tired + overwhelmed = the usual, right?*

Mommy2X: *Amen, sister. Wouldn't trade it, tho. U know?*

StorkHopeDlvrd: *I can't remember life b4 DD. DH and I r already talking bb#2.*

Mommy2X: *Arms r full with these 2 boys. I think my family of 4 is complete. Have you posted pics? Haven't seen any.*

AdGrl: *No, still need 2 upload them. Haven't found the time.*

StorkHopeDlvrd: *Remember when we thought we were busy b4 bbs?*

Mommy2X: *No kidding. I had no clue.*

AdGrl: *Actually, I've been having a rough time, too. Maybe just the rough delivery still has me worn out.*

Mommy2X: *I was a little crazy there for a while. Weepy. Exhausted. And it took me time to heal from my c-section, too. I was myself again around two weeks. Ur almost there, right?*

Lara was two weeks out but feeling less herself than ever. But these ladies were thriving. AdGrl: *Bb's up. Gotta go.*

But the only sound from Auden was the rumble of her deep sleep breath, almost a growl or purr.

Lara clicked open another browser window. In the Google search window, she typed, *symptoms + postpartum depression.* The right side of the screen filled with pharmaceutical ads: Prozac, Paxil, Wellbutrin. Her mother had pens and coffee mugs advertising each drug. She stayed off the ads and clicked on the WebMD link. The first paragraph introducing the segment posed the rhetorical question, how can you be sure that what you're experiencing is more than the baby blues? *Baby blues?* That name fit for a band, maybe, or a line of cheeky military dress-up, not for what Lara felt.

Symptoms: Trouble sleeping. No appetite or insatiable appetite. Irrational fear for baby's well-being. Hopelessness. Despondency.

Treatment: rest (*hah!*) and therapy plus medication. The baby blues resolve on their own, generally after a few weeks.

As Lara navigated to the second page of the article, the image on the page changed from a woman cradling an infant, butt smooshed against bicep, to an unkempt brunette with skeletal wrists and ankles wearing a hospital gown. Fit in on page two and you're Andrea Yates. Lara shuddered. Who could forget those five little coffins?

The bold headline read: *Postpartum Psychosis.* Psycho. Hearing voices. Hallucinations. Pervasive thoughts of infant as source of evil.

Lara wasn't Andrea Yates but she wasn't her mother, either. She wouldn't hop from therapist's couch to armchair, crying on friends' shoulders, her husband's, her kids'. *I'm worrying too much. I can stop that.*

She could do this, would do this. Mind over matter. The alternative was unfathomable deep.

She heard someone at the door. She closed her Internet browser before she finished the article.

Mail dropped through the slot in her door; cardboard, another box, placed against the door. She blew out the breath she didn't know she'd been holding. Lara picked up her cell phone, hit O'Malley in her favorites, tapped in the extension for Brett in IT.

"Brett, Lara James."

"Hi, Lara, how—"

"I'm fine, thanks. Need a favor."

"You bet."

"Tell me how to wipe my browser history clean." She didn't need Will finding any of this.

Chapter Seventeen

Seventeen days old

Will kept Auden downstairs so Lara could hastily shower before the second jaundice recheck appointment. She turned on the exhaust fan, closed the bathroom door, and held her face up to the hot water. Hands dangled beside her thighs, empty of the crying weight of her daughter. She held her breath and then sputtered against the stream of water. It ran from her scalp off her shoulders, splattered on the tile, and swirled down the drain. The mint of her shampoo cut clean into her nostrils, replaced her own two-day-old staleness as it purged the sour milk, the stink of Auden, of screaming, out of her hair.

Lara scrubbed away her own odor, vaguely pubescent, like what had yellowed her adolescent tank tops before her mother handed her a stick of deodorant. She massaged the clumps of milk and saliva from her breasts and soaped only lightly her newly spiky crotch, hair returning and thickening where she'd been haphazardly shaved before her C-section. The prior two days flaked off like sunburnt skin.

She would be clean for *this* doctor's appointment, at least. Like much else, no one had told her how many appointments there would really be.

The door creaked open and Auden's cries, though far away, spilled through the crack and into the steam. "Lar, I hate to rush you," Will said warily as he stepped into the bathroom.

She turned the showerhead off and pulled open the curtain. Her skin was tight, dry, and hot from the water. Will stared at her breasts and arms, crimson with heat. "I'm done anyway. It's amazing what a shower can do." She smiled. He pulled a towel off the hook, hugging it against his bare chest.

She winked at him as she pressed the towel against her. "No time for me to get dressed but time to gawk?"

Auden's cries climbed the stairs.

"What a surprise," Lara answered, her voice light. "I'm naked. Might as well feed her and then get dressed."

"Lucky kid," Will muttered as he took off his boxers and stepped into the shower, no effort made to hide his erection.

Auden shrieked the entire ride to the doctors' office. Again.

Lara and Auden saw yet another member of the practice. Dr. Thompson was older than Lara, though it was difficult to pinpoint his age, hair more white than gray, face deeply lined but elastic and firm. Cat blue eyes clear, even behind glasses. He was a senior member of the practice; however, two of the doctors had only finished their residencies in the last year, so that could mean anything. He wore a light blue polo shirt, no lab coat, no name tag.

"Please call me Dennis," he said.

She could have kissed him hard and long when he called her Lara, not "Mom" like every other doctor and nurse since she'd given birth. His burly fingers, wide palm gripped her hand, a long, firm hello. The thin white hairs tickled. Thick biceps strained the short sleeves.

He cupped a stethoscope in his hands, warmed the metal with his breath. Lara shivered. Auden hollered anyway when he placed it on her chest. He picked her up to reposition the instrument on her back. He didn't make Lara hold her.

"Lusty little gal," he said. "This is a good workout for her lungs and heart, believe it or not."

Lara grimaced.

"Murder on your ears, though," he said, chuckling. He flipped off the light switch, muting the fluorescent light overhead, clicked on the reading lamp at the small desk and twisted the blinds open.

Auden continued to cry, but the pitch changed, backed off of desperate.

"I hate those lights," he explained. "Why wouldn't she?"

Lara wanted to press against him, pin him to the wall.

"Lara, Auden is developing perfectly well. Look at the curve on her growth chart, smoothing out beautifully." Finally she'd done right. "Now, for the colic," he continued. "She's great at making sure her needs are met. Fifty thousand years ago, she would have stood a better chance of surviving than one of those bucket babies in the waiting room."

Those babies, the calm quiet ones, were supposed to be the prize. And their mothers the victors, or so she'd thought. He'd shocked her. Lara's breasts rose, fell, heavy with breath. Throaty, she said, "She'd scare off any predators."

The deep lines beside his mouth curved as he smiled, formed one deep valley on either side, corner of eye to edge of lip. Lara smiled, too.

"Right. It's rotten, but you can be confident there isn't anything wrong with her."

Lara nodded. Her daughter was healthy. Over and over she'd said while pregnant, "I just want a healthy baby, ten fingers, ten toes." She'd asked for too little.

"It certainly takes a toll, doesn't it?" Dr. Thompson—Dennis—brushed her knee with his palm. Lara dropped her eyes. She'd cried in front of the rest of them. Not him.

"Doctor," she said, her voice shaky, his hand still on her knee.

"Dennis."

"If you say so, I . . ."

"Auden is lucky to have you."

Lara's mouth swung open and closed.

"You're doing a better job than you think."

She looked up. "Really?"

"Auden's eyes are shaped just like yours. Did you know that?"

Lara shook her head and then smiled. "I think she looks like her father."

"She's got a lot of you, too. Even in her mouth, her lips. She's going to be a heartbreaker."

Lara tucked a wisp of hair behind her ear. "Thanks, doctor. I mean, Dennis. You really think she's doing all right?" She was doing all right.

"I think you're both going to be just fine," he said. "Stop being so hard on yourself."

"That is so nice to hear," she said, smiling shyly. Relieved. He squeezed her knee, gently.

"You really are a beautiful woman, Lara."

Her dry lips peeled apart. Finally, someone who didn't think she was a fuck-up of a mother, and a pediatrician at that. He used her name. He saw her as more than a creature who had given birth.

When she checked out, Lara scheduled Auden's next appointment with Dr. Thompson.

Chapter Eighteen

Twenty-four days old

"Didn't anyone ever tell you about the first three months?" Brian asked as he painted dark dye on the roots of Lara's hair.

His voice was flippant but his eyes held dark concern beneath the contrived flop of blond bangs. His long, crisp sideburns moved with his mouth. Before Auden, Lara had always booked Brian's last appointment on Saturday evenings, every ten weeks. He was full of gossip by then. Their friendship had sprung from talk of celebrities and his clients as though they were celebrities, who was sleeping with whom among the salon staff, who had to scale back from a full to a partial foil.

Brian's unlined forehead, green eyes bright, his frame, face, hands were large and animated beside her reflection. Lara's eyes, the deep, dark recesses beneath them, looked like banged-up knees. Concealer hadn't done the job. Perhaps she should start wearing glasses.

"What do you mean?" Lara stammered. She tasted tears as her voice broke. Karen had tried to tell her.

Clearing her throat, she looked away from the mirror over to Auden in her car seat atop the next stylist's chair. Asleep. Impossibly asleep. She hadn't planned to bring Auden to the salon. Certain places were for adults only. Chignon, where a partial foil started at $175, was one. But Brian, the owner and the man who had done her hair for the better part of a decade, had assured her it was permissible to bring the baby in when she couldn't find a sitter.

"Babies love me. And they love the noise in the salon," he'd said.

Lara had helped Brian launch Chignon. He trouble-shot her events around town by pinpointing themes that worked or didn't. She included him on every guest list. They met for postmortem briefings over cocktails. Brian never held back.

When she walked into the salon, Brian had reprimanded, "Girl, we've got some work to do." He'd leaned over to see Auden, then lifted her car seat gently from the crook of Lara's arm and placed it into the chair beside his own, swiveling it so that Auden faced them. Lara had wished he'd turn it around.

"Look at her, Lar," he said now. "An angel. Good enough to know when Mama needs her root-be-gone."

Lara forced a smile. Each time Auden kissed or pursed her lips in sleep, each time her eyelids fluttered, Lara's muscles tensed. Her heart beat faster, prepared to flee. Her jaw ached as she ground her teeth, her vigil of tension, rigidity.

Brian caught her eyes in the mirror. "She's asleep. Relax. How about we brighten you up with a few highlights?"

"I know, I know. Sounds good. I could use a pick-me-up. So, what's new around here?" she asked, though she knew to relax would undo the spell. Enjoying the feeling of Brian's hands on her scalp, the grown-up chatter would be asking for it. Was he always this meticulous, painting each strand once, twice, three times before slipping the long tail of his comb into the center of the foil square, then folding it in half, crimping the edges shut with his fingers? *Then I have to sit under the dryer for fifteen minutes.*

"You look like you're in pain."

"I think pregnancy made me more sensitive. Or maybe you've just lost your touch," Lara said and softened the straight line of her mouth.

"Ouch," Brian said. "Anyway, she's being perfect. Just enjoy it."

Calm the fuck down. She sought a glossier version of herself to greet in the mirror and wasn't she getting just that? The timing was perfect: fresh cut and color before the luncheon at her neighbor's house.

"You're right," Lara said. "I'll take it." Still, her mouth had sharp edges.

This baby, asleep in the bucket of her car seat, this was the baby Lara had imagined. What happened to the baby who refused to be put down, to be out of Lara's arms for any amount of time during the day? The woman in the mirror looked crazy, eyes flashing back and forth to the baby she knew would be wriggling and blubbering each time she looked away but wasn't.

"And of course, you see she's made my wall of fame," Brian said, pointing with the tail of his comb to the corner of his mirror, which was covered in baby pictures and birth announcements, including Auden's. In the last week of her pregnancy, Lara had deliberated for hours over which announcement she would send to celebrate the birth of her baby, and had finally selected two—one for a girl and a more masculine color for a boy.

Though the announcement hung more than a foot outside her reach, Lara's skin knew the heaviness of the cream-colored card stock. The tip of her index finger had traced the embossed lettering countless times. Her fingers bumped up and over the pastel pink and chocolate-colored polka dot border.

Auden Beatrice James
May 5, 2009
1:34 p.m.
7 lbs 5 oz; 19 ¾ inches
To that strength belong,
As through a child's rash happy cries
The drowned parental voices rise
In unlamenting song—W.H. Auden

Lara's eyes and cheeks smarted as with cold or after a smack.

Our miracle has arrived!
Love, Auden's proud parents,
Lara and Will James

Everything about the design, the layout—Lucida Handwriting font, size 18.75—the photo—the silky dark curls on Auden's round head, swollen slits of her eyes, doughy curves of her cheeks, and her twitching, sleepy half-smile—were familiar to Lara. Even the edge of the polka dot receiving blanket. The cardstock was antiqued, exquisite. Her choices, perfect.

"You sure you're up to this?" Will asked the next morning as he slung his battered leather messenger bag over his shoulder.

Lara had arranged three different tiny dresses for Auden on their bed. She swapped hats and socks between the dresses, moving the booties back and forth, then shook her head at each combination. Three stain-free burp cloths stood folded and ready to be packed in the diaper bag.

"Of course. It's a chance to get out, be dressed up. And she's cooking, and I have no responsibilities but to show up. They all just want to see Auden."

Lara had never heard of a sip-and-see before the last month of her pregnancy. Despite living in the neighborhood for nearly three years, Lara didn't know her neighbors well. She hadn't baked breads or casseroles when new families moved onto the street. Instead she slipped bottles of wine into black bags embossed with the words *Cheers! Will and Lara* and left them on the neighbors' doorsteps.

But when Barbara, please-call-me-Barb, from the end of the cul-de-sac, at the center of the four largest homes in the neighborhood, introduced the idea of a ladies' lunch shortly after Auden was born, Lara found it hard to argue. It was the perfect way to get to know the other ladies in the neighborhood, a celebration of her new adventure. More importantly, added Barb, the lunch would cut down on the foot traffic through Lara's front door for the first few weeks of Auden's life, with everyone wanting to see the baby:

"Let me get my house prettied up so you don't have to worry about yours," Barb had said.

Lara found it odd that people would show up unannounced to greet a stranger's baby, despite the fact that infants had held Lara in their thrall the last three years. Maybe that was one of the instinctive, animal drives enmeshed somewhere deep in women.

"All they do is sleep at that age," Barbara said. "I'll bring my granddaughter's bassinet down. We all know never to wake a sleeping baby."

Lara limply agreed. "What can I do to help? What can I bring?"

"Nothing. Just the baby."

Lara shimmied into the two-sizes-over-her-normal Trina Turk wrap dress. She blew her hair dry and wrapped a handful of face-framing strands around a thick curling iron, muscle memory intact. Tendrils frizzed at the crown. Curls stuck to her sweaty temples and unraveled. Her cheeks, in the mirror, stayed red from the shower water, the dryer heat. Hair stuck to the back of her neck. Concealer dabbed under her eyes swam beneath her fingertips.

Still, she achieved a more normal peach color, more uniform, muted the blowsy blotches. While Auden slept across the hall, Lara brushed eye shadow across the crease of her lids; dark eyes reemerged from the flesh of her face. She thickened her eyelashes and smiled. *I know you.* She tightened the knot at her waist or, more exactly, where her waist had once been: a mother who still made an effort, still as much woman as mother, and her baby not yet three weeks old. She looked more like herself than she had since the day her water broke.

On the way to Barb's, the incision ached with each step. It was only her second outing with the stroller she'd coveted during her pregnancy. Lara loved the smart, navy sun shade, the thick wheels, white rubber doughnuts in the middle, and the thin metal spokes. The gleaming chrome handlebar was wrapped in white leather to match the lining of the bassinet, the tires.

The day of her first walk, Lara had just maneuvered the stroller onto the sidewalk when Auden started to cry. The baby had two speeds: comatose in sleep or screaming. Sometimes the screaming preceded sleep. Often, though, it just led to more screaming.

Lara had jiggled the pram handle, clucked her teeth, *shuuush shhuuush shhhhuuuushed* herself light-headed. She prepared to admit failure and turn around when Mrs. Everett exited her house with a bang of her storm door. Her neighbor, two doors down, was infamous for watching people make their way down the street, walking dogs, steadying wobbly five-year-olds on two-wheelers, and pretending that she just happened to be coming out at the exact moment they were passing by.

"Who's been pinching that baby?" she asked.

Tears had burned in the corners of Lara's eyes. Failure bloomed in her throat.

"You can hear her howling from a mile away."

After that, the pram languished ten idle days in the front hall.

Today, she pushed the pram with Auden still sleeping soundly, wearing a white linen bishop dress with two delicate rosettes embroidered in the center and the monogrammed diaper cover—Auden's initials in pale pink cursive, a gift from her host. Lara studied her reflection in the storm doors of the houses she passed. A put-together woman pushing a posh stroller with a dreamy baby inside. She walked in step with her fantasy.

There were more women inside Barbara's imposing Tudor-style home than Lara had expected; Karen, the one she'd so hoped to see, was absent. Lara had never met several of the women. Her elderly next-door neighbor Clara waved from across the room. Virginia, in a child-sized, coral-print Lilly Pulitzer shift, flitted around just inside the door. Lara should've been relieved to see someone familiar, her own age. If she'd seen Karen, she would've been.

Lara could only give Barb a one-armed hug, one cream silk sleeve brushed cool against Lara's cheek, Auden cradled hot against her. Her eyes widened when she saw the pile of gifts inside the living room. There weren't supposed to be gifts. Virginia stacked the boxes, arranged the pastel bags. Her bracelet flashed as it slid up and down her forearm. The ends of her blonde hair curled up where it bounced against her shoulders.

"Look at you, putting us all to shame," Barb said. "You're just too lovely to have a newborn. You look so fresh and slim." Lara smiled wider and thanked her.

"And this little angel is Auden, right?" Barbara asked as she lifted Auden from Lara.

"Yes." She felt the baby's absence from her skin as a shock and almost reached for her.

"Is that a family name?"

"Oh, no. She's named after a poet. A favorite of my husband and my father."

"How lovely." Barbara's voice was a coo but her face was too close to Auden's. Barb huffed Auden's baby smell. Lara wondered if she'd try to eat her. "Heavenly," Barbara said, her voice breathy as reeds. She laid Auden in a white wicker bassinet in the center of an enormous Oriental rug in her living room. The baby was a display, like a terrarium deer at the museum with marbles where its eyes had been, embedded in soft fur stripped from the carcass and reassembled.

A woman whose hair resembled stiff whipped cream and who smelled of bottled gardenias, lots of them, intercepted Lara. She introduced herself as Ronnie Tunstall. "Isn't it amazing how your life changes, just in an instant?" Lara recognized her last name. She had often studied the museums' marble donor's walls. The VMFA recognized Veronica Tunstall as a Founders Society level patron. Today, though, she was Ronnie.

Lara nodded and smiled. "Yes. I had no idea I could love someone so much so fast." The words surprised her but they tasted true.

Virginia, a brushed-twill angle over the bassinet, called, "Lara, she's grown so much. Just since the other day!" Had she?

"Such miracles," Ronnie Tunstall said. "They really are." Lara glanced around Ronnie's confectionery hairdo. Four women stood hunched over the bassinet, conversing loudly. *Please don't wake up.* How alarming it would be to stare up into eight alien eyes in a house that isn't your own.

A knife tinkled against glass, then Barb's voice: "Ladies, now that the guests of honor have arrived, let's move into the dining room for lunch." She swung her arm wide to indicate the direction. Lara stepped closer to Auden.

"You, too, now," Barbara said, making a shooing gesture. "I'll wheel her in there with us," she said as she pushed the bassinet into the dining room, smiling and proud like Auden was her own.

Tall vases, quince for the bottom half, jonquil reaching up and out, and duck-shaped tea lights covered the dining room table. Each place setting held soup spoons, salad forks, and dessert spoons. Nearly two hours had passed since she had last fed Auden.

"As we have our salads, I thought it'd be fun if we shared the one thing we wished we'd known when we had our firsts," Barbara said.

"They grow so fast," a woman in a fuchsia, cap-sleeved dress said, her drawl stretching out *grow* and *so*.

"Sleep when the baby sleeps." Virginia nodded heavily.

"Cherish every moment."

"Don't wish this time away."

Either these women have read my mind or Virginia told them. Had these strangers connected the polka dots? Auden slept through the soup course, chicken salad, and decaffeinated lime tea. By the time Lara's fork scraped the plate, her breasts were full and tight, the pads scratchy as steel wool against her engorged skin.

The woman seated directly across from Lara, Deidre Wells—still Dee Dee well into her fifties—gaped at Lara's cleavage. Dee Dee's studies were unladylike, but the topography of Lara's body changed, visibly, with the milk it made. The fourth time Lara's eyes locked on Dee Dee's and she quickly looked away, Lara checked, certain she had dropped chicken salad. Instead, the fabric of her dress had darkened with milk over the left breast. Either she had leaked around the pad or already soaked it. She gave Dee Dee a tight smile and a nonchalant, or so she hoped, *whatcanyoudo* shrug of her shoulders. Her neck was hot.

After Lara's second bite of lemon sorbet, Auden grunted. Auden's dress rustled as she stretched inside the bassinet. *Saved by the baby.* But before she could push out her chair to stand, Ronnie had Auden in her manicured grip, nails long and tapered into severe ovals.

"I've been dying to pick her up," she said. Ronnie lifted Auden up to her pink herringbone padded shoulder. Her rings glittered as she gently patted Auden on the back and rocked side to side. Auden cried and Lara's nipples burned, but she maintained her composure, smiling, even at the woman's efforts.

"She's hungry, I think," Lara said.

"Don't worry. I'll hold her so you can finish your dessert. Every mother deserves to sit through at least one meal. And I had four of my own." Holding Auden when she cried was bad. Being forced to watch, helpless, as Auden screamed made Lara queasy. Ronnie changed her arm positioning, clucked and shushed, rocked faster and slower. The women studied her. Each woman turned to the woman beside her and spoke. As Auden cried, their conversations grew louder, too, though more polite, as if Southern decorum could quiet a wailing baby. *Bless her heart;* they would pretend she was not even there. Lara shoveled the remains of sorbet onto her tongue. Her gag was subtle. After five minutes, Ronnie had circled the table and held Auden out to Lara.

"I guess she does want her mama," Ronnie said. *She wants to eat.*

"Thank you for holding her; this was such a lovely lunch." Lara carried Auden into the living room to nurse her, she had hoped, in private, while the women finished dessert. Discreet and simple. She liked the ease the wrap dress provided for breastfeeding. The unused breast remained covered while the baby nursed on the other side. As she helped Auden latch on, Barbara walked into the room. Barbara draped a lace shawl over them.

"So you'll be more comfortable, dear."

Virginia entered the room and sat on the opposite end of the sofa from Lara. She did not turn to Lara as she spoke. "Did you try those nursing petals I gave you?" The hair at Lara's temples itched.

"I wore them today, actually."

"Oh." Virginia crossed her legs, laced her fingers around her knee.

Within minutes the women returned to the living room. The shawl kept slipping from Lara's shoulder. Auden kicked and squirmed, gumming Lara's nipple, ferocious. They all watched. Each woman's body was angled so they could pretend to chitchat, watching the scene of mother and child out of the corners of their eyes. Teacups clattered against saucers as they lifted, sipped, replaced. Lara kept her face calm and flat; she wouldn't crack. Sweat gathered just beneath her breasts and Auden's head was hot and furious in her hand. The white dress amplified the angry red of her skin, dappled white and purple. Auden kicked hard enough to shove the shawl all of the way off Lara's body, too quickly for her to catch it. Auden cried around Lara's nipple, her breath hot and wet.

"Could I use one of your bedrooms, Barb?"

"Of course," Barbara said. She led Lara and Auden to a guest room. Lara's body temperature dropped ten degrees as soon as Barbara closed the door.

Through the door, Lara heard Dee Dee ask, "Doesn't she carry a bottle?"

"They really are a bunch of biddies, Auden. Thanks for getting me out of there." Auden ate with gusto, but she didn't doze off. Milk flowed.

While in the guest room nursing Auden, Lara heard the continued conversations and the clinking of tea cups on saucers. No one had left.

It wasn't until she had to open gifts that Lara suspected that the women and Auden were working together, hunting dogs flushing the quail from a roost. Auden was quiet, navy eyes watchful, fists balled loose. The blood had receded from her skin and remade her face lineless and smooth, cream-colored again. Back in the living room, the stack of gifts had been moved to surround the striped-silk wingback chair that stood by the front window.

"Lara, we've got you all set up here for presents," Barb said.

"She's full now. Hopefully she'll just drop off to sleep," Ronnie suggested, nodding. "Can I try holding her again?"

Lara couldn't refuse. "Please take one of my burp cloths, just in case."

Ronnie waved her concern away. "If you relax, she'll relax."

It was strange but nice to have two functioning arms for a moment. Barbara gestured for her to sit, and all of the women perched in a tight semicircle around Lara. Wrinkled cleavage and expensive necklaces formed a horizon. She inhaled tea breath mingled with dentures. Barb winked at Lara. Virginia waved a notepad and pen. Thank you notes.

Since she was a child, Lara had felt awkward being inspected while opening gifts, so careful to try and give the perfect response. Women grew strange about how small infant clothes were or wanted to reminisce about whatever memory an item triggered. She had avoided a baby shower for just this reason. Lara's fingers fumbled with the bows. The ripping of wrapping paper felt violent, the torn edges savage and rough.

The first box she opened was from Ronnie, a monogrammed linen bib with delicate eyelet edging, stiff and formal.

"How beautiful," Virginia said. "And if you ever need it, I know the best embroiderer." Lara leaned to set it down beside her and move on to the second, but Barb pulled out the bib and passed it from woman to woman. No one could resist rubbing it between their fingers.

Sweat dripped from Lara's nose, darkening the lavender tissue paper of the second gift, from Barb. As soon as Lara's hands emptied of one gift, Barb placed another in her arms or lap.

Auden's face closed in on itself like a flower past dusk. Her legs flexed and then curled. Ronnie adjusted her hold and then swayed side-to-side. Ronnie raised Auden's head above her shoulder, just as Auden spit up. Vomit spilled over Ronnie's shoulder and down the back of her jacket. Auden screamed her Auden scream.

"That is some cry," Dee Dee said.

Lara stood too fast, and the skin around her incision pulled. Barb's gift, a silver-plated music box, slid from her lap to the floor, landing in mechanical lullaby. She pushed air out through her teeth so she wouldn't groan. "I'm so sorry. Let me take her." Why wouldn't they let her leave? Dee Dee's crepey eyes stretched wide, the whites overwhelming the brown irises. Barb blotted a linen napkin dipped in club soda onto Ronnie's jacket. Lara dabbed at Auden's mouth, then held her against her shoulder, bouncing to try and calm her. She stepped over the gift bags and wrap and tissue paper on the floor before her, ready to carry the baby out of the circle.

"Mine next," Virginia called, as though nothing had happened. She was enjoying this. "It's the one in the toile bag." Lara smoothed her dress and took her seat, tucking a sweaty lock of hair behind her ear. Only three gifts left: she would open them one-handed. A smocked bathing suit, blue and white seersucker with ruffles and multi-colored sea horses, hung from a silk-wrapped hanger. It was enormous.

"Oh, isn't that to die for?" Barb nearly swooned.

"For next summer," Virginia explained. "She'll be such a little beach babe."

Next summer. The Auden that fit that bathing suit would be monstrous. Uncontrollable. It would never end. Lara choked on her thank you. Barb placed a glass of water on a coaster beside her. Lara rubbed the bathing suit's string ties, trying to control her panic. Each day was impossible. Another year. An entire lifetime. The knot fell untied in her hand. She couldn't re-tie it.

"Pass that darling suit around," someone suggested. Virginia picked it up off of the floor and passed it to the woman beside her. Lara wished she would never get the bathing suit back, but knew it was unavoidable. Two boxes remained. One contained a large fleece blanket with a silk border. The last held a small silver cup and spoon.

"Thank you all, so much. Your generosity is truly overwhelming," Lara said once the items had circled the room. The tears in her eyes, she hoped, would make her look sincere.

Chapter Nineteen

Twenty-seven days old

Clara and Chuck Vale, neighbors long retired, broke from gardening for lunch by 11:40, followed by *Antiques Roadshow*. If she waited till then, Lara would not see the Vales' crimson and white gingham shirts and brimmed canvas hats through the latticework separating their backyards. She stayed inside when the Vales were out, though the air was cooler and lighter in the morning. When Lara ventured out in the morning with Auden crying, the Vales' pruning and weeding and transplanting suffered. Their shears stilled, companionable chatter quieted. Mrs. Vale: "Wouldn't the poor dear take a pacifier?" Then she'd resume clip-clip-clipping.

At midday, Auden's skin stuck to Lara. Still thin and whiskered with purple capillaries, Auden's translucent flesh reflected Lara's freckles. Both arms were waxy in the heat. Lara bounced Auden, body against her chest, supported head at her shoulder, naming the holly bushes, the gardenias, back into the shade of the sweet gum tree whose gnarled roots veined the yard.

The azaleas bloomed against the rear fence and behind the tree, a riot of purple and fuchsia for three weeks a year. She preferred the vibrant green leaves to the flowers. Fingers of grass pressed up between the brick pavers she and Will had arranged in a semicircle two years before. She bent down to uproot them, captivated by the curious angle Auden's neck assumed in the bend of her elbow. A startling contrast— the small, pale face, thin strands of blue veins curlicuing up her temples, iridescent strands of hair above the deep red brick.

Lara ran her hand over the rough texture of the brick; her dry-skinned palm caught on the grit. She wiped her palm on her thigh and then laid it over Auden's head, blood moving, pumping against her lifeline. Auden's skull was an eggshell above the dense weight of the brick. Lara stood.

What would happen if I dropped her? She swallowed the thickness in her throat, but it rose again. She'd tripped up the front steps that morning as she went out to retrieve the paper. A rolled ankle, a missed step. How far could Auden fall and survive? Lara shifted her weight, a spiny sweet gum seedpod from the tree underfoot.

A laboring knot pulled, pumped in her chest; the blood it moved, viscous. Her breath stuttered. Again the image formed: Auden falling, arms splayed. The cruelty of the infant startle reflex. No matter how gently Lara laid her down, Auden's arms flew to her sides, tense, fists wide, grasping, eyes dark and wild. Her skull would strike the unforgiving brick first, faster than her torso. Her brain wouldn't speak to those arms flapping useless, telling them to brace her. Then her spine would hit. Her toes, long and purple and straining, didn't know how to stand. Lara could feel more than hear Auden's body smacking solid ground. On the sidewalk as a child, Lara had tried to reassemble the yolky blue robin's eggs she found. The cracked shell had crumbled between her fingers. Yolk and blood stuck under her nails. A cinematic trickle of blood from Auden's ears.

"Stop." Her own voice broke the trance. Lara clenched her jaw. Her mouth was the only part of her she risked moving. She pressed her fingertips together to stop the trembling. Auden's tiny hand held on to her. *Just a few steps and I'll be off the brick.*

Red fluttered in her periphery. Mrs. Vale stood at the fence, two bumpy white fingers curled through the diamond-shaped opening. "You feeling all right, Lara?"

Lara blinked, remembered to nod.

"You've lost all your color."

"Uh—yes. I think I just stood up too quickly." Lara twitched her lips like a smile. Both arms pressing Auden to her chest, Lara walked gingerly off of the brick, over the grass, and up onto the back deck. Never looking back, she slid her finger from inside Auden's sweaty grip to pull open the storm door into the kitchen and let it slam behind her.

She put Auden more forcefully into her bouncy seat than planned. *Hot potato.* Her fingers fumbled the plastic safety clip. When the safety restraint clicked, Lara exhaled with a sob. Auden stared up at her—or at the giraffe mobile on her bouncy seat. Eyes and nose running, Lara lunged for the half-bath off the hallway.

Auden cried, too.

Later that afternoon, the shrill clang from the phone in her hand buzzed through Lara. Will must've turned the ringer back up when she wasn't looking. Why was it already in her hand?

"Hello?" Lara barked into the phone, the harsh tone of voice more strident than the ringing in her ears.

"Hey, it's me. Is now a decent time to talk?" Will's unsure inquiry reminded her of a dog at its master's feet, cowering in hope of attention, fear of punishment.

"Your guess is as good as mine." Lara attempted a laugh but it fell flat.

She paced in front of the fireplace, walking the outline of the stone hearth. Will had arranged the "Welcome, Baby!" greeting cards they'd received in messy rows on the mantel. Their bright colors and brighter sentiments were out of place in the sleek living room, the last adult space in the house.

"All right, I'll be quick." Lara's thoughts bubbled with venom. *He has no idea. The most disruptive thing that will happen to him all day is a faculty meeting will run long. The Diet Cokes might sweat on the conference room table.* "Do you think you can be ready at 6:45?"

"Ready for what?"

"*Jules et Jim* is showing at the Landmark—we can eat while we watch."

"Auden can't sit through a movie." Oh, how she had loved that film: the flirtations, Catherine's power. She'd seen it for the first time on a screen the size of a ship's sail in Central Park.

"I called your mom."

"Beth. Christ."

"She's been dying to help. She even offered to stay a few days."

Lara didn't answer.

Resentment: *(noun)* the need to explain (again) that Auden was still eating every two to three hours, sometimes more. The muscles running up and down her arm tensed. She smacked the cards, the sharp points welcome. The cards toppled, scattered and fell. Lara left them.

Will continued, "There's plenty of frozen milk. And if it made you feel better, you could pump a little before we leave. Beth can come whenever you want."

Lara walked into the hall. The string from a helium-filled balloon bumping along the ceiling stuck to her shirt. She jumped. Lara yanked on the curled ribbon, the balloon sank, rose again. "Why tonight?"

"The movie's tonight. I know how much you love it and—"

"Don't you even want to see your daughter?"

"What?" Will's tone was low, dripped from the phone. Gone was the pleading softness.

"You'll be gone all day today and then just swing by to pick me up and leave again."

"Lara, of course I want to see her. You're being crazy. I just thought—"

"I didn't know I would be alone in this." She couldn't stop herself. Words she needed to say mutated and twisted shape as they passed through her mouth. The more she attempted to clarify her thoughts, the more misshapen they became. She couldn't stand the sight of her home anymore, the feeling of the couch or the rocker below her buttocks.

"It certainly wasn't my idea for you to quit your job. I thought you'd want to get out. That's all."

"I do. You're right."

"Tell me what you want me to do. I'll call your mom and tell her to forget tonight. I'll stay with Auden."

"I'm not going to a movie by myself."

"So, call a friend."

"Who the hell would I call, Will?" Her voice broke on his name.

"You could hit the museum or something. There are so many things we used . . ."

She knew he realized his mistake, but he'd already opened the door. "Before Auden? Your life hasn't changed at all. What don't you get to do?"

She could picture him sitting at his desk, thumb and middle fingers massaging his temples. *Remember the beautiful women on campus.* How many times had she watched this scene play out with men she worked with? She had laughed at the nagging wife who dragged the kids into the office, watched the men slip wedding bands into their pockets when they took clients out for drinks.

"I'm sorry, Will," she attempted. "I really don't mean to be this way."

"I'm not trying to be insensitive." His voice was softer again. "I thought it would be nice to do something together to ward off cerebral atrophy."

"Let's give it a shot, see how tonight goes." She pulled the balloon into the kitchen, dragging the ribbon in the same angry-relieved grip Beth had used when Lara would go missing at the fair as a child. The pink circle with the cartoon diaper pin and stork bobbed behind her. She grabbed kitchen shears from the knife block and punctured the balloon. Once. Twice. The point of the scissors bit into the countertop. The balloon shrank, slid off the counter, to the floor.

She could breathe.

At the movie, Lara crossed and uncrossed her legs. As soon as she set her wine glass on the table, she reached for another sip. Her skin ached for air and freedom. Will's arm scraped her shoulder as he tried to massage her back. She glanced at him. He caught her gaze and smiled. Rubbed harder. She savored the French, ignored the subtitles and Will's skin against hers. She swapped her feet for Catherine's, barely pedaling; hair, coat flying; center spoke of the triangle.

Will's phone lit up. He read the screen, shoved it into his pocket. He shifted his weight before getting out of his seat and exiting the theater. She gathered her purse, his sport coat. Who the hell was texting him?

"I waited to call as long as I could," Beth's voice loud over the phone in the lobby. The baby spit up most of her bottle and was inconsolable.

Being ripped from the trance of the movie was worse than sitting it out entirely. This must be what the phrase *nothing will ever be the same* actually meant. Glimpses of your old life last just long enough to tempt you, and then hot, curdled vomit on your neck, down the back of your shirt reminds you, this is your life now.

"I knew this was a mistake," Lara said as she slammed the car door closed. The view outside Lara's window was streaked, tear-smudged. She wouldn't face Will. She calmed herself and sighed. "I just need some sleep, Will. I'm sorry." She did need sleep. He had no idea how badly.

He sighed, said, "It was probably too much. Why don't you head straight up to bed? I'll thank your mom and get Auddie down."

"You handle Beth. I'll feed the baby and go to sleep."

Will pulled the car into the driveway. Each of the front windows was a bright rectangle of light in the darkness. At this hour, the houses on either side of theirs had porch lights on and upstairs, the muted blue flash of a television screen. There was crying, muffled by brick and windowpane, the exhausted *waaah-waaah*—Auden's relent after hours of raging lament. She had to wear herself out before she sounded like a normal pissed-off baby.

Beth, in a robe, was in the front hallway when Lara walked through the front door. Beth had spit-up on her collar and shoulder and a little on her slippers. Beth's blue eyes widened, expecting silence, as Lara took the baby. Auden kept screaming.

"I'm sorry I had to interrupt the movie," Beth said. "It'll get better. We just have to get to know one another better."

"Things will settle down in a couple of days. Thanks, Beth," Will said.

"Shh," Lara whispered, to Auden, to Will, to Beth. *Please recognize me, baby.* "Mommy's here," Lara said. Auden screamed a fury. "We should have hired a teenager, like a public service. Auden's the best birth control available." Lara twitched a tight smile. "Bedtime for you too, Beth."

"Let me help," Beth pleaded. "Let me stay a week at least."

"I'm not talking about this right now," Lara said as she walked to the steps.

"Let's get some sleep and we'll figure out how to make this work in the morning."

Shaking her head, Lara carried Auden upstairs to the nursery, fumbling with her bra. She jammed her nipple into the baby's mouth on the top step. By the time Lara lowered herself into the rocking chair, Auden had quieted and sucked and swallowed and snorted. *Take it easy, kid.*

"The girl loves her mama," Will said as he walked past the nursery. *This kid hates everyone.*

As much as Lara would have liked to finish nursing and then allow Will to burp the baby, clean the spit-up, change the diaper, and put her to bed, nighttime was easier for Lara when he was already asleep when she went to bed. The only reliable sleep Lara could count on was while Auden nursed and her body had no choice but to relax. The thought of her quiet, dark bedroom hummed a siren's song. But like the fishermen lured too near the rocks, Lara knew what awaited her beneath the cool cotton sheets, now nicely tucked in and crisp, the way they would twist and dampen with her sweat.

Auden fell asleep latched onto Lara's breast. *You really put up some fight tonight.* Lara said "Shhh shhh" before she began lowering Auden onto the changing table, knowing the baby's eyes would open—sometimes it was a drowsy flutter at first and others she was one of those plastic dolls whose lids rolled closed-to-open, closed-to-open with no in-between. The baby slept. Lara changed her diaper.

Lara tiptoed out of the nursery and into her bedroom. Will sat up in bed, reading. As she walked past him, he rested the book, open, on his lap. "About tonight," he said.

"Don't worry about it," she said, too tired to argue. "I'll give Beth another chance tomorrow." Lara walked into the bathroom and turned on the faucet. She brushed her teeth and flossed, washed her face and moisturized as she would have in her B.A. (before Auden) days. She lingered over her ablutions, certain that if she took long enough Will would be asleep. Even after using the toilet and then clipping her fingernails and changing into pajamas, he'd only just snapped off his reading lamp. Will's glasses held his page in *Chekhov in Hell*. When Lara climbed into their bed, she turned to face the far wall of the room. His body scooted over to hers. He slid his arm around her shoulder. The hairs on his legs grated the underside of her thighs.

"Night," she said and then feigned a yawn.

His arm over her body held her six inches from her alarm clock on the nightstand, facing the lights of the baby monitor. Sleep. The world's fixation on sleep annoyed her. Sleep disorders. Sleep aids. Sleeping pills. Until she could not sleep. Will twitched against her. The rise and fall of his chest against her back slowed. He exhaled heavy and warm on her neck.

Green light. Red light. Glowing numbers. Green light. Alarm clock. Midnight. She peeled his arm off of her. He rolled onto his stomach.

The alarm clock read 3:57 a.m. She turned toward him to stare into the dark. Her eyes closed.

It started with vertigo. Spinning. Her shoulders and torso rocked side-to-side. She stood on a merry-go-round from her childhood playground, the platform a chipped metallic yellow. The pipe handrails had been rubbed to bare, cold steel. The rotations started, slow. *Step off the platform, right now, onto the gravel pocked grass.* She would fall if she did not steady herself with the U-shaped handrails. Why couldn't she use her hands?

Clutched in both of her hands were Auden's tiny fists. Her baby's body flapped like a fish and extended out before her over the grass that now shimmered with shards of glass. The playground around Lara blurred primary colors; children swung on swings that ripped from their carabiners. Shrill laughter morphed to screeching, then moaning.

Lara crushed her inner thighs around the cold railing to hold on as the merry-go-round spun, fast, frantic. Auden's head rolled danger-ously to one side, hands slippery inside hers.

"Her neck!" Lara screamed. "She can't hold her neck up yet." Her baby's head, still face down, lolled, sharp, angled between shoulders. The skin at Auden's wrists choked to an engorged purple.

The merry-go-round lurched up on an angle, spun. Lara's thighs twitched, exhausted, lost their grip as the revolutions ripped, force throwing their two bodies apart. The merry-go-round spun hard, spun loose. Baby eyes, open. What could she see?

Her own voice: "Do you know what's happening?" She hinged over the metal restraint, gasping for air. Auden's fist slipped. She didn't want to wake. Her eyes opened when she dropped the fists, Auden's body hurtled away, curled like a kitten. She slumped against the slowing, spinning platform, heart beating against metal. Black sleep encircled.

"Baby, you look exhausted," Will said as he brought Auden into their bed to nurse at 5:40 a.m. "Was she up that much last night? I never even heard her." Even when Auden slept she kept Lara awake. As Auden ate, Lara fell back under, asleep.

Lara awoke in a puddle, a sharp sting in her nipples as breast milk coursed over her chest and down the bumps of her ribcage. The T-shirt stuck to her chest. Her bedroom was too light.

Will walked in, tangy with aftershave, fastening his belt. "Did you get some sleep?"

"Where's Auden?"

"Napping."

"She needs to eat."

"She's fine. Your mom fed her an hour ago." He gathered the bound play from the bedside table; his glasses dropped to the floor. He hurried to the bedroom door. "Call me later?"

"What do you mean? There's barely any pumped milk in the fridge."

He looked down before answering. "She felt like she was helping. She made a bottle."

"A bottle of what, Will?"

"She mixed the pumped milk with some formula that came. Samples, I believe. Didn't look like much."

"Do you know why the formula companies send free samples?" He nodded, still avoiding her eyes. "For moments like this. When breast-feeding is hard. To get us hooked—Auden on the sugar and fat, us on the convenience."

"Look," he said. "She didn't exactly ask my permission."

"You could have stopped her or woken me up." Had he any idea how hard she'd worked to establish her milk supply? The herbs, the hours attached to the breast pump, the bloody, scabbed nipples?

"You're exhausted. Obviously you need more rest."

"What I *need* is to know you're on my side. That the second I take a nap you're not going to go and do exactly what we said we wouldn't."

"I am on your side, and Auden's. A little formula isn't that big of a deal."

"Do you know what they put in that stuff?"

He nodded. "I also know that Auden is fed, full, and napping. You should be, too."

"You sound just like Beth. I knew letting her stay with us would be a mistake."

"I said I'm sorry."

"No, you didn't."

"You're tired. The baby is a lot of work, much more than you expected. But it isn't acceptable for you to talk to me like this."

"I don't need a second child, William."

"I'll get out of your way," he said, pulling the strap of his bag over his shoulder. She waited for the door to close behind him and called, "Mom."

At first, no answer.

She walked downstairs. "Mom!" She spoke like an angry teenager, jaw tight, bottom teeth hard.

"I'm in the kitchen, dear. I made some muffins, carrot and apple." Even her favorite muffins couldn't temper Lara's rage over their betrayal.

Lara seethed into the kitchen. "I don't want a muffin."

"Here's some water, then," Beth said. Lara took the glass, grip fierce, spilling a few drops. Her mother moved around the kitchen, away from her. She closed doors, wiped down the counter, even swiped a paper towel over the coffee pot heating element, just like Lara would.

"I thought you were going to come help, that's what you said. Why can't you do just that?"

"I'm trying, Lara. You won't eat my cooking—you've got that taken care of. I've never seen a freezer with so many pre-cooked meals. I can't take Auden anywhere, and you won't leave. Go get a pedicure or something. You don't even let me hold her."

"This is so typically you, Mom. Thanks for the rundown of all I've done wrong. How can I go somewhere? The second I turn my back you're jamming a bottle of formula in the baby's mouth."

"She was hungry."

"She's always hungry. I asked you to bring her to me."

"You're running yourself ragged. Always cleaning or using that pump. You need more rest."

"Don't tell me what I need."

"Will's worried, too." Beth's voice shook, broke high on the sharp *t* sound.

"You two were talking about me?"

"I love you. We both do." Her face did what it always did when she was about to cry, the skin fell loose, unanchored. The dark crescents below her nostrils dampened.

"How dare you start crying." The shoulders shook, head wagged back and forth. "Dammit, Mom. Always this."

"Let me help. I'm sorry, Jo-Jo, I made a mistake. Tell m-m-me how I can help."

Lara didn't throw the glass. She let it slip through her fingers, sweaty, wet. It smashed against the tile. Flecks of glass cut into her shins. Water diluted the blood as it ran. "Stop crying!"

Her mother picked up each piece of glass with her fingers. She mopped the kitchen and then, once the floor had dried, vacuumed it. Lara repacked her mother's suitcases and set them beside the front door. Lara wanted to apologize for the cut in her mother's palm, the wince when she picked up the bags. She needed to figure out what to tell Will about why Beth left.

Alone again. She called the pediatrician's office.

"I need to schedule a jaundice recheck and a weigh-in for my daughter," Lara said.

A nurse's voice: "Her chart says that no recheck is necessary."

"Oh, terrific," Lara said. "What a relief." She hung up.

That hadn't worked. She needed reassurance, Dennis's under-standing, someone to believe in her. Lara spun through symptoms, what would be enough to get Auden seen but not sent to the emergency room. Fever over 102, do not pass go, head straight to the hospital. All of the doctors knew about the crying, surely the chart listed that, too.

She dialed again. After four rings, "Hello?" Same voice as before. Lara hung up. She called again. To the new voice that answered she said, "My daughter is having loose stools. I'm concerned."

"The only open appointments are at one fifteen with Dr. Michaels and two forty-five with Dr. Thompson."

"The two forty-five works great."

Lara wore a sundress and earrings to the appointment; Dennis, cologne and a thick smile. Auden's bowels miraculously improved. They would meet for tea, next. Dennis asked if, on his day off, he could make her lunch.

Chapter Twenty

Twenty-nine days old

Lara hand-washed pump parts and bottles with Auden strapped across her chest in a sling, the lapis-colored hemp pulled tight through the shiny steel ring, an ache across her lower back that stabbed down into her sacrum, then to the burning points of her hips.

Auden whimpered and writhed. Lara gave up by the second bottle and left the parts floating in foamy suds. "I'll get to it tomorrow," she'd told Will numerous times, most recently last night, or was it the night before.

Will brandished two days' worth of newspapers from the front porch. "People will think we're away if we let these pile up. And if you're not reading the *Journal*, we should probably just cancel it," he said.

Lara had shrugged, knew herself indulgent and lazy if she devoted Auden's fleeting quiet time to something just hers. It had been obvious, natural, to fire the housekeeper two weeks before her due date. She would be home anyway, with all this new time saved by not working. Cobwebs in the floor corners waved. Her sole stuck in spilled milk.

No matter how manic her need for activity, she couldn't stick with anything for more than a few minutes. Her inability to focus was far worse when Auden slept, stillness intolerable.

Really, though, Lara couldn't read the *Wall Street Journal* because she hated the wider world with its occupation and purpose. The way things happened. Made headlines. Lara couldn't change a diaper without risking her daughter's angry wet mouth, uvula bouncing. She never told Will. No one wants to play the ungrateful lunatic.

She dropped the wiry bottle-cleaning brush into the gray water. She lifted Auden out of the sling and rearranged her face, showing her baby a mother who loved her. One who tried as hard as she could.

"Hey, girlfriend. We've got a long day ahead of us so let's see if we can get along." She carried her into the living room and walked her from photo to photo and painting to painting to explain—in as close to a sing-song as she could muster—who every smiling face was and how they were related. She stopped for a moment by a picture Lara's father had taken of her outside Gramercy Tavern in New York City.

"You probably don't recognize this lady. But that's me. Your mommy. That day I . . ." Lara's tongue was in the way, too large for her to speak. Auden gazed at the black-and-white photo. Lara's father had taken the picture during his last trip to New York. He was sick already, probably. The Lara in the photo smiled. Auden wriggled. Lara thunked the frame back onto the table.

The grandfather clock in the hall chimed. Quarter till ten. She hadn't left the house in days. *Well, we've covered all of the pictures and artwork in the house. Any plants still alive?* One fern hung on despite her neglect. She would empty the two dead ones, later. That left her with the fern and her favorite succulent—spiny green with two delicate buds, savagely sharp, kept up high.

Lara tickled Auden's hands, her cheeks with the fern leaves, but the baby saw only the cactus. Auden's cries jangled and scraped, louder and louder. The baby couldn't reach the spines. What if one pressed into the little flesh wrinkled inside her elbow, the slash of her mouth?

Lara reached out for the cactus, cut her finger on the tip. She backed away until her legs met the couch and she slapped down, busying her hand with unclasping and freeing a breast. Auden tugged at her nipple. *People always think I'm hurting her when they hear her cry.* No mother thinks those kinds of things. Auden sucked harder, wagged her head *nonononono*. Lara squeezed her nipple until it purpled and spit a few droplets onto her fingertips. She smoothed her fingers over Auden's mouth until her tongue poked through white lips. Then Auden's mouth opened, and she latched on. Both felt the oxytocin, the chemical made to force this union, and Lara was no longer so afraid.

"Shhh," she whispered. When her left breast slackened she offered the right. Auden switched placidly. Lara touched her hand with her finger, and Auden held it. The clock chimed again: 10:15 a.m. When she nursed, the world thinned, became hazy. Breaths came. But the minute Auden finished, the room regained its sharp, angular brightness, a narrow box, plaster walls and ceiling too thick and close.

As she raised Auden against her palm to burp her, Lara's panic rose like the gas bubble she could feel in Auden's stomach, up her esophagus, throat, and out of her mouth. Any moment and she would start screaming again. There were so many hours left in the day. Beneath Auden's droopy lids, wrinkles appeared and dark skin. Lara was startled by how young—almost unhumanly so—her daughter could look and at the same time ancient, wizened. So much like her father, when there was so little left of him. She felt the space between her daughter's tiny thighs for a bulge of wetness in her diaper and found none.

Lara didn't change her but swaddled her, laid her on her back, and tiptoed out of the nursery. The door handle barely made a sound as it slid into place, closed. She held her breath. *I could shower. I could make myself something to eat. Healthy.* She padded down to the kitchen and poured a glass of water, chugged it, and poured another. She'd had to move a dirty colander to fill her glass. She paced around the kitchen.

She walked into the family room and turned on the television. She sat. Her feet tapped Morse code. She flipped through all 200 channels, volume down almost to mute. She clicked through people awaiting paternity tests, clownish judges banging gavels and spouting catch-phrases, teen mothers, babies born in toilets, all manner of getting-ready-for-baby shows. She walked behind the couch, remote in one hand, water glass in the other.

The cactus had to go. She grabbed it from its perch on the shelf and shook the terra cotta planter empty into the kitchen trashcan, dark soil, benign roots on top.

After twenty-seven minutes, Auden started crying. Lara was incensed. Her thighs tensed. She took measured steps though her heart beat a sprint. She stomped on the creaky steps. Sweat beaded cold in her armpits, ran icy as she clutched the doorknob.

Surely this is wrong, a mother and child so at odds. Who had sat for the painting of the Madonna? What mother, which child could gaze longingly, lovingly at each other long enough to be sketched, let alone painted? Auden's cries crashed, waves against bulkhead.

"Hey, love," she said, resisting the urge to stick her fingers in her ears, down her throat. "Mommy's here." At those words, Auden's cries grew louder, shorter, with minimal intervals of breath punctuating them. *I make it worse. I should make it better.* "Mommy's here," in Beth's voice chased the panic of childhood nightmares. Or perhaps Lara had always waited for the big soft palm of her father's hand on her back as he handed her a Dixie cup full to the lip with tap water.

One foot out, bootie sock kicking, Auden punched the air. The cotton blanket was soaked, so was the diaper, bunched to one side. Even on the sheet where Auden lay spread a dark, murky yellow against the cream cotton sheet.

Dammit. "Here we go, little bird. Let's get you out of this wet mess." She moved her to the changing table, one hand against her abdomen as the other groped for a fresh diaper, wipes. Pushing those to the side, she unsnapped the cotton onesie. Lara stretched out the neck hole so that she could slide the onesie over Auden's head without smothering her in urine. She threw it in the hall: too wet, too stingingly sweet-smelling even for the hamper. When she pulled open the diaper tabs, the perfect curves of her daughter's labia were an abraded pink. "You were barely in here a half hour, Auden. How'd this get so irritated? Mommy is so sorry."

Maybe Auden took umbrage at Lara's condescending use of the third person. Maybe Auden had figured it out before Lara had fully parsed the idea. Mommy and Lara were two different people who would be, should be, no more than indifferent acquaintances who could no longer exist as two people. Both had birthed a child. Auden made her Mommy.

She grabbed the tube of diaper rash cream before bothering to slide a diaper beneath Auden. As she gently spread that ointment over that most delicate and sensitive skin, Auden's face scrunched. Her stomach tensed and rippled. *Oh no.* The seedy yellow mess—hallmark of the exclusively breastfed infant—exploded from her daughter's anus, covered Lara's fingers, dotted her clothes, the changing pad, table, and wall. Auden kicked her feet, ground the booties into the excrement.

"You were waiting for me to do that, weren't you?" She didn't call her a little bitch.

Her hands sticky and smelly, she could hardly touch her newborn, could she? Unscented wipes would get neither of them clean. She picked Auden up, shitty diaper half-on, and carried her into the bathroom. She saw their reflection in the mirror—her poop-stained fingerprints across Auden's abdomen, the shit-covered booties, shit-splattered tank top—and shook her head.

"Look at us, what a pair we make."

Lara laid Auden on the bathmat on the floor and washed her hands. The little mustardy clumps fell into the drain. She started water for the bath.

Between her thighs, she looked down at her daughter on the bathmat at her feet. Not even the size of half the rug. Auden dragged a fist across her eyes.

Out of habit, she slid the plastic infant bathtub into place, then stopped. *We both need to get cleaned up, and maybe, maybe she won't hate the bath so much if we're in it together.* Into the tub she dropped the plastic ducky thermometer that turned from blue to crimson if the water exceeded lukewarm. She peeled off her filthy clothes and balled them up, shit-side in. Lara dipped a washcloth into the bath and wiped the excess mess off Auden, adding the rank washcloth to the pile.

Holding Auden, Lara stepped delicately into the bathtub. A vision of horror, the naked new mother dropping her naked newborn into a porcelain bathtub full of water that gurgled into the tiny mouth that didn't know how to hold its breath, rushed into the growing lungs. Her mind played the scene in two iterations: In the first, Auden crashed onto the lip of the tub, skull a bruised peach, and slid, wet skin squeaking. The water slurped. In the second, a splash of small body flopping into the bathwater, falling straight, the impact with the bottom splaying her head first up and then down, the arms and legs fluttering. In each version, Auden's eyes stared up, open, at Lara through the rippling water, wide and unblinking. Her face was unlined, not crying, fear and shock pulling skin taut. Bubbled breath to flat water.

The bathwater lapped at her ankles. She lowered her body into the meek warmth. First she dipped Auden's toes into the water, then she curved her body beneath Auden's, settling the baby's head, face up, between her breasts.

"It's okay."

Auden was quiet, calm. Her daughter spread her toes and curled them. Opened and closed, discovering the sensation of water on wrinkled flesh, in the places where all of that new skin met. Lara's body relaxed under Auden's. She let her eyes sink closed but lifted her arms to her sides so that Auden couldn't slip off of her and into the water that barely crested her own abdomen and slipped between their bodies, a tantalizing barrier and a peaceful shared experience. Auden's breathing was shallower and faster than her own. The only other sound was the faucet's slow drip.

Lara's throat was tight with gratitude. Hot tears slipped from her eyes. She ran her fingertip up the length of Auden, from her toes dangling in the *v* of Lara's thighs, around the curve of her rump, firm and flawless, bath pink, up her ribcage and her arms. She felt her daughter's heartbeat with one palm and kissed the fontanel. Barely visible hairs tickled her nostrils. Hair that was new. Even newer than Auden.

Lara sat up and lifted a small, square washcloth folded at the inside edge of the tub, wet it, squirted the all-natural baby wash. She started by washing Auden's toes, each movement certain to break this strange silence, elicit the response to which she'd grown accustomed. But Auden pressed her feet against the washcloth. Lara moved up her daughter's legs to her belly, not so rounded as immediately after a feeding, and soaped her ribs. The square cotton covered the whole trunk of Auden, though even when stretched out, corner to corner, the cloth was the size of Lara's hand. So, so small. She wiped between Auden's legs and then swept the cloth between her own belly and Auden's backside.

Auden squirmed, and Lara pulled in her knees, turned the baby around and rested her back against Lara's legs, Auden's hands in hers. This quiet face, eyes open, was that of a stranger. Her lips pursed and parted like a guppy. Her eyes studied some part of Lara. *Probably these giant nipples*, areolas the size and color of the mahogany coasters downstairs. Auden's cheeks were full and rose-colored, no white creases. Space luxuriated between sparse eyebrows.

Her daughter was suddenly so radiant it hurt to look.

One of Auden's feet pulled up and out of the water and then the next. Her fingers tugged Lara's as they curled. Her pursed lips darkened suddenly, purple to brown. Lara held Auden with one hand, braced herself with the other, and stood. She grabbed the white towel from the hook on the wall and wrapped it around Auden, the edges sharp against Lara's cooling thighs.

Halfway between Lara's bedroom and the nursery, Auden started crying. Wet footprints on the wood floor. "Shh. Shh. Let's get some clothes on you. Shh." From the dresser she selected fleecy-footed pajamas, the warmest she could find. She grabbed a diaper from the still filthy changing table and laid Auden down on the towel on the carpet. She quickly fastened the diaper and then wrangled Auden's stiff limbs into the pajamas. Auden howled. The zipper was archaic and dangerous as she slid it up and closed, terrified that she would catch some small bit of skin in its teeth. Auden was dressed, still screaming, and Lara was naked. The ends of her hair dripped.

She felt the familiar hurt in her nipples. *Auden's twenty-four-hour diner, back open whether it's time to eat or not.* Had it been that long? Only a powder-coated nail remained to mark the spot where the nursery clock had hung. She had removed it nights before while she futilely tried to get Auden to sleep and each tick taunted.

Her breasts were leaking and available. Why dirty more laundry? Shivering, she breathed in her daughter's fresh, clean scent and ignored the cloying stink of drying baby shit in the corner.

When she finished feeding and burping Auden, Lara pulled out the folded baby gym, a mat with fabric-covered arches and dangling animals and shapes, and opened it on the nursery floor. With Auden on the mat and Lara in a robe, she grabbed the bucket of cleaning supplies and attacked the mess on the changing table. She gagged but didn't retch as she scraped off the feces and balled the changing pad cover around the rest of the soiled clothes, towels, and blankets. Auden squirmed on the mat. She shoved the bundle into the upright washing machine and set it to sanitize. The heat and the detergent would bleach all of the colors to a clean, cloudy gray. She opened the nursery window to ease the chemical burn.

Auden made sounds like barking and began crying. Lara picked her up off of the mat. "You just ate, little bird." She lifted Auden higher and sniffed her bottom. Clean diaper. *You've got to be tired*. She walked around the nursery with Auden in her arms. She cried louder. Lara plucked *Guess How Much I Love You* from the shelf and sat down in the rocking chair.

"Let's read," she said, propping Auden against her belly and holding the book before her. Auden was squalling before Little Nut Brown Hare told his mother just how much he loved her. The board book fell to the floor with a clap.

"Shhh! Shhhhh!" She said. *No wonder the sounds of crying were such effective torture devices.* "Please, please stop crying." Lara bounced. Begged. Cajoled. Finally offered her breast. But nothing helped.

Lara patted Auden's back. Smoothed the few hairs on her head. "Shut. Up. Shutup shutup shutup." With her hands beneath the baby's armpits, Lara held her out. Studied her. The wide, purple mouth. Veined eyelids. Balled fists. What if she bounced her in that position? Lara shook her. Just a little.

Suddenly it wasn't safe for her to hold her baby just now. She had to set her down and walk away.

She would be safe in her crib.

The front storm door squeaked, and Will's keys jangled as he entered the house. Auden's screams met him at the door. Lara didn't know what time it was. No sunlight poured into the window. Had she closed it? Were the neighbors listening all this time?

"Lar?"

Will was home. What would he see? She knew he would walk first into the family room, where she usually sat awaiting his return. She was not alone in the house. She was exposed. But she could not force herself out of the corner to pick up their screaming child.

Lara's robe stuck to her. She sat wedged in the corner of the nursery, between the rocking chair and the bookshelf, fingers laced around the knees she had pulled into her chest so long ago that her toes were numb. Her legs would protest when she tried to straighten. Lara was not crying, but her eye lashes clumped. Her face was damp.

Auden was in her crib. Her swaddled blanket, undone. She rocked over onto one side in her fury, but fell onto her back, a beetle, capsized.

Will's voice again. "Auden?"

After sanitizing it that afternoon, Lara resented the nursery she had spent a month converting from a guest room, the unisex yellows and greens counterfeit for their colors in nature. Manufactured. And all the white. White bookshelf. White crib. White rocking chair. White changing table. She could still smell the bleach. It was probably still on her hands, leaching into her skin.

His footsteps on the stairs.

"Shush, please," she begged. Auden raged.

Loafers squeaked on wood as Will pivoted at the top of the stairs, heavy, fast footfalls down the hallway. He pulled the door open. His head shook as he tried to understand. He dropped his briefcase, blazer sliding down his arm. His mouth slackened when he looked at Lara. She pulled her fingers together, knuckles white and locked. Mute. *Pick me up, Will. Help me and I can do this.* His eyes were dark and scared. Disgust darkened the pupils.

Will ran to the crib and picked Auden up. "Jesus," he muttered. He curled her into his arms, kissed her cheeks. "Where the hell is Beth?"

Lara tried to stand, knees locked, fell. She crawled to him. But he carried Auden out of the nursery, closed the door.

Sweaty fingers, slipping. Echoing screams burning her throat as the stretched, panicked eyes pleaded: Hold my hand, don't let me go. Mommy. *The force was so strong, she spun dizzy. Lara hooked her feet around the metal railing, trying to find purchase. Her ankles formed right angles. The baby's arms, already too long for her body, long primate limbs, they stretched, hyperextended, distorted. Elbows bent the wrong way.*

Lara's best friend from second grade, Minnie Chester, moved across the horizon. Cotton jumper. Shiny plastic purple headband. She skipped straight, upright, arms swinging, impervious to the gravity, but barefoot on the field of broken glass. Her feet bled. A thick, straight line of blood followed her movements. A man appeared in the one remaining swing on the swing set. His legs pumping to oblivion. He was too big for the swing set. Also barefoot. He almost smiled at Lara, until one carabiner cracked. Then the other. He hurtled away.

She let go. The baby, gone. Gone away with the little girl, the big man. Past the curve of the earth.

Lara sat up in bed gasping. Her back was headboard straight. Sweaty. Her pupils strained for lights. The images of the playground receded. Slowly. Her maraca heart rattled in her rib cage. She reached for Will. Her hand grasped a curved cotton spine, his sheet twisted, his body, absent.

Her bedroom was so quiet. She rubbed her eyes. The monitor stood in its normal place, a single green dot. On and plugged in. She had to check on Auden. She felt as though she had survived a battle from the afternoon through the end of her nightmare. The baby, after so much crying, might wake up hoarse.

She walked to the nursery expecting to find Will asleep on the floor guarding Auden from all dangers in the dark. In the dim light, the nursery looked as it should, the rocker in the corner, cushion plump and tied around the spindles in bows. The books on the shelves stood in straight lines, waiting to be read: *Goodnight Moon*, *The Runaway Bunny*, *Love You Forever*. Wise Brown, Munsch; all keepsake editions. The dresser drawers were neatly closed. Soft garments, fresh and orderly inside. Clean, perfect, and serene. Two blankets were folded, their satin edges shiny. Ready for Auden's hand around them. Almost as soft as her skin.

Auden was alone in her room. Lara stood in the glow of the nightlight staring down into the crib at her daughter. The baby's tiny hands lay up beside her ears, palms open, fingers relaxed. The fluttering of her eyelashes in dream sleep threw shadows across her cheeks and nose. Her breathing was deep and regular. She showed no outward signs of the previous hours. Lara matched her exhalations to Auden's while she studied.

She wasn't afraid of her daughter now. She wasn't afraid of herself. This was a spun glass quiet. Thin, translucent. She wouldn't move for fear of breaking it. Auden kissed the air, frowned, then relaxed her face. She was bigger than the bundle Lara had brought home from the hospital. She hadn't realized. Auden had already begun slowly stretching her legs for brief periods each day; they weren't always hugged into her chest so tightly, even in rest as they were after she was born, continuing the fetal position outside the womb. She wondered if Auden could feel her, right then, when neither of them cried. When there were no demands to be met. Lara felt deeply unworthy of this peace. How could she have huddled in the corner while her helpless newborn had cried in her bed? She had been unable to pick her up only to fail again to soothe her, but she also hadn't been able to leave the room. Auden's cries were her penance. Lara had refused to muffle her own failure, couldn't turn her back on Auden, had to listen and torture herself.

Drool had dried in a thin line between Auden's mouth and her ear. The dried spittle shimmered in the night light with the baby's sleep movements. Lara was transfixed. She could watch her daughter forever like this, it seemed. Her life could make sense in this moment. But the sensation was a glimpse into a snow globe after it settled, into a nursery of another woman and another baby. She fought to stay on the right side of the glass.

"I'm sorry, baby." Whispered. Knowing that she might never be the mother her daughter deserved, culpable for bringing Auden into this life and failing her so profoundly at each step. The nursery smelled of Auden again, humid and sweet as her breath. Lara wanted to put Auden back inside her, where loving each other had come so naturally. She had to learn how to love her daughter in oxygen.

A shadow caught the movement, a quiver, the wing beat of a thrush, the delicate gulp in her daughter's throat where it met her clavicle, her heart beating. The movement was as small, subtle as water in a tumbler. *Babies should have shells. Exoskeletons.* Auden was all open, unprotected. In daylight those open places—soft skull, limp neck, dancing fontanel—felt dangerous. Tempting and exposed and abhorrent all at once. She needed endless protection. Auden's improbably long eyelashes were extended, thickened in shadow.

But that night, after their shared struggle—Lara's labor had been so one-sided—her role of protector felt like a gift. The day had stripped her so completely. Lara was so spent she had no energy left for fear. Remorse had overtaken anger. This beautiful girl asleep in her beautiful bed. Tomorrow they would start anew. Lara pressed two fingers deep into the well between her own collarbone and throat, her pulse beneath her fingertips. She rested one shaky hand delicately on Auden's chest, hovering it above her before actually making contact, her palm riding her baby's breath, a steady heartbeat, chest inflating, deflating. Lara's eyes closed. She stood with her hand above her daughter's heart. Everything hushed, stilled. She formed a new cord. The moments after Auden was born Lara had yelped when Will cut the umbilicus, the gray, veined length of it, throbbing and wet, pinched between the scissors. That was a cord forged of biology and technology. Tonight's bond would be formed of choice. *Anything, baby.*

"What are you doing?" Will's angry whisper. He crossed the room in three large steps.

241

Lara jumped, startled. He moved quickly. He flung her hand off of Auden's chest. He held Lara tightly at the wrist. She shook her head.

"You're going to wake her."

"No—I." Her touch had been light, loving. *Right?* Had she pressed too hard? Auden's breath was regular and still. He looked so angry. So afraid. But she wouldn't ever. They'd been loving each other. Coming to an understanding.

"Go back to bed. I'll get you when she needs to eat."

I wasn't hurting her. I wasn't hurting her. She followed orders and went back into their bedroom. "There are no monsters under the bed, no one in the closet," she whispered in the dark until she fell asleep. *Goodnight, nobody.*

The dark was softening when Lara awoke to Auden's grunts and stretching sounds through the monitor. She padded into the nursery to pick Auden up before the sweet sounds ratcheted up into angry cries.

Lara would do better today, be better. She had to. Finally, it felt possible.

One breast loose and drained, Lara gently switched Auden to her other breast as she rolled to her side. It was one fluid movement. The baby kept hold of Lara's clothes. After several moments, Auden's latch on Lara's nipple slackened, soft. Milk dripped from the lazy corners of Auden's mouth, dampened Lara's T-shirt. Auden's eyes had been closed. Lara's drowsed low.

She had almost drifted off when Will hurried into the bedroom. "Where is she?"

Through a languid fog, Lara answered, "Right here."

"I'm sorry. I didn't know she'd gotten up."

Lara hadn't yet opened her eyes. "Mmm-hmm. It's fine."

"I meant to wake up with her, let you get some sleep."

"Really, we're great. This is how we roll in the mornings." She slid Auden closer to her and prepared to give into sleep once again.

"I'll take her. You get some rest," he said. His arm slid against Lara's breast as he reached for Auden. "I'll change her diaper and make breakfast. Come down when you're ready."

"Um, yes, sir," she said. She rolled over. Sleep had been so close.

The bed was cool without Auden, the sated warm body nestled beside her. Of course Will didn't understand their morning routine. He was hardly there to see it. But he was just trying to help.

She lay in bed for fifteen minutes reminding herself to enjoy the free time. When she entered the kitchen she found a glass of ice water and a steaming bowl of oatmeal. She hated oatmeal, always had. Food that tasted like someone else had already chewed it held no appeal. She and Will had joked about it at the hospital; oatmeal was the centerpiece of every meal in the maternity ward. High in fiber and fully soluble. "Guaranteed to get things back on track," the nurses had said when she tried to send it back. "Things" = her bowels.

Will had put the baby in her bouncy seat and walked in fumbling with the BabyBjörn straps. He was clipped into it the wrong way. Lara laughed. "Do you know how to attach this thing?" he asked.

Lara could put the Björn on and secure Auden one-handed. The PhD had straps in the wrong places and the baby-holding front flap dangled off to one side.

She unclipped the Björn, straightened out the twisted flaps, and showed him how to loop it around his arms and tighten the waist. She picked Auden up out of the seat and slid her into place, gently tugging her legs through the holes. "There you go. And what's all this?" she asked, waving at the hot bowl of goo.

"I thought you might be hungry. I didn't know how hard it could be to get yourself fed while she's awake. I'm going to go to the store later and buy some meal replacement bars, something quick and healthy you can just grab and eat."

"Thank you," she said, moving the oatmeal around the bowl without ever loading any onto her spoon.

A 1950s sitcom housewife: "Don't let it get cold." He watched her. She took a swallow.

"Would you like tea with that?" He stroked the back of Auden's head, still watching the spoon in Lara's hand.

"I'd love some but I can get it."

"You sit," he said as he rifled through cabinets. "There's got to be some decaf around here somewhere."

"In the cabinet above the coffeemaker." The steam would already be rising from the mug, leaves steeping if she'd done it herself. His every movement was slow and unsure. But he was making an effort. She needed to be patient. "Don't you have classes today?"

"Don't worry about that. I've got them covered."

"But—"

"After—" He stopped, then cleared his throat. He didn't say *last night*. "Well, I realized I needed to pitch in a bit more. Which reminds me, eat up. Then you can go relax. Other than her feedings, you're getting the next couple of days off." What had he told his department head, his TA? *The wifey can't hack it at home, so I'll swoop in for a few days.*

"That's not necessary. About last night, I'm . . ." She needed to translate what had happened overnight. How she no longer felt so afraid. That something fundamental had changed, for the better. She wasn't out of breath.

"I'll hear none of it. Just leave everything to daddy daycare." His cleverness tickled him; he chuckled.

Daycare? You're her father.

Again Will gestured to Lara's bowl of oatmeal. "Eat." The oatmeal was sticky and cold. She wouldn't be able to just swallow it down. She pressed the oatmeal against the backside of her teeth, mashed, and then swallowed. She dipped the spoon into the bowl and started again. Phlegm coated her throat. Anywhere else doing anything else, almost like giving a blowjob, knowing that the end was the worst, the gooey come, but that it was, in fact, over. He was trying. She would try, too.

Maybe he really did want to help. He'd finally noticed how much she needed him and wouldn't make her beg. She forced three big bites, smiling after each swallow, and wiped her mouth with a paper towel.

"Now go, back to bed with you," Will said. "I checked her log."

The breast-feeding log had become more of a diary, not just a record of input and output but of Auden's breath while she ate. Notations about when her belly grew hard and distended after a feeding or did it stay warm and soft though rounded and full? Lara jotted notes of how she felt after feeding Auden. She recorded those blissful moments of calm. She could look at them throughout the day to remind herself they had indeed happened and tell herself those happy, good moments would certainly come again. At least once a day Lara listed for whom and what she was grateful. She wrote out the number of hours Auden cried each day and measured it against the quiet hours, looking for patterns, trends, and triggers that might signal small improvements in the crying-to-quiet ratio. Will's reading of it was a violation.

"You should be able to nap for at least an hour," he said.

She shuffled upstairs and back into bed. Being horizontal during daylight hours was the strangest feeling. The balls and heels of her feet expected wood, not air, beneath them. The baby needed her diaper changed. Did he even know how to get Auden out of the Björn safely? The memory of Beth's trick festered. Was he going to take Auden somewhere? He'd seemed calm if not gentle in the kitchen.

Calm down. He just wants to help.

Lara tried lying on her back first, but her eyelids fluttered as she tried to still them. Then she shifted to her side. Was that sound Auden crying? She counted back from 100, then from 1,000. *Sleep, idiot.* She was still awake when Will cracked open the door to check on her, but she faked sleep like she had as a child when she was up past bedtime. She rolled to the other side. She flipped the pillow over, pressing her cheek against the cool cotton underside. Then she flattened it. She knew he'd be angry with her for staying awake. She could remember, vaguely, what it felt like to be well rested. She'd have given anything to feel it again.

A lazy shower would be almost as restorative as an actual nap. She had tried to sleep. The pretend napping was exhausting and frustrating. She showered and shaved her legs. Then went back downstairs.

"I thought I heard water running," Will said. "You were in there for a while."

She faked a yawn and stretched her arms above her head. "Thank you."

"Tell Mommy no more complaining about how tired she is if she won't take a nap, Auddie."

"Yes, Will, I know." As if it were that easy.

"This girl's looking hungry. Since you're up, how about you nurse her? I have a little reading to catch up on."

"Sure." Apparently daddy daycare clocked out at 10 a.m. "I just need to go to the bathroom first."

"What were you doing up there all that time?"

Her bladder ached, but she held it. As Lara raised Auden to her breast, she was equal parts peeved and relieved. Will walked out. Certainly she could never just hand off Auden to someone. Even for a minute. Nonetheless, it was nice not to be watched for a while, hovered over. She hoped to recapture some of the magic she'd shared with Auden earlier, but the baby was restless and squirmy. She grunted and wiggled. Lara wondered if Will could hear. Was he listening? Lara was keyed up; her milk wouldn't come down. She tried the breathing exercises that sometimes worked, but no luck.

She knew Auden would wail when she burped her, but she had no choice. She rested Auden against her chest, the baby's head just above her shoulder. Lara couldn't summon a burp any other way. With the first tap of Lara's palm to Auden's back, the baby howled. Lara felt the air bubble rising up from Auden's belly. It must have become more painful as it reached the surface, considering the intensity of Auden's cries. It always got worse before it got better. Will hurried into the room.

"How's everyone doing in here?" He looked concerned.

"She needs to burp."

"Ah. How about I give it a go?" he asked. Lara handed Auden to Will. He held her torso against his forearm, cupping her neck in his palm. "She seems to like it this way," he said. Lara didn't roll her eyes. He patted Auden's back. The baby cried but didn't burp. He tried again, looking perplexed. Auden didn't stop crying until finally the gas erupted from her lips, as indelicate as a drunk. Finally.

For two days, Will cleaned the house and he watched Lara. He held Auden and he watched Lara. If she spent longer on the toilet then he expected, his knuckles tapped the door: "Everything okay in there?" She tried to sleep. He would only leave her alone if she slept. But instead of napping, she lay in her bed chasing sleep behind closed lids. The eyes closed part wasn't bad.

Immediately after breakfast on his third day of supervision, Will suggested, "How about we go for a walk?"

"I've been trying to get a morning nap established," Lara answered.

"I thought you said she never napped."

"We're trying."

"Maybe you're just setting yourself up for failure. Not all babies nap at the same time."

She laughed. He studied her. "I'm going to try and lay her down. If she doesn't sleep, maybe."

"I'll take her up," he said. "You can take a few minutes to dress."

"Is there a dress code? I hadn't read that far into the neighborhood rules and regulations." She swatted him on the shoulder. Where would they be taking this walk that a T-shirt and shorts would constitute an egregious fashion faux pas?

"You've always taken care of yourself, but there hasn't been time lately. I get it. Nothing fancy, of course. Perhaps something with a button or zipper."

She sucked her teeth and tightened her jaw. Her neck flushed hot. She tugged the hem of her T-shirt. A fat joke. *Nice.* She tried to ignore the skin pressing below and above the waistband of her shorts. It was empty and loose and shriveled-looking. Similar in a way to Auden's drying umbilicus, except that it wasn't bruise blue or flaky, and she'd have it forever.

It was nice to be outside. But it still hurt a little to walk more than a block, pain that stood between her and the natural world. It was hard to breathe serenely when you never knew when you'd take a wrong step and have to mask a wince.

They walked away from the nosiest neighbors and toward the green space at the edge of the neighborhood. Auden tolerated her stroller for eight minutes, a personal best, but she quickly transitioned from whiny to crying a full-tilt boogie.

"Is the sun in her eyes?" Will asked. Lara had never considered that possibility on their few walks. Why hadn't she?

"Um, maybe." They turned around and walked in the other direction. Even in the shade Auden cried. "It was a good try," Lara said. "We're going to walk right back by the house. Should we quit while we're ahead?"

"Nah. We all need some fresh air. I'll try carrying her in the Björn. You said she liked that better, right?"

"Sure," Lara said, shrugging. "Sometimes." Will had scoffed when she tucked the BabyBjörn into the basket beneath the stroller, thinking it unnecessary, but now Lara helped Will into the straps, lowered Auden into the center.

"There we go." A few scant hairs on her scalp—she'd had so much hair when she was born—two curled up feet, and balled fists; that was all that was visible of Auden from the mesh sling that held her in place against her father's chest. Lara soaked it in. This sight should be mommy porn, the handsome father wearing his baby. She slipped her fingers into his to complete the picture. With his free hand, Will waved at passing cars and neighbors on front porches like a man running for office. Every third house or so, he'd tip his head low and kiss Auden's scalp. His strides were long and fast. Lara had to take two steps for his one.

"I'm sorry. Can we slow down?"

"Words never spoken by your mother before, Auden."

Lara's belly burned and the biting waistband nauseated her. Auden's butt wiggled beneath the mesh. She sighed. A woman walked by with her dog, a shimmering Rottweiler. Its haunches were muscular, tight. The woman stared at Will, eye-fucking him. And yes, on their many nights of scheduled sex during the first year of trying to get pregnant, it had helped Lara to picture Will just like this, a proud papa, their baby in his arms. The fantasy had made her wet.

"Pretty dog," Lara said, peeling the woman's stare off of Will.

Auden whimpered.

"We should probably head back home. We've been out almost a half hour."

"It's beautiful out. We're fine," he said, as he stooped over to pet the dog, one hand on Auden to keep her from falling out.

"Little girl or boy?" the slut attached to the dog asked.

"Girl," Will answered. Auden got louder.

"Well, I won't stop you," the woman said.

I bet she wouldn't.

"I was thinking about this fall," Will said as they continued walking. "We should get out of town over fall break."

"Like where?"

"I don't know." Auden cried louder. He kept talking. "Maybe somewhere close. Or not. We haven't been to San Diego to see my family in years." San Diego. That was at least two flights from Richmond.

Across the country. They hadn't gone a mile in one direction and Auden was crying.

"Maybe something a little closer." Auden crying, Lara's breasts leaking.

"The beach. That could be fun. We could rent a little cottage."

"We'd have to bring so much stuff."

"All you can ever see is the negative. Wouldn't those ladies from the chat rooms, the Infertile Myrtles, wouldn't they trade anything for what we're doing right now? Walking, together, with our beautiful little girl?" He had to raise his voice at the end so he could be heard over Auden's wailing.

It was a shot to the groin. She told herself that over and over, hour after hour each day. *Youwantedthisyouwantedthisyouwantedthisyouwantedthis.* More than anything in the world. It was her private punishment, a mortification of the flesh, this knowledge that she wasn't up to the challenge she'd begged, bought, sacrificed everything for.

"Yes, Will. Of course."

"But you never stop to think, not for a second, about anyone else."

Auden kept crying. Louder and louder. Even the woman with the Rottweiler looked back at them.

"Will, I know. I'm sorry. Can we please turn back toward home? Please?"

The questions of a child seeking forgiveness. Will wasn't her father.

And yet she had begged Ted's forgiveness, once, only once, too. "Come on, honey," her father said, surveying the wreckage of the nursery. His eyes cut from her brothers' room to Lara's guilt-hot face. Lara's father massaged his palm. Her ten-and-a-half-year-old cheek burned. She kept her hands at her sides. "This is beneath you. You're way too old for this."

Baby powder snow blanketed the carpet, the rocking chair, the crib the twins shared. Talc hung in the air. Her mother had asked Lara to get another container. She'd run out.

"Lara, just open a new one and throw the old one out," Beth had said. "Simple. Under the sink, by the baby oil." Yes, it was simple. The fortieth *simple* errand her mother had sent her on that morning: *Grab the bottles. Shake them. Soak the soiled diapers and pants and T-shirts in the sink. Where's Beatrice? Go find your sister.* She had just started watching *Little House on the Prairie*, the return of Mr. Edwards episode, when her mother interrupted.

Lara had twisted the top off the talcum powder. A small puff, a cloud piffed out of the tiny holes. She barely had to squeeze it. *Piff.* She threw the empty container away and walked the new one into the nursery, to the changing table. One more squeeze. Baby smell. Her mother never shut up about it. *Smell the babies, Lara. They're so delicious I could eat them.* She gave another puff and set the bottle down. She picked it back up. She sat in the rocker. Squeeze. Another white cloud. She danced around the room squeezing and turning the bottle upside down. She climbed into the crib. Squeeze. Dump. *Piff.* Her lips were dry, her throat, coated with talcum. She'd used more than half the container.

She ran back into the bathroom and looked under the sink; that was the last one. The powder was almost light as air. Maybe it would just disappear, settle in a few minutes. She was so dry. Every inch of her. She opened the bottle of baby oil and poured a few warm, slippery drops into her palms. She smelled of bottled baby, just like the powder. She dabbed the oil onto her pulse points, the base of her neck, her wrists. Then coated her palms with it. She peeked into the twins' room, hoping the powder would blend in with so much white furniture but no luck. A dusting, almost like snow or ash, clung to every surface and suspended in the air. She doused her hands with baby oil and dragged them through the baby powder. She'd known she needed to stop. Part of her wanted to. Part of her didn't.

"I didn't think we needed to . . . take care of you, too," her father had said. "Your mother and I have our hands pretty full." And they never had to, never again.

—

She'd learned how to calm her father; Lara could do the same for Will. "Can you lower your voice?" Lara pleaded, cowering. They had been partners once, friends and lovers. Now he shamed her like a child.

"Am I embarrassing you?" He leaned over her.

Her chin quivered. Her glottis pushed up and tight. "I'm sorry. We can take a trip. I'm sorry. She's so upset."

"She's a baby. She's crying. You're a grown-up. Act like one." He kept walking away from the house. "All of those hours in the house would make anyone crazy."

She turned the empty stroller around. If he needed to scream at her, maybe he'd follow her home.

"Where are you going?"

"Home."

The faster she walked, the worse her incision flamed. Hot, stinging, wet, too. Could she have popped a stitch? Be bleeding again? She gritted her teeth and kept going for the front door.

He grabbed her shoulder. "Don't run away from me."

"I wasn't," she mumbled, eyes down. When had she become such a failure to him?

"Just be a mother, Lara." It was just that simple, and that impossible.

"I'm trying." He tried to make her turn around. She stared at the door, and his reflection in it. He had no idea.

"Try harder." The anger and bitterness she'd felt toward herself and for Auden hadn't even touched Will. He had no right to treat her this way.

She stood up straight and spun to face him. "You didn't even want a child." *Seventy-two hours hardly makes you Dr. Sears.* "She's mine." Auden wailed louder than ever. "She's hungry, Will. Make your point later."

He looked over Lara's shoulder as she picked Auden up out of the Björn and carried her inside. She brought the baby to her breast before she sat down. She smiled through her tears at Will. *One thing you can't do better than me.*

He returned with her cell phone. "Call your doctor," he said.

"Why?"

"You need help. And I want my wife back."

"I need you to stop all of this. Just stop."

"After you call." Had he always been so nasty?

Lara dialed. "Hello, I need to make an appointment to see Dr. Thompson."

"Her next available appointment is in two weeks."

"I'll take it." What's two weeks? If Will just had a little faith in her, and stopped treating her like a child, she'd be just fine.

"Satisfied?" she asked Will.

Chapter Twenty-One

Thirty-six days old

When Will finally returned to work the next day, Lara waited fifteen minutes after he left to change her clothes, put on makeup, and prepare Auden for drop-off at Virginia's. Virginia had been surprised when Lara took her up on the offer to babysit, one casually made a couple weeks earlier, but she'd agreed nonetheless.

Lara had ordered a new dress for her lunch with Dennis, another brown package like so many others. They had skipped over meeting for tea. Auden wasn't coffee-house quiet yet. Lara had hidden the box beneath the sweaters she'd never moved from her closet back up to the attic. Sleeveless, boat neck, and black, the dress defined a waist and the short skirt flared an a-line. She hoped it would fit; slim arms and legs and a pretend waist visible.

As Lara finished applying her makeup, the doorbell rang. *It must be another package; he'll just leave it outside the door.* The phone had rung earlier, hadn't it, while she was dressing, but she had unplugged it. Lara had stopped charging her cell phone overnight, too. The ringing, the bells, were just too much. Even on vibrate, when it buzzed, she jumped. There was something about how it rattled and shook around on the cabinet or table or countertop, almost like walking into a room expecting no one but catching a shadow in her periphery. The kitchen phone jack was disconnected as well, the cord wound beneath it. She'd done that, too, hadn't she? She hadn't looked at the caller ID before unplugging the phone in her bedroom earlier. Probably just a telemarketer or someone who wanted to see the baby.

At the door, two women, strangers, had arrived uninvited with beige casseroles, a base of canned cream of mushroom soup. Lara had only attended church sporadically during her pregnancy but apparently it had been enough to hit the Casserole Care Committee's radar. She thanked them, several times, but did not ask them in despite their stretching necks, glances trying to reach around the door to catch a glimpse of the baby.

"She's napping," Lara said. The ladies left.

Again the doorbell rang. Auden started crying upstairs. Two sharp knocks on the door.

"Lara?" Bea's muffled voice from outside.

Shit. "Just a minute," Lara said, thankful for the makeup and dress she was wearing. How like Bea to just show up without warning. Lara's family acknowledged no boundaries.

As Lara reached the front door, Bea knocked again, this time on the back door to the kitchen. Perfect. They could sit outside and leave the mess inside. "I'm coming, Bea." *Who's the impatient one now?*

Lara opened the wooden kitchen door to find Bea already holding the storm door open wide. She was alone, no children. Her hair, which she'd always worn too long and rather shaggy, shimmered in a loose side-braid that lay flush over the shoulder of the simple linen dress. Bea's toes, in wedge espadrilles, were a flawless lavender. The only makeup Bea wore was mascara and a sheer pink on her lips.

Her glossed mouth parted. She rubbed her lips together. "Hey, Lar! I felt like I was on a scavenger hunt."

"Have a seat. I'll be right out. I just need to get Auddie. She just woke up."

Upstairs, Lara licked her palm and smoothed it gently down Auden's neck and chest to try and remove the remnants of spit-up and drool as she carried her downstairs and out to the backyard. Auden had been napping in only a diaper, and Lara hadn't bathed her after her first feedings of the day, but this was Bea, who always laughed about looking like an adult form of Pigpen from Charlie Brown, a dust storm of kid chaos swirling around her. Who was she to judge?

"Can I hold her?" Bea asked when Lara and Auden walked out. "She's grown so much!"

She's going to smell the spit-up. Lara always kept Auden clean. She wanted to tell Bea that. "Um, sure." Bea fluidly rested Auden's head into the bend of her elbow and began swaying gently.

"Did you two have a long night? Although you look great, by the way."

"Yes. This kid doesn't want to miss out on anything."

"I know how that goes." Bea smiled down at Auden. It was so odd how when there was a baby in the room conversation among adults always progressed without eye contact.

"I'm sorry, I would have gotten her, the house, more together if I'd known you were coming."

"You know you don't have to do that on my account. I couldn't get you on the phone and I need to head home in the morning. I thought I'd just drop in."

"My cell has been wonky lately. And I had to turn the ringers down on the home phone, because the minute I get her to sleep . . ."

"I remember that, too." Bea clucked softly to Auden, then wrinkled her nose and stuck out her tongue playfully.

"Are you in town for work?"

"Yeah, and the boys are out of school and camp won't start for a few weeks, so I packed us up."

"Camp Beth, huh?"

Bea laughed. "Pretty much." Bea continued to sway and rock as she held Auden. Bea's skin was gold, not how Lara remembered it. Her own calves were the color of winter, even in late May.

Particularly with Bea standing, Lara couldn't sit still, so she began dead-heading dying plants bordering the house. She popped off the head and rubbed the soft petals between her fingers. She kicked leaves off the porch with bare feet.

"Wow," Bea said. "She's lost the last little bit of her umbilical cord already. You're such a big girl, Auddie. In a few weeks you're gonna learn how to smile."

Lara formed what she hoped was a wistful look in response. *Smiles. Right.* She'd happily settle for less crying. A smiling baby might as well be a unicorn. She had to change the subject. "How are the boys?" With just one question Lara knew Bea would be off and running with the hectic mess of her two sons. Bea always assumed that everyone was as enthralled with her offspring as she was.

"They're fine, thanks. Thrilled to be out of school, of course."

"Good," Lara said. "Good."

"The sun's getting hot and high. Can I go snack on your delicious little girl clothes and get her dressed? It's no fun dressing fourth and fifth grade boys. But I swear they were never this small."

"Sure, but Bea, the house is a mess."

"You've always lived in a museum. You know I'm at home in clutter."

She couldn't say no. "Then I'll take you up on it. You know where the nursery is?"

"Come on, little ladybug," Bea cooed to Auden. "Let's go get you fixed up."

With Bea upstairs dressing Auden, Lara sprang into motion. She closed the office door, though she had to push a box out of the way with her foot so the door would latch. She sealed off the laundry room next and started water for tea.

Bea brought Auden downstairs in a frilly pink dress, a miniature leotard and tutu for a tiny ballerina, and a bow. Lara didn't know how Bea had found enough hair to secure it. Lara stared at the baby she had imagined so many months ago, in her sister's arms. Quiet. Angelic. Calm.

"I know you've got plenty of clothes but I couldn't help myself going all girly-girl. I'm relieved, though, that even you had her in just a diaper. I thought I'd find you two in matching mommy-and-me designer wear. You look too put together to be real this morning."

"Thanks. Will and I are both over the stretchy, stained aesthetic I've been working the last month."

The tea kettle whistled. Lara walked to the kitchen. She heard Bea at the foot of the stairs. "I need to check in with work. Do you mind if I get online for a minute?"

"Wait, Bea!" The tea kettle sputtered and hissed. Lara turned the stove off.

Bea gasped.

Lara walked to the office. Her sister couldn't get to the computer. There were six unopened boxes, three opened ones, four dirty bottles littered across the desk and on the floor. Baby books and magazines splayed open. Soda cans sat empty beside the keyboard. Wrappers stuck to the desktop. The room stunk sweet. A brown banana peel hung from the lip of the trash, fruit flies buzzing around it.

Lara wrestled Auden out of Bea's arms before trying to explain. "I—I didn't know you were coming. I haven't gotten in there today to clean."

"Today?" After gesturing at Lara's dress, her hair, she said, "You had time to do all of that . . ." She leaned over to pick up packing peanuts from the floor, tossed them onto the mound in the trash can.

"I know. It's a mess. I warned you." Lara picked up a box, stacked it atop another. She pushed some torn plastic wrap under the desk with her foot.

"My house is a mess. This, this is a little scary." Bea inspected the shipping labels.

Lara lifted *Happiest Baby on the Block* from one open box. She shook the book lightly at Bea. *See?* "I'm getting more organized. I'm going to get through it." She crumpled the packing paper into a tight ball.

"I'll stay and help." Her nose wrinkling, Bea peeled off a piece of notepaper stuck to Lara's desk with a liquid ring. "Beth can keep the boys a little longer."

"I thought you had a meeting."

"Um."

They were working against her. She felt dizzy. "Beth sent you, didn't she?"

Bea stared at Lara. "We all need help sometimes."

"I've got it under control."

Bea shook her head. "I hope so."

"And, actually, Auden has a checkup this morning, so we've got to run."

Once Bea left and she'd dropped off Auden at Virginia's, Lara couldn't get to Dennis's house quickly enough. She hummed with the radio on the way. Excitement was unfamiliar, welcome. He kissed her on the cheek when she arrived. He took her hand and led her inside. She wasn't certain why she was there, except that his eyes looked at her with kindness and a flicker of attraction, not pity or worry. To Dennis, she was a woman.

Dennis Thompson's dead wife did not haunt his home. Lara could barely detect any evidence of her. A small wooden table with a clamp, magnifying glass, and tiny jars of thread and fluff comprised the den.

A sparkling green nymph fishing fly, meticulously rendered, dangled from the clamp's jaws. The chair backs in his dining room held two sport coats and two sweaters. He could pluck one from the chair and be out the door. Chocolate lab hair clung to a flannel blanket over one cushion of the couch, beside the deepest groove. The dog was curled up beside an air conditioning vent, dozing in the corner. A napping house.

They ate at a small wooden table in the kitchen. The chicken salad he'd made was mayonnaisey and bland. But she could eat with both hands, while sitting down, without another body strapped to her own. They were silent, except while chewing. Lara was drunk on quiet.

Inside the faded, flowered wallpaper square of his bedroom, they spoke very little. His lips were thick, plump. Lara expected to squash, flatten them with her mouth and teeth, but they pressed back firm and wet.

Sex with a man who wasn't Will would break her, force her to find new form. Beth would never have done such a thing. Lara, as Auden's mother, would not do it either. But now, she was just any other adult making her own risky choices.

He grabbed her wrist, clutched the bones with his brawny hands. His touch was not lyrical. His callused palm dragged across her clavicle. This hard, weathered skin heavy on hers was exactly what she never knew she needed. She bit his shoulder. He licked her scarring incision, hip to hip. She split open. His knee pushed apart her legs. She howled her pain-edged pleasure.

Dennis wanted to hold her, after, learn about her. He stretched his arm out across the bed, motioned for her to lay her head down. She apologized, flushed away a wad of toilet paper stained pink with his semen and her blood, and quickly dressed. On her way out she pressed open the clamp holding the fly; the nymph fluttered, shimmering as it fell.

Once home, Lara ran the shower water so hot for a moment it felt icy. She had less than an hour before Virginia expected her to pick up Auden. She scrubbed with soap, chafing her skin. If she got clean enough, it would have never happened. She could wash Dennis, her day, her infidelity off if she scoured her skin. *Will's going to know. He's going to know and he's going to leave and take the baby.* She envied the soap bubbles, how they swirled and then popped and were done. She was a liar and a whore, but a clean one. Maybe if she could make herself pretty again everything would be fine somehow.

Her face in the mirror: shiny swollen pores, greasy craters, and blackheads. She washed her face again over the sink, the skin pulled tight and dry as a paper towel. Her eyebrow hairs were curly and unruly, too thick and long. They threatened to overtake her face like a vine. She plucked first the hairs sprouting between her brows. Each hair, plucked to the root, brought a twinge, a burn, and then a *pop*. But it wasn't enough. Years of plucking and waxing her eyebrows had toughened her skin, deadened the nerves. She needed a plan. She could make a plan and make everything right.

She closed her right eye and stretched the lid as though she were to tweeze again from her brow, but instead pulled out an eyelash and examined it perched in the tweezers. As she pulled she experienced a distilled, immediate sensation of pain, and then release and a slight after-burn. New pleasure-pain took the place of old pain, the scary pain that chased her and always caught up.

I should invite Virginia and her girls over for a play date. That would give me something to look forward to.

She plucked another lash from the lower fringe.

When Auden gets a little older, she can start Baby Gym. I'll meet some other moms.

Then she reminded herself that she had to even her eyelashes out so no one would be able to tell the difference. Controlled pain, and then release, and then the absence of pain, crystalline non-hurt.

I should call Kathy at work and see if I can secure some consulting hours. Maybe ten a month to start.

Another pull.

The tsunami of pain, regret, guilt, and fear tossed her again. She met different eyes in the mirror, exposed and frightened. The mascara wand tugged, blackened, and thickened the sparse strands.

She picked her phone up off of the counter. She had to clean up her mess. Cheating was sloppy, and why? Just because Dennis called her a good mother? *Christ.* They just had to pretend it never happened. Will had stopped going to doctor's appointments, so the three of them would never even have to end up in the same room.

Lara texted Dennis: *This was a mistake. Sorry. Can never happen again.* She exhaled a woosh, re-fogged the mirror. Her phone buzzed in her hand before she had a chance to set it back down.

Who is this? If this is a non-emergency patient matter, my office hours are Monday through Thursday, 9-4.

Lara was incensed. He'd nearly begged her for her cell number. He'd asked suggestively, and at least twice, if the "preferred contact number" in Auden's file was her cell phone rather than a home phone. She'd assured him he'd reach only her.

She texted back: *Ha ha, Dennis. Not funny.*

Buzz. *If this is an emergency, please dial 9-1-1 or visit the nearest emergency room.*

What a son of a bitch. How dare he? All she needed was his word, a promise, that neither of them would ever discuss the afternoon they'd spent together. The swelling skin between her thighs.

She called him this time. *No more hiding behind your thumbs, old man.* After one ring she was dumped into his voicemail. The bullshit soothing tones of his voice: "You have reached Dennis, please leave me a message."

"We need to talk," she said. "I'll see you at the office in the morning." She didn't leave her name. Everything was shaking.

After dressing, Lara pushed through the boxes to her computer. Her fingers trembled as she typed into the search screen:

Suicide methods + clean

23,200,000 results.

Suicide Clean-Up Services. Call for professional help and a quote. 800-455-7563.

She didn't erase her browser history.

Another faked symptom and hastily arranged sick baby visit. Lara tarted herself up so that Dennis would have a last long, hot look at what he'd be missing. When Lara arrived at the office the next morning and grabbed the flower-topped pen used to sign patients in, the receptionist stopped her.

"You can go straight to Dr. Thompson's office. He'll go over the test results with you there." The woman folded a piece of yellow legal paper, a brief note, script, in Dennis's cursive. "No exam needed," she continued.

Lara smiled. *Straight to the office is right.* "Ah, okay," she said. "Thanks so much."

"Past the scale and the bathroom on the left. He'll be in shortly."

Lara collected her diaper bag and car seat and made her way to Dennis's office, Auden grunting now, turning her head from side to side, starting to root. Perfect timing. After closing the door behind her, Lara unclipped Auden from her seat and put her to her breast. Both nipples went hard. She unbuttoned more of her blouse than was strictly necessary.

Dennis's office was a mess. Picture collages covered the wall, hundreds of babies and children staring out at her. She read and re-read his diplomas. Still, she felt recrimination from all of the smiling, cut-out faces adorning his office. He still had a picture of his wife and sons on his desk. How sweet.

Dennis's arms were full of books and file folders when he entered. "Mrs. James," he said, not looking at her. "Good morning." He took off his coat and draped it over the chair. His shirt sleeves were rolled up his forearms.

"Dennis," she said. His eyes pulled from the floor to her breasts, his mouth suddenly slack, lips parted, just barely, in the center. She uncrossed her legs so that he could sit in the chair beside her.

He blinked as though trying to clear an eyelash before moving a pile of books from his desk chair to the floor. He sat, the heavy wooden desk between them. Reading glasses on again as he bent over a file thick with papers and tabs. A Bic pen in his hand, he glanced up quickly over his glasses and then down again to the papers before him. "Auden's labs, her growth charts, everything is looking terrific, Mrs. James."

"Good, that's great," she said, offering her other breast to Auden. She'd left the Hooter Hider at home. "But, obviously, that's not what—"

"She's a healthy girl, growing well." His neck and earlobes flushed. He began see-sawing the pen between his middle and index fingers. "And I see no reason why you shouldn't stick to the recommended check-up and vaccination schedule for babies her age."

"Stop pretending it didn't happen, Dennis."

"If you have legitimate concerns about her well-being, of course schedule a sick visit with any of my colleagues. You're well versed in how to do that, yes?"

She stood, Auden still latched to her breast. "Shut up!"

"Please keep your voice down, Mrs. James." He unrolled his sleeves down to the wrist, buttoned them.

"Stop calling me that. I don't want you. I just need to know that you won't say anything. It was a mistake."

Dennis leaned back in his chair; a hinge groaned. "New motherhood can be lonely. And loneliness can give rise to fantasy. To reading more into a situation than there really is."

Auden gummed angrily at her nipple, wagging her head against Lara's exposed breast. "I'm not crazy. You're some kind of a predator, you know that?" She took a step closer.

Dennis stood. "Mrs. James, you're very upset. Is Mr. James in the waiting area? Should I call him to pick you up?"

"It's *Doctor* James," she said. He knew how to shut her up, just mention her husband. "I know who you are," she said, buttoning her blouse.

"I suggest joining some mommy groups. Get out more. Stroller strides, Gymboree, Kindermusik, maybe."

"Fuck you, you lech," she said under her breath as she smoothed her skirt and exited his office. As she click-clacked her way out of the building, she hesitated. His stubble had burned her throat, left her raw. His fingers, his tongue, his dick inside her . . . *Right?*

Chapter Twenty-Two

Thirty-nine days old

For three and a half hours, Lara tried love, sweetness, calm, endurance. Fleetingly, she contemplated a lithe, shimmering bottle of Absolut, the thick glass cool against her palm, cheek. By 10 a.m., she was done. Lara could not breathe through her tourniquet windpipe as she wiped Auden's butt for the second time. The baby, all purple mouth, forehead trenched, balled fists at ears, laid on Lara's bed. *Even she can't stand the crying.*

She needed a distraction, a text to Will: *Hi, honey. How's your day going? Another day in colicky paradise here ;) Just wanted to say hello. XOXOXO*

Her phone buzzed with his response: *XOXOXO to you, too. Control the day. Get out and get some exercise. You don't have to hole up at home, you know.*

She did not text back. *Grammatically correct and utterly unhelpful, Will. Thanks.*

"Shh, shh," Lara said, without intonation, each time meaning *shut up, please, please, shut up*. She dumped out Auden's diaper bag onto the mattress. Auden hushed while she shook it empty. Her inventory: four onesies, three bibs, two knitted hats, three pairs of socks, a dozen diapers, one pack of wipes, four clean bottles. Thirty-six ounces of breast milk sat thawed in the fridge, ready to go, enough for at least six feedings. She plucked the insurance card from the zippered pocket inside the diaper bag and slid it into her wallet. The last time she had used the insurance card was at Dr. Thompson's office. She shuddered.

Wearing yoga pants and yesterday's "Hair of the Dog 10K" T-shirt, Lara faked a lilt and said, "We need a change of scenery, baby girl." She couldn't risk another hour at home. *What mother can't stand being alone with her daughter?*

Two days had passed since she'd last showered. With the brown rubber band on her bony wrist, she twisted her hair into a sloppy bun. Seconds later she yanked the elastic out, ruffled her hair. Twisted, secured again, again let go.

Lara buckled Auden into her infant seat and walked out the front door, not bothering to lock it. Sweat beaded on Lara's forearms. The weather had turned hot, would stay hot through September. Sticky and close, the high and low temperatures separated by single digits. The sun a blistering menace. Oh, but outside was so much better than inside, the sharp heat a ting in her nostrils as she inhaled. Damp at her hairline. Auden pressed her eyes closed against the bright but quieted. Lara contemplated the stroller in the trunk. Another walk? Maybe this time would be different. *No. Not today. No more mommy walks of shame.* They both needed some distance, actual remove from this brick and mortar box. The door handle blazed under her skin as she pulled it open.

In the car, Lara angled the AC vents up to dry out her sweaty pits. The blast of cold on her overheated flesh prickled sharp ridges on her skin and somehow more sweat trickled down her sides. It was so humid, the windshield fogged up. She backed out of her driveway like a fugitive, head darting from side to side, despite the sleepy block. Her tongue was sandpaper. Surely she'd drunk some water this morning. Hadn't she? Water and a little gas, that would be their first stop. Richmond had countless Wawas. She had to pass one. The cool of the refrigerated plastic bottle against her cheek, the cold swallows, a new fantasy as she drove.

She fled, weaving through a blur of obstacles. Honor roll student bumper-stickered Suburban parked on the right, a lawn service trailer on the left. She tapped the brake, then barreled through the crosswalk painted to protect the child she'd dreamt would attend the school on the other side. Finally, the reassuring yellow and red, orderly rows of gas pumps.

She double-checked the seal on the windows before filling up so that Auden wouldn't inhale the deliciously noxious gas fumes. Ten and a half gallons later, Lara lifted her wallet from the passenger seat. *Beep beep!* The remote lock, key fob smooth in her hand, wallet tucked under her armpit. She walked to the wall of refrigerators and stood transfixed. So many bottles: some tall and aquiline, painted with hibiscus flowers or wild game peering out from the logo. Lara's mouth dripped. The beautiful bottles cost twice what the squat, ridged bottles cost, of course, and the water they held tasted exactly the same. Still, she deserved a little extravagance. As she reached for the refrigerator case handle, the front door to the store opened with a signaling beep and slam. Lara held the bottle to her throat.

"There's a baby at the pumps! Pump four," a woman sputtered. "A baby's alone in a parked car."

Even as Lara heard the woman and her distress, she couldn't connect the words or make any sense of them. How could someone forget their own baby? *Jesus.* Then her fingers loosened, the bottle slipped, thunked on the industrial flooring. Next a clatter of keys and the thud of her wallet. Lara's shoes squeaked as she scrambled to collect her things, left the bottle splayed on the ground.

She ran out the door, past the frantic woman and her wild, searching eyes. *I forgot her. I left my own baby in a sealed car in the early summer heat.* "Oh my God," Lara said. "Thank you."

As she fumbled to unlock the car, her fingertips throbbing, she pressed her palm to the shiny black car body, so hot she hissed.

"Auddie," she said. Her daughter looked up at her through the window, calm for once. Fine, or at least unharmed. Door opened, she quickly unbuckled Auden and pressed her against her shuddering chest. It had only been a couple of minutes, couldn't have been more than that. *She's okay. I'd be able to tell otherwise.* She collapsed with Auden into the driver's seat, turned the AC on full blast, Auden at her breast, calming them both down; her mouth as rough as Lara's pulse. It happened every summer, a baby left in a sweltering car to die. A tragic accident. How long would it have taken? Five more minutes? Twelve? She couldn't even remember to get her daughter out of the car.

Would suffocating feel like drowning? An anvil pressing down or a clean, neatly bored lack, an empty space where oxygen belonged? Would the lungs collapse or explode? Lara hugged Auden against her breasts, the only place they both seemed safe. She was exhilarated with relief. Thankful, but—it had been an accident. She hadn't wanted to walk away alone. It had to be. She had forgotten, sleep-deprived, that her baby was still in the car. A terrible mistake.

She'd seen a book once, photographs of dead things, babies and adults and animals made to look like they were sleeping. Of course you couldn't tell by the pictures that the subjects weren't breathing, would never breathe again. The softly closed eyelids—had they stayed closed on their own or had the photographer needed an adhesive of some kind? She knew all the lies a picture could tell. The artifice that food stylists performed to make sesame seed hamburger buns glisten, how to manipulate temperature so that coffee steamed in perfect, lazy spirals. Lighting and chemicals and tricks. The way she could pretend to be a mother, in well-lit, fleeting moments.

An insistent rustling against her abdomen, a wriggling. Auden's heel pressed firmly against Lara's palm. Insistent little strikes, almost like when she was pregnant. The baby's head twisted beneath Lara's other hand, breaking the latch on Lara's nipple. Auden's skin was red where Lara had been holding her, indented like a watchband worn too tight or hair elastics on Lara's chubby preteen wrists. Her own grip had caused it on Auden; she'd held on too tightly. Auden was suddenly feverish in her embrace, Lara's forehead an icy ache from the air conditioning.

She didn't want to be in the car. No more car, no more driving. The stroller was in the trunk. She could just walk away. But she could feel the stares of the clerks from inside. She had no choice but to get back on the road.

She burped Auden, relieved as her skin color evened, and dabbed the corners of her mouth with her T-shirt. A deep breath and ballerina posture, and she managed to walk Auden back to her car seat and buckle her in. She gave an exaggerated smile of relief and mouthed *Thank you!* at the blinding Wawa windows before climbing back into the Volvo. She pulled out of the parking lot, unsure where they would end up.

Lara clutched the steering wheel, knuckles points of exposed bone against the black leather. She stayed in her lane, just beside the yellow lines on the roadway. People obeyed the two thick strips of paint. Bright lines kept people moving in the right direction, on their prescribed sides. So much traffic, so close. Window down, she could graze her fingertips against semis, buses, behemoth SUVs that cast shadows on her midsize Volvo, with the highest safety rating in its class, as they hummed by. Perhaps it would all end in this car. Maybe she wouldn't need the stocked diaper bag on the passenger seat. Maybe life could return to normal.

To cross the yellow lines, she would have to let go. A slip more than a nudge. Her forearms trembled. *If there's an accident, everything will be like it was before. The driver is most likely to survive.* Her father had said that while teaching Lara to drive, made her promise to always be the one in control. She clamped her bottom lip between incisors, bit, and tasted blood.

Tears pinched, blurred the view. She fumbled with the radio, sought distraction, something inappropriate. She would not look at Auden, properly restrained and rear-facing. She pretended she wasn't there. Auden, quiet in the car for the first time since they left the hospital thirty-five days ago. Her daughter's sudden silence, unnoticed. Will, Dr. Wohlleben, Dennis, her mother—she could hear them in her head. All her failures, all of Lara's collateral damage.

Brake lights flared ahead. Lara stomped on the Volvo's brake. The car skittered, a one-ton shudder, then stopped. She'd avoided the bumper in front of her but was caught in the reflected glare of the driver.

I need to get us out of the car. There was no room to merge. She had to keep the car straight or she would surrender, stop it all. This hysterical, impregnable fascination; cars careening toward her, the damage they could inflict.

Tick, tick, tick. Her tires on the yellow line crunched reflectors beneath. She counted the ticks as she would on the swings as a child: *one . . . two . . . three . . .* Summoning the confidence to jump. She snapped the radio off. Silence, shallow infant breath. *Tick, tick, tick.*

A public place. There, she wouldn't be alone with the dangerous impulses, odorless as carbon monoxide. Her home wasn't a toxic prison. She was the problem.

She drove on.

Three miles with her arms held tree-trunk straight, eyes forward. Finally, a brown sign on the shoulder directed Lara: SHORT PUMP MALL. She swerved right and waved off a chiding honk. She parked in the first open space, at the far edge of the parking lot's maw, nowhere near the reserved "mother with child" spots, signs with the image of a stork's beak holding a tied, innocuous bundle. Her Volvo lurched back and forth as she slammed the gear shift into park. She pulled the key from the ignition and threw it into the passenger seat foot well.

Squinting, her eyes hurt. A parking deck would have been better, more anonymous, with a flickering fluorescent bulb overhead. Never daylight or full dark. The blank cinder block walls would be homey. Lara collapsed on the steering wheel, sobbed, choking on tears, mucus, and shame, shaking. Acid burned up her throat. In the full mid-morning sun she flung open the door and vomited on the shiny black asphalt, on the pockmarks of blackened chewing gum. She spat, couldn't remember when she'd eaten last. Her breasts hardened with milk.

Auden's face reflected in the rearview mirror and the plastic mirror mounted on the passenger seat. Lips twitched in a sleep smile, neck curved, ear rested on shoulder.

Lara picked her raw, pink cuticles. One large step over the puddle of bile to the trunk, she clicked it open to remove Auden's collapsible stroller. As she wrestled the stroller out, she swallowed acid picking its way up again. Cars rumbled on the nearby highway overpass.

"Do you need some help with that?" asked a deep voice behind her.

With the weight of the stroller in her hands, Lara looked over her shoulder. A man in a French blue Oxford shirt and jeans stood several feet away. One cuff-rolled-up arm extended, his eyes hit the open car door, Lara, the vomit. He swallowed, his ears flushed. He looked away.

She shook her head. "No, I've got it." Tears on her scalding cheeks; snot pooled under her nostrils. She wiped her face on a sleeve, then removed the stroller, opened and locked it.

His Cole Haan long wings grazed a pool of oil and cigarette butts.

"Really." She cleared her throat. "I've got it."

He opened his mouth, nodded, and stepped back.

"It's all right, Auddie. Shhh. Shhh. I'm here." But Auden was silent, sleeping, so she spoke for the man, for the concern in his gray eyes as he approached. Could he detect the poisonous saccharine of her words? The baby was quiet in her arms. Car tires on the highway, the ramp close enough for her to hear the rubber's rhythmic *thwump thwump thwump.*

Lara began walking, her feet unsure on the white stripes painted over the asphalt. Was he still watching? In the stroller, Auden's fingers lay flat in her lap, relaxed, one crossed over the other. The skin over her fontanel kept time. She sighed. *Don't wake up, baby.* Not once did Lara check the row where she parked.

Inside the posh mall that wasn't supposed to look like a mall— *Open-air! Hard-to-find escalators and elevators to maximize traffic past all stores!*—neon signs blinked. *It's a town center, not a mall,* she had reminded her staff in meeting after meeting as they outlined the PR campaign. *You want to attract the people who wouldn't dare set foot in a mall.* Blinding, the letters flashed sales, pretzels, brand names. The hard slap of shoes against brick pavers echoed against low ceilings. She walked several feet from the gaping mouths of store entrances. The pungent odors of scented candles, carousels of body lotions, assaulted. Lara tried to outrun the cresting panic, adrenaline tight in her muscles, sharp. She wove between the crowds. Grinding her jaw. Stuttered breaths. Forms, head to toe in black except for white name tags, popped out from behind well-heeled kiosks and store openings. They thrust round, black trays, miracles in plastic ramekins, at her face.

"Try!"

"Smell!"

"C'mon in! Terrific sale on summer."

She flinched each time.

Children's cries and laughter from the play area in the center of the mall ricocheted loud and sharp inside the plastic mini-houses, from the miniature seats on the model train. They cut.

I shouldn't be here.

A man sneezed; she felt it on her neck. Lara glared at him. She stretched the shade of Auden's stroller down, farther, as far as it would go. Auden's seal-blue eyes blinked open wide. Her hands curled into fists beneath her chin. She licked her lips like a lizard. Lara pushed faster.

People everywhere, too close, always leaning over Auden's Peg Perego stroller, cooing, clucking teeth. Their chins cocked to one side, pressed lips formed a *u* of a smile. Sweat rolled from Lara's armpits; her fingertips were ice. She hated shopping malls as a rule. And Auden was so little. She had no idea why she'd thought this outing was a good idea, why she'd put her newborn, the one she had prayed for, mourned, and wept for, thought she would never have, at risk. But Lara herself felt more dangerous than any infectious disease.

She steered wide around a small raised platform surrounded by onlookers, her gait slowing as she passed a chintzy replica of an old-timey marquee. DOLL DIZZY IMPERSONATORS: PERFECT FOR WEDDINGS, PARTIES, ANY EVENT! On the small stage were a cluster of men and one woman clad in '40s postwar fashions—double-breasted jackets with peaked lapels, cap-toe shoes on the men. Gelled hair, artful smirks, fake cigarettes, and cocktail glasses. Rat Pack phonies crooned alongside faux Nat King Cole and Mel Tormé. The woman—bouncy, Hollywood girl-next-door bottle-blonde—wore a slim-paneled jacket, belted at the waist, a long skinny skirt: Doris Day. She smiled down at Lara. Offered a wave and a wink. Lara steadied herself against the stroller and walked on. The clash of time and place, of memory and reality, her father's favorite music, disoriented. Lara wouldn't stick around to hear her sing.

On the walkways, mothers pushed empty strollers. Each had black mesh compartments overstuffed with white and beige plastic bags. Some of the mothers used the seats where their babies weren't to showcase the statelier stand-up bags from Nordstrom. They wore their babies on their chests, floppy starfish in BabyBjörns or lumps beneath paisley fabric slings. Babies demanded holding, instinctively eschewed strollers, high chairs, anything designed to free a mother's hand or lift the pressure on her back. Lara hadn't realized.

Before Auden, she'd had no sympathy for grin-and-bear it mothers, women whose babies came so easily they couldn't appreciate them. *I can't even pretend that much.*

A handful of women power-walked, clad in ill-fitting, faded black Capri pants cut to highlight pale, chubby calves and shins, too-white sneakers. Hair cut too short, angled to expose full cheeks, unmade-up faces. Heavy breasts bounced under polyester tops in prepregnancy-sized bras. Yet compared to her, the women were supermodels.

Why can they do this when I can't? She memorized the uniform, the markers used to recognize one of their own. But a trail of holes ran up the forearms of Lara's T-shirt, on both sides of the seam. Picking dried spit-up off of her clothes was how it started. She had rubbed or peeled off her fingernails. She could still dig holes in her clothes. Still, however snarky her inner monologue, Lara ached to speak their language, ape their stride.

A brunette made eye contact with Lara as they passed. The woman's dark eyes, the matte map of her face realigned as she looked from Auden to Lara and back. Her thick eyebrows pulled together, a furrow of worry. She stopped mid-conversation, mouth agape, and stared. The woman then wiped her face blank, spoke loudly to her friend.

I'm here. I'll just buy something. A plastic bag would camouflage. Looking right could mean feeling right. She decided against the women's anchor stores: too many mirrored columns. She passed Gymboree and Baby GAP, as repelled now as she was once desperate to enter. The bright, coordinated colors singed like an unobstructed view of the sun. Stride Rite? The anxiety to buy heightened.

Hallmark. She could make a photo album for Will or her mother. He'd been asking for pictures to add to his desk, and maybe it would make Beth forgive her. She timidly navigated the stroller around the large plexiglass display cases full of plush hearts, floozy reds, purples and pinks, white stitching in front, *M-O-M*. SALE ON ALL MOTHER'S

DAY ITEMS. 50 TO 75 PERCENT OFF. Lara almost ran into an overweight man in tight chinos and a purple and gold Hallmark shirt.

"Hi there!" The man said. The name tag identified him as Hal. Lara tried to walk past him. "What can I help you find today?"

"I—"

"Have you seen our selection of baby books? They're beautiful. Have you started one yet?"

"No. I—"

"It's not too late. Here, let me show you." He turned, waved for her to follow to the rear of the store. She obeyed, though saliva flooded her mouth, and her throat widened. "It's this half of the wall," he said, with another sweep of his freckled hand.

Wedding albums and baby books, half-and-half, covered the back wall. First comes love, then comes marriage. Then. The mass of creams and pastels, ribboned and framed black-and-white images of bliss undulated.

"Little girl, right?" Hal asked.

Lara nodded, grabbed a book to steady her hands. "I came here to buy my daughter's baby book. I've needed one."

"Excellent choice," Hal said. She walked to the line at the register in front. "We have stationery to match, ma'am. Can I show you anything else?" She kept walking. Auden whimpered as Lara took her place in line between an elderly couple and a teenage girl, feverishly texting.

"We're going to pay for your baby book, cutie," Lara said to Auden, a stage whisper. On stage, the mother would trace a loving arc down her daughter's cheek. She couldn't. She looked at the baby, spoke to the baby. Lara would not touch. *You break it, you buy it.*

"She's so beautiful." The unsure, female voice came from behind Lara. Behind Lara stood a petite woman with a black pixie haircut. Lara stiffened, anticipating the words that would inevitably follow: "What a miracle. I hope you're enjoying every minute." But those words did not come. Lara recognized the hesitancy she'd hated in herself the years she thought she'd never have a baby of her own, when a human smaller than a puppy could take her breath away.

The woman's brown eyes muddied and rippled. A man's forearm, the husband's no doubt, turned her away from the baby or comforted her, or both. He whispered, "I know."

Lara knew those eyes, that look. The same eyes Lara hadn't been able to control, the same faithless hope, singular sadness. The envy— the way the woman's hands, entire body, gravitated to Auden and stung Lara, implicated her. The woman hadn't even been talking to Lara. She wanted Auden. She might not have known she'd spoken.

Lara plopped the book down on the corner next to the register and jerked the stroller out of line, jogged out of the store. The stroller slowed her down. The band around her throat and chest strangled.

Her teeth were slick, sweating. She stopped between the two-story clock tower and the mall's center fountain, large as a pond, but perfectly round. From the air, the architectural drawings she'd studied before ground had been broken, it looked like a Vitruvian water wheel. She wanted to peer over the edge of the fountain, maybe show Auden her reflection. The water was deep. At least a foot.

Karen. She would know what to do. Lara dialed with trembling fingers. No answer. Redialed. Voicemail, again. She threw the cell phone into the basket at the base of the stroller. Her hamstrings twitched. She had to move.

The fountain burbled and splashed. The large pump in the center, though decorative, slurped water onto the stone steps. At the edge, a child cranked a smaller black pump like a whining, squealing air rifle, up and down, up and down, and down-up. Screaking and twanging over and over. The pump and the music from the speakers hidden in corners clanked together. Lara's head buzzed.

"What a sweet baby girl," a woman said. Lara looked up from her feet. How long had she been standing there? The powdered peach face, framed by spun cotton hair, hadn't moved. The woman's eyes, the clear green of a glass bottle, did not avoid Lara's. The woman stepped closer. Her face was so lined Lara did not have to watch concern or fear or horror etch the skin.

"Thank you," Lara responded.

"How old?"

"Um . . . she's almost six weeks."

"That's about what I thought," the older woman said. "May I? I'm a grandma wannabe." She smiled and shrugged her shoulders.

Lara nodded. This woman touching her child felt right, somehow. Auden's fist softened under her caress. The baby blew spit bubbles. Gurgled. She would be safe. *This woman will love her.* Already she felt lighter. The moment between "The Star-Spangled Banner" and the shotgun start, nerves chilling to calm. Her breaths were shallow puffs.

"Ah—actually, would you just watch her a moment?" Lara asked. "You can even hold her if you want. I—I need to use the bathroom. Get some air." Her voice faded, but she kept mumbling. Lara stepped back. She blew a kiss to Auden and held both hands up, palms forward, saying she meant no harm, she'd dropped the weapon as instructed. Auden blinked, flesh and then those dark irises, the Jennings eyes. *Look away.* The baby's eyes were as dark and deep as Lara's father's had been just before his death. They were focused on Lara, not wild and unseeing. *She can't know me yet. She won't miss me.*

The woman studied her. Green seared between heavy lids. One hand clasped in Auden's, the woman reached out to Lara. "Are you sure?"

"I'll be right back. I know you won't hurt her. Please. I'll be right back." She had practice lying; her tongue tasted fallacy. If she avoided Auden's face, those eyes, she'd be able to do it. She could escape. She wouldn't have to face Will. She could start over.

"Are you okay?"

Lara shook her head. *I can't breathe.* Backed away. She turned around; all she saw before her was ground to cover. Lara stretched her stride, drove her knees high, quick, fast.

"Wait!" The old woman behind her. *Don't look back.* Dennis's dry fingers could catch her if she stopped. He would confuse her, again.

A phone rang. Lara's phone. Delibes's "Flower Duet." A phone under a diaper bag in a stroller. The sound nipped her eardrums. Lara slowed to a jog. Her wallet lay flopped open, unzipped, lay on the top of the diaper bag. She had left her phone. And a bag, in a stroller. A baby stroller.

Keep going.

Ahead of her, not far, an exit sign burned above a dark hallway to the outside. Less than one hundred steps would carry her out into the sunny day. She would be a woman on a walk, a woman without house keys, without a husband or a name. No baby. No daughter. No Auden. No, Auden. She had to flee. But where? Her life was a smoldering ruin; she'd lit the torch herself.

Just a little farther.

Movement in front of her. She couldn't see the door anymore, but she had to be close. Dead singers blocked her way. Cheap polyester stage fabric. Makeup that swapped one person's face for another. She tried to squeeze through the line. Dean Martin 2.0 put a hand out.

Doris Day gasped, "What are you doing?"

Lara paused. *Mine to have when this moment and this place fall away.* Her father had belonged to her in just that way. Was she running away from her chance of belonging so singularly to her daughter? "Doris Day is still alive," Lara mumbled. "You haven't quite got it." The fake blonde sighed and moved away.

A trance broken.

No way out. A face she couldn't erase. Eyes she couldn't outrun. While he hadn't decided to fight his cancer until the very end, her father had never chosen to leave her. What would she have become if he had walked away from her? Nothing, or even less, perhaps.

"Wait!" Lara said, standing still, her back to the stranger holding her baby. The impersonators shrank back.

"Wait!" Lara spun around. The woman holding the baby, they hadn't moved. So many people watching, Lara tripped over her flip-flops and fell upward, into the air, and then down. Lara smeared against the gritty brick, scalped her knees, shins, the tops of her toes. Her forehead rapped the brick last. Her grated palms bled.

Lara picked herself up and walked the rest of the way back to the old woman and her baby. The woman smiled, raised her arms and the baby they held to her.

Lara shook her head. She stepped back.

The woman nodded. She walked slowly to a bench, pushed the stroller. Lara followed. The woman sat first, Auden horizontal in her lap. Lara collapsed beside her.

Auden's foot tickled Lara's elbow. She stroked her sole, ridges under fingertips.

"Please don't leave," she said.

Lara wiped her bloody palms off on her pants. Her thighs were tight, tense, ready. She sat still. Her phone rang again. She couldn't move her arms to pick it up.

"I think you should answer," the woman beside her said.

"I can't."

With Auden cradled in one arm, the woman picked Lara's cell phone out of her diaper bag and flashed the face to Lara. Three more rings. One missed call. Karen. No voicemail.

Then a text message flashed across the screen: *R U OK?*

The woman held the phone in front of Lara and gestured once for her to take it. It was cool in her shaky hand. Lara typed: *No. I need some help.*

The phone rang again. Lara looked at the woman who took the phone, answered Karen's call.

"No, this isn't Lara. She and the baby are at Short Pump Mall with me. In the center. I won't leave until you get here."

Auden twined her fist around Lara's index finger. She waited.

No more running.

Acknowledgments

A book belongs to its writer, and it does not. This book would not live in the world without a tremendous number of people. My heartiest thanks go to Peggy and David Sokol, my parents, for loving me when I was difficult even to like and forgiving me when I gave up on math in high school. I owe you countless sleepless nights and a ready shoulder. You instilled in DJ and me the luxuriant hubris to dream big. Thank you, DJ. I will always be looking for ways to make you proud.

My dedicated and tireless agent, Michelle Johnson and her team at Inklings Literary, never lost faith in this narrative or in me. Chelsey Emmelhainz at Skyhorse Publishing, thank you for both taking a chance on this story and pushing me to better each draft.

Between the Muse Writers Center and the Goddard College MFA program, I have benefited from the most generous of mentors including Janine Latus, John McManus, Ellen Bryson, Tim Farrington, Rahna Reiko Rizzuto, Douglas Martin, and Darcey Steinke. I have fervent literary crushes on all of you. Fellow Goddard graduates Kenny Tomasits, Castle Yuran, Joslyn Robinson, and Nik Shier, you inspire me across time and space. Gretchen Gillen, Tammie Elliott, Kate Copeland, Cindy Carlson, Michael Withiam, Michael Khandelwal, Lisa Hartz, Jane White, and everyone at the Muse, I don't know what I would do without our community.

Finally, for the people in my life with "real jobs" who fanned my goofy, creative flames, attended reading after reading, and wouldn't allow me to give up, my life is infinitely richer with you in it: Jessica Kliner, Katie Fletcher Creech, Kerri Furey, Kelly Robbins, Lindsay Burrell, Margaux Karagosian, Elizabeth Shumadine, Sherri Stein, Anne Mueller, Jessica Chesson, Braden Wicks, Betsy Hnath, Clark Avery, Susan Twomey, Randy Sokol, Linda Graham, Lee Ann Avery, and Patricia Kantor.

The words thank you just aren't big enough.